ESCAPE WITH ME

KRISTA LAKES

ABOUT THIS BOOK

"I gave it all up to be happy. I'd give it all up again for you."

Cassie is bored with her predictable, rule-filled life. When on a tropical beach for a destination wedding, she decides to cast those rules aside, let her hair down, and be a little unpredictable.

That's when she meets a handsome bartender, Wyatt.

Wyatt knows the island like the back of his hand. And after sunny days spent breaking all the rules on the beach together, Cassie realizes that nobody has ever listened to her the way that Wyatt does. His carefree life is enviable, his kisses are intoxicating, and she can almost imagine a life with him.

But all vacations come to an end. And when Cassie invites him to visit her hometown, Wyatt reveals that he can never go back. Not to her town. Not to America. Not to civilization.

Cassie leaves, confused and heartbroken, wondering just who she got herself involved with. Suddenly, her predictable life gets turned upside down when she sees her picture splashed across the Internet. And when the tabloids come looking for the woman who found the lost billionaire, she has no idea what to do...

...until he comes back.

To my family
Thanks for believing in me

1

Cassie

Cassie couldn't believe it.

The guy at the bar just looked at her.

Not just looked, but did a double take and then a full body check out.

And then he smiled like he liked what he saw.

It wasn't something Cassie was used to. It certainly wasn't anything she expected, and to be honest, something she hadn't had in a long time.

She was sure it had to be an accident. She checked her clothes and didn't see any embarrassing stains or funny marks. Her hands immediately went to her hair and face to make sure nothing was wrong. Her long dark hair seemed to be still neatly up in its ponytail, and nothing was sticking out. She didn't feel anything strange on her face. Why else would he be looking at her and smiling like that?

"Psst, Brianna," Cassie whispered to her best friend. They stood next to one another in the line to check into their hotel. "Do I have something on my face? Anything in my hair?"

Brianna set down her suitcase and carefully evaluated her friend. "Nope. Not even a gray hair. You look good. Why?"

At least her hair dye job was working.

"I think that guy over there is checking me out." Cassie motioned with her head, trying not to be too obvious. The line to check into the hotel moved up slightly, and Brianna took the opportunity to look around without it being blatant.

"The tall guy by the bar?" she asked. "With the beachy hair and rocking body?"

"Yeah," Cassie said with a nod. She had to resist the urge to turn and look. Instead, she stared at the island-themed wallpaper behind the check-in desk. They had some lovely flowers in a vase on the counter as well.

"He is definitely checking you out," Brianna replied.

Cassie started to grin. "Really?" She'd been on an airplane all morning and didn't feel cute. She felt tired, hungry, and sweaty. Cute, let alone sexy enough to check out, felt crazy. "What should I do?"

"This." Brianna raised her arm and pointed to Cassie, looking directly at the guy. "She's single!" Brianna yelled out.

Cassie felt the entire hotel lobby turn and look at her. Brianna's voice echoed down the hall, and so the people at the pool probably heard her too. The whole Caribbean resort now knew that Cassidy Turner from Phoenix, Arizona was single.

Great. What a way to start a vacation.

Cassie winced and instantly felt her cheeks burn. "Brianna, what are you doing?" she hissed. She wished she could disappear into the floor. Risking more humiliation but unable to stop, she quickly glanced over at the guy to see him grinning. He winked at her and her blush deepened. He shot her a knowing smile and then walked out of the lobby bar and disappeared.

"What am I doing? I'm trying to get you a date," Brianna replied, shrugging like she hadn't just completely embarrassed her friend. "Remember what we talked about on the plane? You're going to have fun. You're going to relax. You're going to let loose and be a little wild."

"And what does that have to do with shouting that I'm single to a random guy in the bar?" Cassie asked. She tugged angrily on her suitcase as they inched closer to the check-in desk. "That isn't fun. It's embarrassing. Everyone here is looking at me."

Brianna sighed. "How many people do you know here?" She waved her arm, indicating the hotel lobby.

Cassie glanced around, counting heads. They were at the end of the short line to check in. A couple of people in shorts and tank tops sat at the bar on the opposite side of the room watching some sort of sports program. Other than that, the lobby was fairly empty. Maybe ten people. Tops.

It wasn't enough people to be angry over, but there was now way she was going to tell Brianna that.

"That's not the point," Cassie replied, crossing her arms and flipping her hair over her shoulder. Her face still felt hot, but she tried her best to ignore it.

But Brianna wasn't finished. "How many people do you know on this entire island?"

Cassie shrugged. "I don't know. It's a big island."

"How many?" Brianna crossed her arms and raised her eyebrows. She was determined to make some kind of a point.

"Fine. There's you." Cassie held up one finger. "Janessa and Kyle." She held up two more fingers for the bride and groom whose wedding they were attending. "Julia's not here yet, but she counts," Cassie continued, naming the fourth friend in their friendship group. "And Lorna."

"Lorna barely counts as a person," Brianna informed her with a grimace.

They both chuckled, breaking the tension between them. Cassie wasn't a fan of Kyle's cousin Lorna either. Lorna was self-absorbed and caused trouble everywhere she went. She was a classic "mean girl" and loved to rub it in everyone's faces how much better she was than everyone else.

Cassie tried to always be friendly, but Lorna definitely rubbed her the wrong way.

"So, you know five people, most of whom would love for you to let loose and have a little fun." Brianna motioned to the empty lobby. "This is the place to be 'Vacation Cassidy.' You can be the fun-loving, crazy girl I know is locked deep inside of you."

Cassie frowned. "I'm fun."

Brianna crossed her arms and gave her a wry look. "Right."

Cassie sighed and fidgeted with her bag. The truth was, Cassie herself thought she was boring. She was just over forty, but behaved like an eighty-year old. Cassie was in bed by eight every night. She hadn't been drunk in years. Her car oil was changed early, and she never left clothes in the dryer. Cassie flossed every night and always ate all her vegetables, even the ones she didn't like.

She felt old, even though she still had most of her life ahead of her. She'd fallen into a rut.

She followed her company's work manual to the letter. She wore only company approved clothing and hadn't changed her hairstyle in years. Despite wanting to on many occasions, she never broke corporate policy. She was the perfect little corporate employee who always willingly worked overtime.

Her divorce a few years ago was the only interesting thing about her, and that just made her feel more pathetic. No one should have a divorce be the most interesting thing about them.

She had fallen into a monotonous life, and she knew it. She'd been fun once. She wanted to get back to the person that laughed more and went on dates. That wasn't over-worked and underpaid. That had hobbies other than working and wore things other than dark, conservative office wear.

This week was the chance for her to be the Cassie she wanted to be again.

The line moved forward, and it was their turn to check in.

"Brianna Fuller and Cassidy Turner," Brianna announced to the check-in person. "We're with the Barnes/Frankson wedding."

The man at the desk typed something into the computer. "Excellent. We have you in room seven-thirty-two. Two queen beds and an ocean view."

Cassie grinned. Coming from Arizona's parched land of desert heat and sun, the ocean was something magical to the both of them.

"Welcome to the Ocean Key Resort." The man handed Brianna two keycards. "Enjoy the island."

Together, Brianna and Cassie grabbed their bags and headed up to their room. Cassie could feel her spirits lifting. She could be young here. She could be fun. She was sure of it.

The Caribbean resort was gorgeous. The hallways were wide and spacious with beautiful artwork hanging on the walls. Cassie caught a glimpse of the ocean through a window and had to control the urge not to drop her bags and just sprint outside. It was such a perfect shade of blue that she had a hard time believing it could be real.

Janessa and Kyle were going all out for their wedding bash. They'd paid for airfare and hotel rooms for everyone in the wedding party. There was no way Cassie would have picked, let alone been able to afford, something this luxurious on her

own. Kyle and his family owned the three biggest car dealer-
ships in Arizona, so they could afford the nicer things in life.

This all-inclusive resort with beautiful turquoise waters
and white sandy beaches was definitely one of the nicer
things.

Their room was a standard hotel room. Working in the
hotel industry, Cassie tried not to judge the thread-count or
the quality of the TV, but they were on the pricier end. It felt
like an upgrade. Back home, Cassie managed a large-chain
hotel for middle-class and business travelers. StarTree Hotels
had over six-hundred properties in fifty countries. She
managed the one in downtown Phoenix.

"They have the remotes out and linens nicely placed,"
Cassie remarked as she looked around the room. Having the
remotes out was one of the corporate mandates this year. All
remotes needed to be easily found.

Brianna rolled her eyes and threw open the gauzy curtains
to reveal their ocean view.

"Look at that," Brianna said with awe. The view was spec-
tacular. Palm trees, white sandy beaches, and pale blue water
that slowly turned into cobalt waves stretched out before
them.

It really was paradise.

"Ian would love this," Brianna said softly, looking long-
ingly out the window. Ian was Brianna's eight year old son. He
was staying with Brianna's sister for the week, but Cassie
knew Brianna would miss him. Being a single mom meant she
was used to having him with her all the time.

"Someday, you'll bring him to the ocean," Cassie assured
her, putting a hand on her friend's shoulder.

"Yeah. Someday. It would help if my awful ex paid for
anything." Brianna took a deep breath and forced a smile.
"But, we're not talking about him. And Ian is having fun with

his cousins. Right now, I am kid and responsibility free. Today, I am having fun."

"Heck yeah." Cassie grinned and went to unpack. Her bridesmaid dress needed to be hung, and she had a couple of shirts that she wanted to iron before they went out to dinner. Plus, there were a couple of dry-clean-only things that she wanted separate from her more casual wear.

"What are you doing?" Brianna asked, lounging on the bed and watching Cassie put things away.

"Unpacking. If you give me your dress, I'll hang it up. I'm going to ask the concierge for a steamer so we can get the wrinkles out," Cassie said, carefully hanging the blue satin dress in the closet. "If you have anything that wrinkled in your suitcase, I'll be ironing later."

Brianna sighed and shook her head. "You brought clothes that need ironing to a tropical vacation?"

"Yeah. So?"

Cassie could feel the disappointment in Brianna's slow head shake.

"Let me see what you're wearing to dinner tonight." Brianna motioned to Cassie's half-empty suitcase.

Cassie pulled out a sensible pair of khaki shorts and a button-up silk shirt. It was a pale pink.

"That's what you're wearing?" Brianna asked, wrinkling her nose.

"What's wrong with it?" Cassie asked. "I like the color."

"It's sensible. It's plain. It's one of your work shirts. It's not letting loose and having fun. Did you bring anything remotely fun?" Brianna got up and started pawing through Cassie's things.

"Hey!" Cassie shouted. "You'll mess up my system."

Brianna stepped back and gave her a sad head shake.

Cassie sighed. "Fine. I just have this." She held up a maxi

dress with blue and red flowers. It was the most "fun" dress she owned.

"We're going shopping," Brianna announced. "If we can't find anything, you can wear that, but not the shorts. Those are old-lady shorts."

Cassie frowned. She liked the shorts, but as she looked at them, she realized that she could easily see her uptight grandmother wearing them. They were old person shorts. A fun-loving vibrant woman that liked to be spontaneous and flirty wouldn't be caught dead walking down the beach in those shorts.

"Okay. I'll let you pick for me," Cassie told her. "I can't seem to pick anything that isn't for work."

Brianna grinned. "This is going to be fun."

And suddenly Cassie was nervous again.

Two hours and more money than Cassie planned later, she was the proud owner of cute clothes. They'd found a fun little shopping area near the beach and Brianna did her thing. Cassie currently wore a flirty little sundress with strappy sleeves and cherries printed on it. She had short shorts and cute tank tops in one bag. In another, there were two more sundresses made of a light silk material that made her feel almost naked wearing them. Brianna had insisted she get both.

"Just imagine dancing on top of a bar with this on," Brianna told her when she'd hesitated to buy one.

"People would look up my skirt," Cassie replied, putting it away.

Brianna rolled her eyes and had stuffed it back into Cassie's hands. "Fine. Imagine dancing on the floor. You'll be the hottest girl there."

Cassie did feel different wearing the dresses. They were sexy and fun. She still had long legs and the dresses were flattering around her middle. She liked the idea of being the hottest girl, rather than just an old lady. The dresses were who she wanted to be this week. She was letting her hair down, and these dresses with their short hems and low cut tops were the first step.

So, she bought the dresses. All of them. She bought clothes she would probably only ever wear here on this island. These were entirely against corporate dress code. It wasn't like Cassie to buy things that she couldn't reuse a million times.

It felt liberating.

Brianna and Cassie hurried from the shops and back to the central tower of the hotel. It was almost time for dinner and Brianna still needed to change. As they entered the main building, that's when Cassie saw him again.

The guy from the bar. He was headed toward the hotel lobby again, walking across the entrance.

Somehow, in the two hours since she'd seen him last, he'd gotten more attractive.

He saw her, grinned, but kept walking toward the bar. Cassie paused for a moment, trying to figure out what she should do. Should she follow him? Talk to him? Give him her room number?

"Cassie?" Brianna called. She was already at the elevators. Cassie glanced back toward the lobby, but the man was gone. She'd missed her chance.

Cassie hurried over to Brianna and made it right as the elevator arrived. She didn't tell her friend that she'd seen the hot guy again. Cassie knew Brianna would push her out of the elevator and tell her to go catch him and Cassie wasn't ready for that. Besides, what would she even say?

It was for the best, Cassie decided. Baby steps on this

going wild thing was a good plan. She wondered if there was something in the corporate handbook she could use.

Corporate handbook?

Cassie sighed internally. Here she was coming up with *responsible* steps on how to go wild. She really did need a break from her rule-filled life.

Still, she hoped she'd run into the handsome man again. Cassie could do big girl steps then. Maybe even be spontaneous. She was "Vacation Cassidy" after all.

2

Cassie

The sound of lively conversations filled the restaurant. Friends and family sat around six large tables in a small party room set off from the main seating area. The big ocean facing windows stood open, letting in the last sunshine of the day as well as a cooling sea breeze.

Cassie felt naked in her thin dress. Her shoulders were bare and her legs exposed. Despite the tropical heat, she wished she had a sweater. Or her long sleeved pink work shirt. She missed the safety of her work clothes.

"Oh my gosh, Cassie. You look amazing," Janessa announced, hurrying across the room to greet Cassie and Brianna.

"You like it?" Cassie asked, looking down and inspecting the cute little cherries on her dress.

"Like it? I love it," Janessa told her. "Brianna has great taste."

Cassie tried not to feel hurt that Janessa knew Brianna

had picked it out. Was it really that out of character for her to wear a cute dress?

"I definitely have great taste, but Cassie's got the legs for it," Brianna agreed, giving Janessa a hug. "Sorry, we're late. It was my fault. Too much great taste and not enough shoes."

Janessa chuckled and showed them to their table. Cassie and Brianna were seated with the bride and groom. Janessa's teenage daughter sat next to her mother. Cassie sat down in her chair and took a sip of water. The glass was slippery with condensation, but the cold felt good on both her hands and her throat.

"Where's Julia? Is she here yet?" Brianna asked, looking around the room. Brianna, Julia, Cassie, and Janessa had been roommates in college. They were still close friends, despite life taking them in different directions.

"Her mom's sick, so she's not coming for a couple days," Janessa replied. "She'll be here in time for the wedding, but she's going to miss the bachelorette party tomorrow."

"Darn." Brianna frowned. "She was supposed to help Cassie be wild."

Cassie rolled her eyes. "I don't need everyone's help."

Janessa made a cough that sounded suspiciously like an attempt to cover up a laugh.

"What?" Cassie asked her.

"I am excited to see you let loose and relax," Janessa replied diplomatically. "I hope you get drunk and at least flirt with a sexy guy. You've been so stressed lately. You deserve some fun."

"Get drunk and flirt?" Cassie said, sarcasm dripping off her voice. "Wow. The bar is set so high. How will I ever accomplish that?"

"Baby steps," Brianna told her. "We have faith that you can do far more, but this is a good place to start."

Cassie rolled her eyes at both her friends. Was she really

so lost in her job and being responsible for the hotel that she'd forgotten how to have fun?

"I'll be right back," Janessa said as more people came into the dining room. She stood gracefully, walking to greet the newcomers. She looked beautiful, Cassie thought. Janessa was thin with light brown hair that was tucked up into a neat bun at the nape of her neck. Her simple sundress was cornflower blue, and Cassie knew Janessa had picked it to match her eyes.

Kyle, Janessa's fiancé, caught Janessa by the door and gave her a quick peck on the cheek. She grinned at him, her smile warming her entire face with love. He said something to her, and she nodded. Together, they both came back to the table. Janessa sat, while Kyle remained standing. He picked up a water glass and tapped it with his butter knife.

"If I could get everyone's attention," he called out. His voice carried well in the small room. He waited patiently for the murmur of voices to die down. "First, Janessa and I would like to thank you all for coming. We're so glad we have family and friends willing to travel for our big day."

There was a slight smattering of applause.

"I can't wait to marry the love of my life," he continued, making Janessa smile. "I know that I'm not the most attractive man in the world or the richest, but when I'm with her, I feel like I am."

A chorus of awws went through the crowd. Kyle was an average looking man with moderately good looks, but would never be movie star handsome. He had gone the route of shaving his head rather than trying to hide the male-pattern baldness that most of the male members of his family shared. It suited him.

"I'd like to thank Katy for bringing her mom and I together," Kyle said after the pause.

"And thank you for my new car!" Katy shouted back. "Best

trade in offer ever!" The crowd chuckled and Kyle winked at his soon-to-be step-daughter.

"Anyway, I hope you enjoy dinner tonight. The bachelor and bachelorette parties are tomorrow. Make sure to see Janessa or me if you have any questions on those. The rehearsal has been moved to five pm on Friday, rather than six, so make sure you're on time if you are in the party." He shrugged and glanced around the room. "That's it for announcements. Thank you all for coming."

Light applause filled the room once more. Kyle sat down with a smile for his bride, and the hum of conversation resumed.

"How are you, Katy?" Cassie asked, reaching for another sip of water.

"Great. This place is amazing," Katy replied. She was the spitting image of her mother, just thirty years younger. "Nice dress by the way, Aunt Cassie. It looks great on you."

Cassie beamed. Teenager compliments were the real deal.

The doors to the private dining room opened with a slam that made everyone turn and look.

Lorna had arrived. She sashayed in like she owned the place. At least she'd waited until the speech was over. She hadn't at the last family dinner Cassie shared with Lorna.

"Sorry I'm late everyone," she announced. She posed for a moment at the entrance, her skin-tight black pleather dress hiding nothing of her perfectly plastic-surgeon sculpted body. Cassie wondered how Lorna could wear pleather in tropic humidity like this. If Cassie were wearing that, she'd not only melt but have the pleather squeaking with her every movement.

Lorna was in her early forties and currently between rich husbands number three and four. Number three had been a plastic surgeon, and she'd utilized his services well. She had curves in all the right places and better than nature could ever provide. Her dyed blonde hair hung in graceful curls down her back, and her makeup was perfect. Her blue eyes looked around the room, judging the women for competition and evaluating the men for their net worth. If Cassie ever needed to describe what a gold-digger looked like, she planned on simply describing Lorna.

Lorna walked over to Cassie's table, passing up several empty seats. "Kyle, dear, where am I supposed to sit?"

"We have you at the table over—"

"I'll just pull up a chair here," Lorna cut him off. She grabbed a chair and scooted between Cassie and Janessa. "I'm family after all."

"Everyone here is family," Janessa muttered under her breath, but luckily Lorna didn't hear her.

"I'm glad you made it, Lorna," Kyle told her. "I knew you said your flight was coming in late."

"Oh, the nightmare at the airport. It's why I only fly first class these days. It was simply horrid." She sighed dramatically. "But, I'm here now. My little cousin is all grown up and getting married. I couldn't miss this."

You couldn't miss meeting wealthy husband number four at a place like this, Cassie thought to herself. It wasn't a kind thought, but she only felt a little guilty about thinking it.

"Wine, please." Janessa motioned to a waiter. "I was planning on taking it easy tonight, but now I feel like I need a glass."

"Can I have one?" Katy asked hopefully.

"No," answered Janessa, Kyle, Brianna, and Cassie at the same time.

The waiter came over, and Janessa ordered a glass of white. Cassie motioned to him to make it two. He nodded and quickly returned with two glasses of white wine.

"Where's mine?" Lorna asked him, looking up.

"Ma'am?" The waiter frowned.

"Where's my wine?" Lorna smiled, but it wasn't a warm or a kind smile.

"I didn't know you wanted one," the poor waiter stammered.

"Well, obviously I do." She shook her head. "I want a red. Not the house red. A good red. Something with body."

"Of course, ma'am." The waiter nodded quickly and disappeared to get Lorna her wine.

"You just can't get good help these days," Lorna said with a shrug, smiling around the crowded table.

Cassie bit her tongue. This was what Lorna did. She was the queen of making things uncomfortable.

"So, Kyle, this resort is beautiful," Cassie said, trying to change the conversation. "The wedding is on the beach, right?"

Kyle nodded. "We have a private area of the beach booked. It's absolutely stunning. Janessa picked it out."

"You'll love it," Janessa gushed. She flushed with excitement, and maybe the fact that she'd downed almost the entire glass of wine. "It's got this crystal clear water, and we're having this little arch thing put up. The reception is going to be outside in the main courtyard where you can see the ocean and--"

"Where is my wine?" Lorna demanded, interrupting the conversation.

"Lorna, it's been thirty seconds," Cassie said without thinking.

Like something out of a horror movie, Lorna's head slowly turned and faced Cassie, her eyes mean and cruel.

"Excuse me?"

Cassie swallowed hard.

"I just meant that it's a busy room. He's probably making sure you get the best wine they have," Cassie quickly stammered. Corporate rule number seven: always make a problem sound like a positive.

Lorna's lips narrowed, and she flipped her golden hair over her shoulder. The woman knew how to hair flip effectively. "It's lazy is what it is."

She rolled her eyes dismissively at Cassie before turning away and starting a conversation with Kyle. Cassie let out a small sigh of relief. Being in Lorna's cross-hairs was never a pleasant experience.

"Don't aggravate her," Brianna whispered. "You know the drill. Smile and nod. She'll get bored and go bother someone richer than us."

Cassie took another sip of her wine. It had been a long day of travel, and she was tired. A good night's sleep would make it much easier to deal with Lorna. Lorna did have the ability to be funny and pleasant when she wanted to be. Maybe tomorrow would find her more agreeable.

At least, that's what Cassie hoped.

The food arrived shortly after Lorna's wine. Cassie had a delicious looking white fish with fresh mango salsa. It smelled wonderful and tasted even better. Cassie nearly moaned with the first bite. She couldn't remember the last time she had fresh fish that tasted this good. It probably was due to the fact the ocean was just steps away.

"I ordered my steak to be medium-well. This is medium."

Cassie internally sighed as Lorna's shrill voice broke the once happy silence of people eating. This poor waiter, Cassie thought, looking over at Lorna's plate. The steak looked perfect to Cassie's eyes. Granted, it wasn't the way Cassie would order a steak, but it looked like a solid medium-well done steak. There was nothing wrong with the food. It was just Lorna being difficult because she could be.

"I'm so sorry, ma'am." The waiter wiped his hands on his apron. "I can take it back to the kitchen for you."

"Yes. You do that," she told him, tossing down her fork and looking annoyed.

Cassie shook her head slightly and took another bite of her fish.

"Oh, you all go ahead and eat without me," Lorna announced sadly. She sighed, looking like a true martyr. "I'll just sit here and wait."

Janessa sighed this time.

They were now in the awkward position of eating and making Lorna look like an angel for letting them do so, or not eating and showing solidarity with her. Kyle set down his fork.

"We'll wait for you." He smiled at his cousin and she, in turn, beamed at him. It was easy to see that Kyle didn't see Lorna's true nature.

"You've always been the best cousin," she cooed.

Brianna made a slight gagging sound, and Cassie had to stifle a laugh.

Luckily, the waiter returned quickly with a fresh plate of food for Lorna. It was another perfect steak that looked nearly identical to the previous one.

"There. That's a medium-well steak," Lorna said as he set it down. "That wasn't too hard, was it?"

"Anything else, ma'am?" the waiter asked, giving her a fake smile. It made Cassie wonder if maybe the chef had spit in Lorna's food. In fact, Cassie sort of secretly hoped he did.

"No. But your manager will hear about your poor service," Lorna informed him. She looked pointedly at his name tag. "You'll be hearing about this, Fernando. If that's your real name. I'm going to have you fired."

The poor man took a step back with a shocked look on his face.

"Seriously, Lorna?" Cassie couldn't help herself. Maybe it was the wine giving her liquid confidence. Maybe it was the new dress. Maybe it was just a death wish. "The guy didn't do anything wrong."

Lorna's blue eyes flashed. "Excuse me?"

"The waiter didn't do anything wrong. He brought you the wine you never ordered. He fixed your meal. He's been nothing but polite."

Two pink spots bloomed on Lorna's cheeks.

"Oh? So because you're some hot shot hotel manager, you think you know better than me?" Her eyes narrowed as she focused on Cassie. "You work in a crappy hotel. You wouldn't know customer service if it slapped you in the face. You don't have any class. If you did, you'd understand why I want to speak to this man's manager. It just shows how terrible you are at your job. No wonder no one important stays at your hotel."

The table gasped and went silent. Hot tears stung at the back of Cassie's eyes. She was proud of the job she did. Cassie was damn good at it, and she was the reason her hotel was rated the best StarTree Hotel in the Phoenix area.

But Lorna wasn't done.

"I don't even know why you're here, Cassie. I get that you're friends with the bride, but you're going to ugly up the pictures, and you don't fit in with the type of people here. You're low class. We're high class. You don't belong with people like us."

The table sat in shocked silence for three heartbeats. Even the other tables had quieted. Cassie put on her manager's face. It was the one she used when dealing with difficult guests and vendors. It was firm without showing emotion.

"Wow, Lorna. You're right. If you're class, then I don't want any." She stood up, carefully placing her napkin on the chair behind her. "Excuse me. I need to use the restroom."

"Running away solves all your problems," Lorna replied.

She leaned back and crossed her legs, daring Cassie to respond.

Cassie nearly sat back down, but she knew it would just be proving Lorna right. So, Cassie turned and left the table. Her hands shook as she headed out of the dining room and into the hallway leading to the bathrooms. Her face ached with the heat of her blush and her eyes stung with tears she refused to let fall. Not while Lorna might see.

She wouldn't give Lorna that satisfaction.

3

Cassie

Cassie entered the bathroom and found it blissfully empty. Leaning against a stone tile wall, she let the hot tears escape. There weren't many. She didn't usually cry. She was typically strong and steadfast. She didn't let people get to her.

Cassie blamed it on being tired. She blamed the tears on traveling all day. She blamed it on the stress of her job. She blamed it on Lorna knowing the exact buttons to push to make her doubt herself.

She wiped her face off, checked the mirror to make sure she didn't look like she'd been crying, and went to order more wine. She found their waiter in the hallway putting orders into a computer.

"Fernando?"

He looked up with a start and then relaxed when he saw it was just Cassie.

"I just wanted to let you know that if Lorna does speak to your manager, I'd be happy to speak to them as well. You've been great. She's the customer from hell, and I want to apologize to you for her. I don't want you getting in trouble with your boss because she's awful."

Fernando smiled, his shoulders releasing from around his ears. "Thank you, ma'am. That means a lot."

"I'm happy to do it." Cassie shrugged, but inside she felt a little bit better. "And when you get a chance, I'd love some more wine. Me and everyone sitting at our table. Except the teenager. Don't bring her any no matter how much she asks."

"Of course." He nodded, then paused for a second. He glanced around and then leaned forward. "We didn't recook her steak. Chef just moved the potatoes around. Same exact plate."

Cassie's eyebrows raised.

"I also would recommend not eating anything from her plate. Just in case Chef did something else. He doesn't like when orders get returned for no reason."

Cassie had worked in hospitality and food services long enough to know you don't anger the people that make your food. They had all the opportunities to put things like bugs or food that had fallen on the floor onto your dish without you ever knowing about it.

Lorna apparently never had that lesson.

Cassie thanked Fernando and headed back to the table. Luckily, Lorna had moved on. She now sat at a table with a wealthy looking man who was currently trapped in a conversation with her. The poor man had no idea what he was in for. Cassie felt bad for him, but not bad enough to rescue him. She didn't want Lorna to come back to her table.

"You okay?" Brianna asked when Cassie sat down. Janessa and Kyle were making their rounds around the room talking to guests. Katy was off talking with her grandparents. The other guests had finished dessert and were chatting among themselves.

Cassie nodded. "I got us more wine."

"Good." Brianna looked over at Cassie, appraising her. "You sure you're okay? That was brutal."

"I think so." Cassie gave a small shrug. Her eyes darted over to make sure Lorna was still occupied at the other table.

"You know it's not true what she said, right?"

"I know. It's just..." The threat of tears tightened around Cassie's throat again. She swallowed hard and wished the wine was here already. Her ex-husband used to say similar things.

Brianna gave Cassie a quick side hug. "She just enjoys pushing buttons. She's evil, and I hope a shark eats her this week."

"Poor shark."

"Yeah." Brianna paused for a moment. "Actually, I don't know if a shark would eat her. She's too bitter."

Fernando sat two big glasses of wine in front of Brianna and Cassie with a smile. They were bigger than the ones from before. Cassie took a sip and felt her shoulders relax a little.

"On the upside, we may have discovered an effective shark repellent." Cassie took another sip. The bittersweet liquid was soothing to the soul.

Brianna chuckled. She took a sip of her wine and then set her wine glass down hard, nearly spilling it in the process. "Oh, I almost forgot. We're going dancing after dinner. There's supposed to be this amazing dance club here."

Cassie could feel the tension increasing in her shoulders again. "I think I'm going to pass tonight," she told Brianna. "I'm tired. It's been a long day."

Brianna pouted but didn't push. "Okay. If you change your mind, come find me."

Cassie nodded, and Brianna gave her another a quick hug.

"I'm going to go change," Brianna said, standing up and taking her wine with her. "These aren't dancing clothes."

"I'll walk up with you." Cassie grabbed her wine glass. They both waved to Janessa and headed out of the dining area.

Brianna started telling Cassie all about the dance club, obviously trying to entice her to come along. They walked across the outdoor pool area, and Cassie let her talk, nodding and making the appropriate noises, but secretly looking forward to cuddling up in her bed and watching some bad hotel TV. Mario Lopez was her plan for the night.

But then she saw him. The guy from earlier. Sexy short blonde hair, broad shoulders, and sun-kissed skin. He stood behind the outdoor tiki bar serving drinks. She stopped short.

"You can wear those shorts with the black tank-top we got... and why are you stopping?" Brianna followed Cassie's gaze to the tiki bar. "Oh." She looked back over at Cassie and smiled wider. "*Oh.*"

"I think I'm going to have another drink before bed," Cassie told Brianna. She chugged most of the rest of the wine in her glass. Partly so that she would have an excuse to be at the bar for a new drink and partly for courage.

"Hold up," Brianna said, pulling out her phone. She snapped a picture of Cassie looking confused with a mostly empty wine glass.

"What's that for?"

"So I have proof you can let loose," she replied with a smug grin. She gave Cassie a gentle push toward the bar. "Go get 'em, tiger."

Cassie rolled her eyes and took a confident step toward the bar. And then a not so confident step. Was she really ready to do this?

"If you bring back a guest, just put the privacy card on the door," Brianna told her. "I can bunk with Janessa. She's in a room by herself until her wedding night."

Cassie glanced back, and Brianna was grinning at her. She looked like a proud parent sending her kid off to school.

"You know what?" Brianna grinned a little wider. "I'm just going to stay with Janessa anyway. You go have fun, party-girl."

Brianna started walking again, leaving Cassie just steps from the bar. It was time to put this vacation on the right track. Time to let the fun Cassie out for a bit. What was the worst that could happen? If she made a fool of herself, no one here knew her. She wasn't at work. There were no corporate rules here. She could be the confident, charismatic, fun woman that she knew herself to be.

She could do this.

Cassie took a deep breath, lifted her chin, and walked over. She took a seat at the end of the bar and drank the last of her wine.

Time to turn on her best flirting abilities and try and earn a vacation fling.

4

Wyatt

Wyatt noticed her immediately.

How could he not? She was gorgeous in an innocent-yet-sexy kind of way. She kept fiddling with the thin straps on her dress, and he couldn't help but want to be the one to slide them off her shoulders. He kept imagining his fingers sliding through her dark hair as he laid her onto his bed.

He could just imagine the way her beautiful red lips would look gasping his name. Her body was made for loving. Those long legs peeking out of the sheets... The way her hips would rise to his...

He needed to get a hold of himself. He was supposed to be making drinks, not imagining guests naked. Even if it was a really lovely image in his head. He should at least learn her name first.

He quickly finished pouring the last few mai-tais for the tourists in front of him. While he set the drinks out, he carefully checked out her left hand. No ring. That was a good sign. Thoughts of her in his bed once again filled his thoughts. He pushed them away, trying his best not to spill the mai-tais. She was distracting.

Luckily, it was a quiet night. The first few nights of the week always were. All the guests were either settling in from their travels or going to the club to start their vacation out right. He was glad that she wasn't at the dance club.

He slid down the bar and made eye contact with her.

Damn.

Those eyes. Dark and warm like hot chocolate on a winter's evening. She chewed on her bottom lip and all he could think about for the next ten seconds was what he would like to do with that lip.

"What can I get you?" His voice nearly cracked.

Usually he was smoother, but for some reason, she had him nervous. He hadn't been nervous about a woman in a while. That was a good sign. If anything, it meant that this would be a good week. He hadn't been really interested in any guests recently, but he wanted to change that with her.

"What do you recommend?" She smiled at him, and once again he found himself imagining her in his bed.

"Do you like sweet or not sweet?" he asked, giving her a smile of his own.

"I like strong," she replied. She readjusted herself on the bar-stool. "And sweet."

"You ever have sex on the beach?" he asked, already pulling out a shaker and the bottle of vodka.

"Well, I'm from Arizona, so no." She frowned slightly, her brows coming together in confusion as her cheeks pinked slightly. "Isn't that a little personal?"

He couldn't help but chuckle. "I meant the drink."

The pink spots on her cheeks blossomed into red. He wondered if that was her reaction to other things as well. He wanted to find out.

"Oh, right. Duh." She sighed and gave him a self-depre-cating smile as if disappointed with herself. "I'd love some sex on the beach."

He raised his eyebrows provocatively at her as he added peach schnapps to the shaker. "Is that so?"

The blush intensified. He found he rather liked the look on her.

"I mean... I.. uh..."

He let her fumble for a moment as he quickly mixed, shook, and poured the drink into a glass.

"Sex on the beach for the lady," he said, sliding it in front of her.

She gave him a bashful grin and took a sip. "It's good," she said.

"I am the best," he told her.

"Well, then I'll just have to get all my sex on the beach from you," she replied. She took another sip. "You know how to make screaming orgasms too?"

It was his turn to grin. She kept a straight face, but the blush in her cheeks gave her away. She was trying to flirt with him, but she was nervous.

She liked him.

Wyatt was used to that. Women always liked the attractive bartender, especially after a couple of drinks. That was why he was here. That was why he picked this job out of all the possible things in the world he could do.

It was easy to pick up women here. And he was going to pick her up tonight.

He leaned forward over the bar, whispering in her ear. "I make the best screaming orgasms."

She shivered as his words tickled the small hairs on her neck. A nervous giggle escaped her mouth, and she quickly downed most of the drink. He raised his eyebrows.

"Slow down there, slugger," he advised. "I'm here all night."

"Then I'd like another," she replied. Her words slurred together slightly, but her eyes were still focused. She was tipsy, but not drunk.

So he made her another.

"What brings you to the Caribbean?" Wyatt asked, setting down the drink in front of her.

"One of my best friends is getting married," she replied. "He's a great guy. I think they'll be really happy together. Although, If they have kids, I hope they get her hair and not his. He's balding. Bad."

Maybe she was a little more tipsy than he thought.

"How long are you here?" He picked up a cloth and began wiping down glasses. He did it because it was his job, but it also kept his hands busy, which helped keep the temptation to slide those dress straps off her shoulders away.

"Just a week. I couldn't take more time off work." She shrugged and took a sip of her drink. It was a smaller sip this time.

"And what do you do? Model?"

"No." She laughed and shook her head. "I manage a hotel. Well, I'm one of the managers. The head manager. I'm important."

"I could have told you that." He loved the smile she gave him at the compliment, but she was definitely heading towards drunk rather than tipsy. How much had she had to drink before sitting down at the bar?

"What's your name?" she asked him.

He pointed to the name tag on his chest. "Wyatt."

Her smile warmed, her eyes drawing him to her. "That's a nice name."

"Thanks. What's your name?"

"Cassidy. But everyone calls me Cassie." She shrugged. "I

actually like being Cassie better than Cassidy. Cassidy sounds like I'm a cowboy. Like Butch Cassidy and the Sundance Kid." She looked up at him with big eyes. "You probably get that a lot too. Not the butch part. Just the cowboy part."

"If I had a dollar for every time someone said, 'like the cowboy,' I'd be a millionaire."

Not that he needed the money. He was technically a millionaire already. One thousand times a millionaire. This job was just for fun. It was a way to meet women and give himself the life he'd always wanted. She didn't need to know that though. None of the women he brought back with him did.

He was just the sexy bartender fling they told their friends about without knowing who he really was.

"Well, we can be friends then," she told him. "Just don't bring anyone named Sundance or Tonto next time you work, and we'll be fine."

He chuckled. She was cute *and* funny. His own personal brand of kryptonite.

Unfortunately, new customers arrived, taking their seats at the other end of his bar. He wished they would have picked another bar for their drinks as he was enjoying talking to her. She was tipsy, but still in control. If anything, the liquor was giving her the courage to flirt with him. From the way she gripped her drink and the flush in her cheeks, she wasn't used to flirting like this.

"I'll be right back," he said.

"I'll be here." She took another sip of her drink and bit her bottom lip in a nervous smile.

He quickly poured the beers and margaritas for the new patrons. He knew the bar would only pick up for the rest of the night. The tiki bar by the pool was a spot everyone wanted to get a drink.

Wyatt kept an eye on Cassie. He made sure to fill her

drink as often as he could, even at the expense of other patrons. He didn't need the tips, so it didn't really bother him too much. Besides, the smile she gave him every time he came near lit up the night. That was more than enough tip for him.

Even though he'd done this routine a thousand times, tonight felt fresh. She gave him butterflies in the pit of his stomach every time he caught her looking at him.

It was probably just his imagination. He hadn't worked this bar in a while, preferring the lobby bar with air conditioning. It had been a while since he'd picked up a date working the tiki bar. Any bar really. He'd lost his taste for random women the past few months.

But she was different. She was something new. That was it. That was where the excitement came from. He just hadn't done this pickup routine for a while.

Or maybe, it was her smile. The way she played with the straps on her dress like she didn't know what to do with them. Perhaps it was the way she grinned and joked with him, unsure of herself but trying anyway.

It was flattering in the most sincere way possible.

An hour later, she was still sitting at his bar. She'd had more drinks, and although he started watering them down, she was no longer tipsy.

She was drunk.

"You are cut off," he told her when she slurred his name when he approached.

"I never drink this much," she confided. "You just make them so tasty."

"Well, no more for you." He poured a glass of water and handed it to her. "Drink this."

"I thought I was cut off." She looked at him with those big brown eyes, not wanting to get in trouble.

"Just from sex on the beach," he told her. He nudged the glass. "Drink the water."

"Can I have sex on the beach later?" She grinned at him and giggled.

"We'll see," he replied. He wasn't sure she'd want another fruity drink after this. How had she gotten so drunk? He'd barely given her three light drinks over the hour.

He silently chastised himself for not paying better attention. He'd been enjoying their flirty banter and making her smile. He didn't want her to be hung over in the morning.

He refilled her water glass. "Drink this one, too."

She nodded and dutifully began to drink the water. He hurried over to pour some more beers for another customer. When he came back, the water glass was empty, but she was starting to sway on her chair.

"Here," she said, sliding a napkin across the bar. She slipped off the bar-stool and caught herself with a nervous giggle. "For when you get off. If you want to get off. If you know what I mean."

He looked down at the napkin and saw a room number. Seven-thirty-two. It was seared into his brain without even thinking.

But she was drunk. Some nights that might have been acceptable. But not with her. He wanted to see her sober. If she was this smart and funny while drunk, he could only imagine how amazing the sex would be sober. He didn't want drunk Cassie.

"You're drunk," he said gently, sliding the napkin back to her.

It was the wrong thing to do. Her face crumpled and tears formed in her eyes.

"Oh god. I screwed it up," she whimpered. Her whole body went from excited to dejected.

Wyatt felt like the world's biggest idiot. He was usually much better at this.

"No, Cassie. It's not like that." He reached out and took her hand. "I really would like to. I just think you should have less alcohol in you."

She sniffled and tried to hide wiping a tear off her cheek. "You don't have to sugar coat it. It's fine. I suck."

She turned and started to leave. He had really screwed this one up.

Wyatt hopped over the bar and stood in front of her. She bumped directly into him and looked up, utterly surprised to see him suddenly there. He put his hands on her shoulders.

"I would like to see you again," he said, making sure to speak slowly and clearly. "Have lunch with me tomorrow."

Hope slowly brightened her eyes. "Really?"

He nodded. "Really. Please have lunch with me tomorrow."

"Okay." She nodded, her head going faster than her body could react. She put both her hands on either side of her skull to make it stop. "Where?"

"Castaway Cantina," he told her. "Noon."

"Castaway Cantina. Noon. Castaway Cantina at noon. Castaway Cantina at noon," she repeated. She looked up at him and grinned. "Castaway Cantina at noon."

"That's it." He gave her shoulders a gentle squeeze. "Now go to your room and get some sleep. And drink another glass of water before you go to bed."

She nodded, but he wasn't sure if she really heard him. She was still repeating "Castaway Cantina at noon."

Wyatt stepped out of her way and gently directed her toward the tower her room was in. She took a couple of unsteady steps before starting the drunken weave down the pathway. He watched her for a moment, wishing he could go with her.

"Dude! Drinks!" Someone called from the bar.

Wyatt sighed. He hurried back to the bar and poured the beer as quickly as possible. It had way too much head, but he didn't care.

He picked up the bar phone and called security. "This is the tiki bar. I want to make sure a guest makes it up to her room okay. Her name's Cassie. She's coming up to the main tower. She's in room seven-thirty-two."

Security promised they'd look after her, but his stomach still twisted. He should have just abandoned the bar and walked her back. It would probably have cost him his job, but he didn't need the money. He liked this resort a lot, but there were others just like it all over the islands. It would be an inconvenience, but to make sure Cassie was safe would be worth it.

The thought surprised him. It had been a long time since he'd felt a connection like this with one of his flings. He'd had his share of women, yet he hadn't ever felt the need to abandon his bar to walk them home. Telling security had always been enough. The resort was one of the safest places he knew.

Yet, for some reason, he worried about Cassie. He wanted to make sure she was safe and that she had that extra glass of water. He wanted to make sure she was tucked carefully into bed, not just deposited inside her room. He wanted to take care of her.

Eight long minutes later the phone rang. It didn't even finish the full first ring before Wyatt had it to his ear.

"Cassidy Turner is safe in her room. Thanks for letting us know," the security guard told him. Wyatt's shoulders relaxed and his stomach no longer felt like solid ice.

"She didn't have anyone else in there, did she?" he asked, feeling a little dumb for asking. She didn't have a ring, and she was flirting with him, but that didn't mean anything.

He didn't want to get his hopes up only to find out she was here with her boyfriend who was planning on proposing. That had happened to him once. He didn't want a repeat.

"No one was there," the guard told him. "It's rented to her and another chick."

Wyatt's chest loosened and the ice in his stomach finished melting. He smiled, feeling like he could breathe again. "Thanks."

The guard hung up, and Wyatt went back to pouring drinks. Another woman tried to flirt with him. She was just his usual type, beautiful and long-legged, but he wasn't interested. Two drinks later, she too slid her napkin with a room number across the bar. It went in the trash without a second glance.

He was too busy thinking of the woman in room seven-thirty-two.

5

Cassie

Cassie woke up with a headache the size of New York.

Luckily, it was just New York City-sized and not the entire state, but still a pretty horrific headache. The only reason it wasn't worse was the two glasses of water Wyatt had her drink at the bar as well as the one before bed.

She didn't remember much about coming back to her room, but she did remember that she needed to drink a glass of water. It was one of the very few things that she remembered.

"Did I really do that?" she asked the empty room.

She groaned as she remembered sliding the sexy bartender her room number. Her head ached, and her mouth felt like it was stuffed with cotton. It took more effort than she expected to roll over and check the little alarm clock to see what time it was.

A little after ten in the morning.

Not only had she gotten drunk, propositioned a bartender and failed, but she had also slept in.

Brianna would be so proud of her.

There was a soft knock on the door.

"I don't need any housekeeping!" Cassie yelled, but it came out more like a croak. She needed another glass of water and a new head. This one hurt too much.

The door cracked open.

"No housekeeping!" Cassie called out again.

"I need to grab my swimsuit," Brianna said through the crack in the door. "Is it safe to come in, or can you just hand me my suitcase?"

"You can come in," Cassie told her. "I'm all by myself."

Cassie heard the Brianna push the door open further and then the soft thump as it shut behind her.

"Are you hungover?" Brianna asked upon seeing Cassie still in bed.

"Maybe."

"You are!" Brianna clapped her hands with joy. "I'm so proud of you!"

"You're proud of me having a raging headache and feeling like I want to puke?"

"Yup." Brianna grinned at her. Cassie pulled the pillow up and over her face.

"I want to hear all about it," Brianna said, sitting on the foot of Cassie's bed. When Cassie didn't say anything, Brianna poked her foot until she groaned.

"If you get me a water and some aspirin, I will tell you." Cassie's voice was muffled by the pillow.

"Done." Brianna got up, pulled a tepid Gatorade from the mini-fridge and a bottle of painkillers from her own bag. She unscrewed the lid and handed the bottle to Cassie.

Cassie slowly sat up and took the pain meds with a sip of Gatorade. It felt good on her throat. Thank god Wyatt had gotten some water into her last night. Now that she was sitting with some liquid in her hands, she didn't feel as bad as she had been afraid she would.

"So?" Brianna bounced on the edge of the bed like a little kid.

"So, his name's Wyatt." Cassie took another sip of Gatorade. "I totally embarrassed myself. I gave him my room number, and he didn't take it."

"Seriously? That jerk." Brianna crossed her arms. "I'd have taken it."

"No, I think it's actually good," Cassie said thoughtfully. "I was pretty wasted. He wants to meet me for lunch."

"Wait, you didn't say anything about lunch." Brianna's anger dropped and was quickly replaced by a smile. "You have a date!"

"I guess I do," Cassie replied slowly. Her eyes went wide. "What the heck am I going to wear? What if he doesn't like sober me? What if I embarrass myself again?"

"First, you'll wear the blue sundress we got yesterday. Second, if he liked drunk you, he'll adore sober you. And third, who cares?" Brianna asked. "He's one guy on an island you won't be back on for a long time."

Cassie considered that for a moment. Brianna was right of course, but the nervous butterflies and tightness in her chest didn't really let up. She liked Wyatt. The alcohol had undoubtedly helped her confidence, but she'd felt comfortable around him. She'd actually flirted with him. It was some of her best flirting if she did say so herself.

It didn't say much for her skills that she knew it was terrible. She'd made jokes about screaming orgasms and sex on the beach. It was low hanging fruit, but it had made him laugh.

That laugh was the thing that had her getting out of bed.

The way he smiled at her, his green eyes full of light. He'd made her feel beautiful. Even if he'd turned her down.

"Okay. Blue dress. Strappy sandals. They're feminine, but not slutty. And they're easy to walk in." Brianna went to the closet and started pulling things out. "Sexy undies. You can pick those out."

Cassie sipped on the Gatorade but otherwise didn't move.

"You should probably shower, too," Brianna said, crinkling her nose. "You smell like fruity booze."

Cassie gave her a slow blink.

"I mean, I guess he's a bartender. Maybe he's into that kind of thing." Brianna shrugged and managed to dodge the pillow Cassie lobbed at her head.

With a groan, Cassie swung her feet off the bed. She was definitely hungover, but the Gatorade was helping. She was still wearing her cherry sundress from the night before. It was all wrinkled now, and there was something pink spilled down the front.

Cassie turned on the shower and ran cold water in the sink to soak her dress. She hoped the stain hadn't set. She was rather fond of the cherry dress. It was her brave, fun, flirty dress now. Even if she never wore it out again, just knowing it was in her closet would give her confidence.

She'd been flirty and carefree once. She could do it again.

The hot shower water felt like life flowing back into her, and when she emerged twenty minutes later, her skin was pink, and she actually felt a little hungry. It was a freaking miracle, and one that Cassie wasn't about to waste.

Brianna had left her blue sundress out on the bed. Hotel stationery sat next to the dress with Brianna's curly, loopy handwriting.

Have fun. Be crazy. The room is all yours for the rest of the day!

PS. Bachelorette party tonight! Don't be late!

Cassie shook her head and slid into the silky blue dress. The fabric hung to her curves and felt see-through. Brianna had assured her that it was not see-through under various lights, but Cassie still felt naked.

She brushed her hair and let it air dry while she put on a light layer of makeup. Just some smoothing sunscreen, mascara and eyeliner. And a little lip gloss. Lip gloss with color was always a good touch. It was also one of the few makeups encouraged by corporate.

Cassie finished three minutes before she needed to leave in order to get to the Cantina by noon.

She stood in front of the full-length mirror, making sure the dress really was opaque and that her mascara was in place.

"You can do this. You are fun. You are cute. You are sexy," she told her reflection. Her stomach was twisting, and it had nothing to do with the drinks from last night. She was nervous. "If it's awful, you leave and never see him again. No one is judging you here."

She took a deep breath, put her room key in a small beach bag, and headed down to the Castaway Cantina. It was almost noon.

Cassie walked quicker the closer she got. What if he didn't show up? What if he wasn't so attractive without two glasses of wine in her? What if he realized just how boring and old she was?

What if she had said something super dumb while drunk?

Cassie tried not to think about it. She told herself not to worry. There was no real consequence here. Unlike at home

where she had her job, her reputation, and her hotel's reputation all on the line. This was her chance to try something
new. She didn't have to be perfect here. She could
be human.

Castaway Cantina came into view. It was a small building
with large open windows to let in the sea air. It was a buffet
style eating area with seats both inside and outside. The
atmosphere was relaxed and soft music played overhead.

Cassie checked her watch. It was ten seconds past noon.

She didn't see him in the restaurant. She didn't see him
walking up the path or sitting at a chair near the entrance. He
wasn't here.

She tried to tell her self that it didn't matter. She'd been
drunk, and he had been kind. It wasn't a big deal. It was no
huge loss.

Yet the ache in her chest and the burning in her eyes said
otherwise. Deep down, his rejection hurt.

"You came."

She turned to see him walking up the path to greet her.
Today he wasn't wearing the employee outfit. Instead, he
wore a pair of dark blue swim trunks and a really nice short
sleeved shirt that showed off his broad shoulders and lean
waist. He pushed a pair of sunglasses up into his windswept
hair.

Her heart skipped a beat, and the tightness in her chest
changed. Now it was nerves instead of heartbreak trying to
strangle her.

"Hi." It was probably the lamest thing she could have said,
but seeing him standing there, she didn't know what else
to say.

He smiled, and her heart went into overdrive.

"How are you feeling?" he asked.

Having him on this side of the bar was almost overwhelming. He had such presence that it was hard not to get drawn

into his orbit. Cassie found herself unconsciously stepping toward him, wanting to touch him.

"I'm actually feeling pretty good," she replied. "I have a feeling it's due to the water you had me drink. Thank you. I'm not usually a drinker."

He grinned at her. "Could have fooled me."

"No, I didn't," she replied. "I didn't fool anyone. I'm a lightweight. And I apologize if I said or did anything inappropriate last night. I'm not used to being drunk."

"If you're used to being drunk, that's typically a problem," Wyatt replied. His eyes crinkled in a smile as he looked at her. "You were fine last night. A real lady."

She scoffed. "Real ladies don't give out their room numbers."

"The kind of ladies I like do." Light sparkled in his green eyes, and Cassie felt her knees go wobbly. Suddenly she was thinking of screaming orgasms that had nothing to do with alcohol.

"So you like your ladies dirty?" Her voice wavered a little bit. The heat curling up around the base of her spine from the way he looked at her was affecting her vocal cords.

He grinned. "Dirty. Clean. I like them all."

Cassie's brain drew blank. This flirting thing was hard and she wasn't sure she was doing it right. Was she dirty enough for him? Was she getting in way over her head with trying to flirt with a man like this? He had experience with women. She had corporate policies memorized.

Was she really what a man like Wyatt would want?

"Lunch?" she asked, changing the subject to something she was more comfortable with. She could handle lunch.

"I'd love to." He offered her his arm like a knight in shining armor. She laughed, and he escorted her into the buffet.

Cassie picked out fruit and a baked fish dish. She only

took one of the coconut macaroons and felt guilty about ruining her diet the entire way back to their table.

Wyatt on the other hand, chose a cheeseburger, fries, and a small side salad. He had three desserts set off to the side on a separate plate.

"You know you can eat anything you want here, right?" he said, eyeing her healthy plate.

"Vacation calories definitely do count," she told him. "Besides, I have to fit into my bridesmaid dress in two days. After that, I can eat whatever I want."

"I'm sure you'll look great in the dress," he said, his eyes going over her body as she sat down. The gesture was intimate in a way that made Cassie want to blush and at the same time stick out her chest to give him a better view.

"You can't possibly eat like this every day," Cassie said, picking up a fork.

He shook his head. "Only when I eat here," he admitted. He took a big bite of hamburger. "So, where are you from?"

"Arizona." She nibbled daintily at her fruit. "You?"

He shrugged. "The easiest answer is California. I was born in Kansas, raised in Utah, and went to school in California. Now, I'm here."

"What brought you to the Caribbean?" Cassie asked, genuinely curious. She placed him in his mid-to-late forties, but incredibly fit. Something about him spoke to education and life experience that didn't fit with his current job description. He wasn't just a beach-bum bartender. There was too much age around his eyes.

"This is where I want to be," he told her. "I spent enough time in offices and sales meetings to last a lifetime. I hated it. I wanted to be here every second instead. So when I got the chance, I ditched my modern, high-stress job and ran away to the beach."

Cassie had often imagined running away. She'd wanted to

open a small hotel that was all her own. The big chain was so corporate and demanding. They wanted her to always be presentable and ready. There were rules for everything. She lived and breathed rules at work. It was a big part of why her friends wanted her to relax this week. When she let herself, she'd daydreamed of running away from it all just like Wyatt said he did.

"Do you regret it at all?" she asked, her fork hovering over her plate.

His green eyes met hers and held.

"Never for a second. Best decision of my life."

Something inside her trembled. A possibility was forming in her mind, but she didn't dare let it grow. Just because he escaped his life didn't mean she could.

"What do you do now?" She didn't look away from him. She couldn't look away from him. "Just serve drinks at the resort?"

One side of his mouth curved into a smile. "I do whatever I want," he replied. "Right now, that's serving drinks. Tomorrow, it might be teaching surfing. I've been considering expanding my horizons. Maybe even deep sea fishing."

"That sounds wonderful." Cassie sighed.

"What do you do?" He finished off his burger and leaned back in his chair.

"You mean when I'm not getting drunk at hotel bars?"

Wyatt laughed, and Cassie felt a little pride. She was getting better at this flirting thing.

"I run a hotel. A StarTree in Phoenix." She shrugged and picked at her fruit.

"Do you like it?" Wyatt asked. She felt his emerald eyes on her, even as she stared at her fruit.

"Sometimes," she admitted honestly. "I like the hotel part. I like setting things up and making sure everything runs smoothly. I'm always busy. For the most part, I like the customers. I like interacting with them and fixing things, so their trip is better."

"And you don't like?"

Cassie sighed. "It's corporate. There's no flexibility or freedom. I have to present the StarTree image at all times. I have to live, think, and breathe StarTree rules. It's a little stifling."

She was surprised she was admitting to that. Especially without alcohol in her system. It had to be Wyatt. He was the reason she was spilling her guts. He probably had bartender magic. Everyone spilled their secrets to the bartender.

She cleared her throat. "Anyway, thank you for taking care of me last night. I'm really sorry about getting so drunk."

He let her change the subject. "It was a pleasure last night," he assured her. "I wouldn't have asked for lunch if it wasn't."

Warmth filled her chest, and Cassie smiled. "So, what would happen if I gave you my hotel number now?"

The corners of Wyatt's mouth turned into a confident smile. "I'd teach you how to make a screaming orgasm."

Cassie's heart pitter-pattered out of control. Her girl parts reacted in ways she wasn't used to. Her nipples went hard. "Wow. Okay."

Wyatt chuckled. "I don't think you're ready."

"I'm very ready," Cassie protested. "I'm beyond ready."

"And that's why you're blushing?" He tipped his chin and waved to someone behind Cassie. "By the way, you have someone watching you."

For a moment, Cassie thought it might be Lorna. Lorna would be the worst person to see her while talking to a hot man. Lorna would tease Cassie. She would mock her. She would then attempt to steal Wyatt away just because she could.

Cassie turned, bracing herself for the worst. Luckily, it

was just Janessa. Relief flooded Cassie. She waved, and Janessa gave her two big thumbs up.

"Friend of yours?" Wyatt asked, chuckling softly.

"Yeah. The bride."

"When's the wedding?" Wyatt asked as Cassie turned back around.

"Tonight's the bachelorette party, tomorrow is the rehearsal. Saturday is the big day," Cassie replied, going through the schedule in her head. Corporate rule number three: always know the schedule and stick to it.

"So, are you free until the party?"

That too warm, blushing feeling washed over Cassie again when he looked at her. He wanted to spend time with her. It made her light-headed and giddy.

"Yeah. I am. You said I'm not ready to bring you up to my room, but maybe we can go to your place."

"Slow down, tiger," he said gently.

Cassie felt her cheeks heat. She was pushing this too hard. She needed to slow down and enjoy herself. The point was to have fun this week. Not just to get laid. She was supposed to let loose and be a little wild, not sleep with anything that showed the slightest interest. She didn't have to be like her ex.

"Right. Um, an activity then? Outdoors, so I can't tempt you," Cassie replied. "Or you tempt me."

"You ever go jet-skiing?"

Cassie shook her head. "I'm not even a hundred percent sure what that is," she admitted.

Wyatt grinned. "I'm guessing you're not wearing a swimming suit under that dress." He eyed the dress appreciatively, and Cassie felt that familiar heat creep up again. "Meet me by the dock in fifteen minutes with your suit on. You can swim, right?"

"Of course I can swim," Cassie replied indignantly, crossing her arms.

Wyatt grinned and stood from the table. "I'll see you in fifteen then."

He winked and walked away, leaving her at the table. She sat there blinking for a moment, still trying to figure out what was happening.

Was this really happening? Had she managed to flirt herself into a date? Was this even a real date? She wasn't sure, but she wasn't about to waste the opportunity.

There was too much at stake. She might actually have fun.

6

Wyatt

Wyatt couldn't believe he'd turned her down. Again. She'd offered him another chance in her bed, and he'd said no. That he wanted to wait.

He was an idiot.

His body wanted her. He'd been glad that the table hid his obvious attraction to her. She was made for loving with her soft curves and warm smile. Today's dress was worse for his self-control than yesterday's dress. The dress was practically see-through, and he kept staring, hoping that he'd catch a glance of something.

It was a beautiful kind of torture.

And then she'd offered herself to him — screaming orgasms in her room.

Usually, after a suggestion like that, he would be the one dragging the girl up the stairs to her room. But those dates always ended with him leaving before she fell asleep. He didn't remember their names. They blurred together. While fun, they went quickly. They didn't mean anything to him.

He didn't want Cassie to blur. He wanted her to remain crisp and perfect in his memory. He wanted to take his time. He wanted to enjoy this.

It was different than his usual seductions.

It felt better.

Wyatt paused as he walked the length of the dock to where the jet-skis waited. What was he thinking? Cassie was just another tourist. She would leave in a couple of days. She would fade into another happy memory just like the rest. So why was he trying to make this last? Why did he want to take his time and actually get to know her?

He didn't have an answer for that.

You're just making it last longer, he told himself. That was the reason. He was making the seduction last. He was enjoying her and this way, he would have more time. She wouldn't just disappear after sex. This was a way to get three days instead of only one. He was trying something new.

Sure. That was it.

He put a mini-cooler from the bar and a hotel beach towel into the small storage area of the jet-ski he'd rented. He tried to wait patiently. To any observer, he looked calm, but inside, he was all butterflies and electric energy. Every person that stepped out onto the deck caught his attention. He checked his watch every thirty seconds, each time surprised to see that only half a minute had passed. To him, it felt like hours.

Finally, she arrived, right at the fifteen minute mark. She wore a long t-shirt and sandals. Her hair was pulled back up into a ponytail. She chewed on her lip as she approached the dock and then broke into a full-fledged smile as soon as she saw him.

"Hi."

It was the same greeting as before, and it made his stomach do happy cartwheels again.

"Hey. You have a swimsuit on?" he asked, hoping she'd show it to him.

"Yup." She nodded but didn't lift her shirt to show him. "That's the jet-ski, right? I've never been on one."

She stepped past him to look at the vehicle. The ocean breeze tugged at her shirt, exposing the curve of her butt and giving him a peek of her swimsuit. She was close enough to touch, and he had to take a deep breath and control himself. They had the rest of the afternoon. He could enjoy this and take his time.

"You ready?" he asked her. He handed her a life-jacket.

"I don't know how to do this," she replied. "I mean, I know how to put on a life-jacket. I don't know how to ride a jet-ski."

"Don't worry. I'll drive." Wyatt chuckled as he put on his own orange vest. He deftly swung a leg over the jet-ski and then motioned her to join him.

She swallowed and then tried to mimic his movements. She succeeded in nearly knocking them both into the water. The jet-ski rocked dangerously, and her arms flailed until she wrapped them around him.

He liked the way she felt wrapped around him. Her arms were stronger than he expected, but it could also be that she was afraid of falling in the water. She was warm and soft, pressed up against him. It was a good thing she sat behind him, or she would have something poking into her back for the rest of the ride.

"Sorry," she murmured. Her voice was soft in his ears. She shifted, keeping her grip tight on him. "Where are we going?"

"You'll see," he told her and started up the engine.

The jet-ski roared to life. He revved it a couple of times, feeling the vibrations rumble through the both of them. One of his previous dates had told him this was the best foreplay she'd gotten in years. That was before he'd had his way with her.

He moved slowly away from the dock before gaining speed. The open ocean beckoned to them. Caribbean blue water shimmered in the bright sunlight, and Wyatt hoped they would run into dolphins. Women always loved to see the dolphins.

Once they were in the open water, Wyatt opened up the engine. Cassie shrieked and held onto him, but when he risked a glance back, she was grinning from ear to ear. Her eyes sparkled with enjoyment. So Wyatt went faster.

He played in the waves, catching them to get air. She whooped with delight every time they went up in the air. Wyatt found her enthusiasm contagious. He sped across the water, giving her a fun-filled ride.

He wasn't just showing off. He actually had a destination in mind. There was a small sandy island just a few hundred yards from shore. It was usually used for private weddings or romantic picnics, but since it was an afternoon in the middle of the week, the island was empty.

It was the ideal spot to woo a woman.

"Oh, there's an island," Cassie said as they approached. She rose slightly on her feet to get a better look. "It's beautiful."

Wyatt beached the jet-ski on the soft white sand, making sure that he accounted for the tide. They wouldn't be here long, but the last thing he wanted was to lose a jet-ski. It wasn't that he couldn't afford to buy the resort another one, it was that he would never hear the end of it. Plus, they needed a way to get back home.

"Wow." Cassie stood looking along the beach. The place was more sand bar than an actual island. There were four palm trees and just a couple of shrubs in the center, but the tourists loved to have their own 'private' island for a few hours.

"Want a tour?" Wyatt asked, taking off his life-jacket.

"Sure," she replied with a grin. She carefully removed hers as well, setting it neatly in the sand beside his life-jacket. The edges of her shirt were wet from sea spray and clung to her skin. It was nearly impossible for Wyatt to pull his eyes away. All he could see was her curves and hints of smooth skin calling for his touch.

They walked along the small beach, with the trees to their left as they walked the circle of the island. The sand was warm beneath their feet with the sun hiding behind a small group of clouds.

"So, here we have some palm trees," he said, motioning to the small grove. "They provide shade and are the main attraction here on the island.

Cassie giggled. "How interesting!"

They walked for a bit, making small talk. She was so easy to talk to that he didn't mind that they kept circling the island.

"I don't have any kids. Janessa and Brianna do, but it never happened for me. It's part of the reason I got divorced," she was saying. She looked over at him and blushed crimson. "And now I'm being boring and just talking about myself. Sorry."

"Definitely not boring," Wyatt assured her. The fact that she was divorced didn't bother him. Many of the women he met were divorced. He grinned over at her. "You have any siblings?"

"Why? You want to know if I have a younger sister you can date?" she teased. She grinned at him. "I don't have a little sister. I have a little brother, but he's married."

"Aw shucks," Wyatt replied with a fake disappointed look.

"You?" Cassie asked. "Any siblings? Divorces?"

"No divorces and I'm an only child," he replied. "My mom died when I was little, so it was just my dad and me for a long time."

"That sounds like you are close," she said, looking down the beach like she was looking for something.

He nodded. "We were. He died when I was in college." His throat tightened, but he kept his head up.

"I'm sorry," she said softly.

"I wanted to be just like him for a long time. He was everything I wanted to be, and then he was gone." Wyatt didn't usually tell people this. He didn't talk much about his dad. The man had been a force of nature. He was always moving, always working. Wyatt had tried to do that for a long time, but it only burned him out.

That was why he was here. He wasn't his father. He didn't want to work himself into an early grave like his father had. He had to learn from his father's mistakes.

She looked thoughtful, taking him in again. "What kind of business did you have?"

"A small one," he said, waving his hand like he could brush the question away. He'd given her too much information about himself without realizing it. "I sold it."

"And now you're serving drinks in the Caribbean for fun. You just keep getting more interesting," she told him. "Layers and layers."

"Like an onion or a parfait?" he asked, referencing the movie Shrek.

"Parfait." She grinned at him. "You like making waffles?"

"You saying you want a sleep-over?"

"Maybe." She flushed a little bit and looked down at her feet. They'd walked the whole of the island several times, and they were back where they started with their life-jackets.

Wyatt grabbed the small cooler and towel from the jet-ski, took off his shirt, and sat in the warm sand. "Come sit with me."

She hesitated for a moment. Her face said it all. She didn't hesitate because she didn't want him, but because she couldn't believe this was real. He'd seen that look before, but it had never looked as good as it did on her. Her expression was innocent and excited. There was wonder in her face that made him feel like a god among men.

She settled in the sand beside him. Close enough that it was flirting, yet still enough distance to show she was nervous. She didn't do this kind of thing. She was a good girl, and the idea that he was helping her be bad was a powerful aphrodisiac.

"Here." He handed her a bottle filled with pink liquid. She held it and took a cautious sip.

"Sex on the beach." She grinned and took a bigger sip. Her eyes narrowed, and she looked at him. "Are you trying to get me drunk all the way out here on our own little beach?"

"Maybe," he replied with a shrug. Her eyes went wide, and he chuckled. "These are virgin drinks. I have to be able to drive you home."

She laughed and drank again without hesitation. "When you said we'd have 'sex on the beach,' this wasn't quite what I had in mind. It's good, just not quite what I was expecting."

"And what were you expecting?" This was the part where things got good. He could feel it in his bones. His voice came out low and deep.

She chewed on her bottom lip again. Desire flared up in her eyes, and he could see it battling her self-control. He hoped she would let the desire win.

"I was hoping for some sex on the beach like this." She leaned forward and kissed him on the lips. It was more peck than kiss. It went so fast that it didn't even register in a kiss in his mind before she had already pulled back.

7

Wyatt

Her lips pressed together, and her eyes were full of nervousness as she waited for him to respond. He could tell she wasn't used to being the one to initiate. If anything, the fact that she would do something so far out of her comfort level made it clear how much she liked him.

She swallowed hard, still waiting for his reaction.

"I think we have more time than that," he said, reaching a hand out and cupping his fingers around the back of her neck. Slowly, he pulled her to him, giving her a real kiss this time.

Her lips tasted of the drink and her own blend of sweetness. He teased her closed lips with his tongue, and slowly she opened to him. Her soft moan sent shivers of desire down his spine that had him wishing they had a bed and not just a sandy beach with a towel.

He pulled back to see her sitting in the sand with her eyes

closed. Her cheeks flushed such a pretty shade of pink, and her chest heaved up and down.

Slowly, her eyes fluttered open, and she looked at him with those big brown eyes of hers. Long lashes framed their warmth. Chocolate wasn't an accurate description for them. They were warmer, more delicious. There was a hint of gold and green near her pupils that hinted at depths still to be explored.

And he definitely wanted to explore her depths.

She moved slowly, as if unsure of what she was doing. She sat up and then proceeded to straddle his lap. Her eyes stayed on him, watching for any hint that he was going to pull away. At this point, the only thing that would be able to pull him away was rampaging sharks.

And they were firmly on dry land.

Her weight settled on his lap, her arms going to his shoulders. Her breath was quick and nervous, yet the smile on her face said it was the good kind of nerves.

She moved her hands down to the hem of her long shirt and pulled upward, taking the shirt from her body. She paused when it was free of her and then carefully tossed it to the side. In front of him was a glorious sight.

She wore a deep burgundy-colored bikini top. The halter-top design held everything perfectly in place. It wasn't skimpy or sexy, but classy. The swell of her breasts barely peeked out from the dark fabric to give just a tasteful hint of what was underneath. She could have worn it to a family-friendly resort, and no one would raise an eyebrow. It was stylish and wholesome, yet with her breasts right in front of his face like this, he would have said it was the sexiest bikini he'd ever seen.

"Wow," he whispered, forcing himself to look up from her chest. "Are you sure you don't do this all the time?"

"I don't," she assured him with a nervous laugh. "You just make me feel comfortable."

"Good." He wrapped his arms around her and drew her in for another kiss. This time, she was more open. Her tongue found his, and she let him taste her. She nibbled on his bottom lip, making him groan with pleasure.

She rocked her hips into his lap, enjoying the hardness that was growing between her legs. She released him from the kiss, pulling back just enough so that she could see his face. Her bottom lip went between her teeth as she took a deep breath.

And she reached up and undid the tie to her swim top. The top stayed perfectly in position, but the two neck straps fell to the side. Her eyes lingered on his face as she reached behind her and undid the bra-strap.

Her elbows held the top in place for a moment, as if she were debating really doing this. She stopped biting her lip and tossed the top to land on her shirt.

"Wow." He was at a loss for words. She was stunning. Gorgeous. Perfect.

His hands cupped her perfection, thumbs grazing the perky nipples. Her breathing was fast and shallow, but she wasn't pulling away. If anything, she was pushing into him. She rocked her hips against his, making him groan again.

"And you say you haven't done this before," he whispered, ducking his head and taking a nipple into his mouth. He loved the small shudder that ran through her body. He loved the way her hands went to his hair and pressed his face into her chest. He loved the low moan she made when he flicked his tongue against the tight little nub in his mouth.

"Don't stop," she whispered, arching her back and letting her head fall back. Grinding hips, whimpers, and the grip of her fingers in his hair all told him he was making her feel good. The sensation of her grinding into him and the soft skin of her breasts was making him feel good as well.

With his mouth still on a breast, he moved his hand from her hip forward. His thumb ran along the edge of her swimsuit bottom. It too was burgundy with a conservative cut. His fingers slid across the slick fabric of her suit, moving lower with every stroke.

She froze when he brushed her middle. He pulled away from her breast, looking up at her. She stopped breathing for a second and looked down at him.

She nodded.

With a slow grin, he brushed that spot again and was rewarded with a low whimper. He licked his lips as he slid his hand inside the swimsuit bottoms. His fingers found what he was looking for and began to stroke and tease.

Her stomach tensed and her hips rocked against him without her realizing it. He watched her face loving the way she twisted her mouth in pleasure. Her eyes closed, but her lashes fluttered as he gave her the path to ecstasy. Her breathing came fast and hard, and her arms tightened around his shoulders. He moved his thumb just a little bit faster.

Watching her come was nearly as good as an orgasm for himself. She cried out, her voice filling the air as she shook and fell into him. He almost lost it himself watching her. Every shiver and whimper was a glimpse into what heaven looked like.

Her forehead came to rest on the curve of his shoulder. Her breaths were hard and fast. Every once in a while she would still shudder slightly.

"I've never..." she gasped. She raised her head, and their eyes met. "I've never had one that good."

"Just wait for what comes next," he promised. He loved the way her pupils dilated, and another shiver rippled through her body.

"Oh boy."

He grinned at the way she said it. She sounded almost reverent.

He kissed her again, taking his time. He figured they had all the time in the world.

Which was a mistake.

The radio on the jet-ski started to squawk. "Jet-ski One, Jet-ski One, come in."

She pulled away, her eyes going to the beached jet-ski. "Should we get that?"

"Just ignore it," he told her, pulling her back into him.

"Jet-ski one, jet-ski one, come in," the radio continued to screech. "Cassie, are you there?"

Upon hearing her name, her eyes lost the bedroom look, and her body went rigid. The post-orgasm relaxation disappeared entirely. Wyatt shot daggers from his eyes at the radio.

"I need to answer that," she said, rolling away from him. She grabbed her swim top before going to the jet-ski radio. She put it on before she answered as if the person on the other side would be able to see her nakedness.

She fumbled with the radio for a moment but quickly figured it out. "This is Cassie. Over."

"Are you okay?" a female voice asked over the radio.

"Yeah," Cassie replied. "Janessa?"

"The jet-ski guy said you went off almost two hours ago. You were supposed to be here twenty minutes ago, and it's not like you to be late. I was half afraid you were dead. You sure you're okay?"

Cassie scrunched up her face and looked down at her watch. Her eyes went wide. "Wow. I lost track of time. I'll be there as soon as I can."

"Okay. I'll tell the jet-ski guy," the radio crackled. "Hurry back. There's a couple that wants to rent it."

Wyatt looked down at his own watch. He couldn't believe

so much time had passed. They must have spent more time talking than he'd thought. Which never happened. It was always physical with the women he brought here. Yet, he'd spent the majority of his time with Cassie just enjoying her company. Learning about her. It had felt like no time at all. And now all he wanted was more. One taste of her was not enough.

She walked across the beach to him and picked up her shirt. She shook the sand out and slid it over her body, hiding her glorious curves from him. His body ached with need for release. He half wanted just to grab her and take her right there on the beach.

But he didn't. Instead, he stood up and gathered up their drinks and the unused towel.

"I'm sorry," she said as he opened up the storage area and put everything away.

He looked over at her to see remorse on her face. The responsible part of her was warring with the fun-loving side of her. It was clear the responsible side was winning. He had a feeling the responsible side had a lot more practice.

"It's okay," he told her. "Rain check?"

"Yes, please." The grin that blossomed onto her face made his knees go a little weak, and once again he considered just tackling her into the sand and making her his.

She helped him push the jet-ski around and into the shallow water before the two of them got back on and started the engine. She looked back wistfully at the spot on the beach with the sandy imprints of their bodies and sighed.

Wyatt took the direct route home rather than the fun-filled zig-zag one he'd made to the island. Cassie had her cheek pressed into his back, her arms wrapped around him. They didn't say much, which was fine as it was hard to talk over the roar of the engine.

He slowed down as they approached the dock and she

pulled away from him. He missed her gentle warmth against his back. He let the engine sputter and die at the pier.

He got off first and offered her his hand. She took it with a smile, their eyes meeting. Her dismount from the jet-ski was much more graceful than her climb on. No one even came close to falling into the water.

"Do you work tonight?" she asked, standing close to him. She didn't let go of his hand.

"Yes. But, I'd love to see you after."

"I might have a couple of drinks," she said. "You know, bachelorette party and all. You aren't going to turn me down again, are you?"

The ache in his pants made that a big no. "Room seven-thirty-two."

She grinned wide and went up on her tiptoes to kiss him. This time, it was sweet. Her tongue caressed his for only a second before she pulled back with a grin.

"I'm going to hold you to it," she told him, taking a step down the dock.

"I certainly hope you do." He grinned at her.

She did an adorable little happy wiggle before turning and heading down the dock. Her friend from earlier appeared and motioned to her. The other woman looked down the dock and gave him an appraising look before the two of them left.

He let out a long sigh. He missed her kisses already. He wished his shift was already over so that he could find her and finish what they'd started on the beach. Although, he had a feeling that even if they had finished on the beach, he would still want her just as much.

She just had that effect on him.

8

Wyatt

The jet-ski guy was not pleased with Wyatt for being so late. Luckily, it was nothing that couldn't be fixed with a little bit of money and a promise to never do it again. It was a false promise, and they both knew it. Wyatt always did it again.

Wyatt headed back down the path through the pool area toward the employee locker room. There, he would change into his dark polo shirt and khaki slacks work outfit and head to the bar for his upcoming shift.

His phone chirped in his pocket, and he pulled it out to see a message from his boss.

Scheduling change. See the front desk.

Wyatt groaned. Scheduling changes were never good. It usually meant he had to change to the pool bar. He liked working at the tiki bar or the lobby. He didn't like working the pool bar nearly as much because all his tips came back wet. He didn't need the tips, but carrying wet money around was never pleasant.

He veered from his course, changing direction to head to the front desk rather than the employee area. He cut through one of the hotel's lush gardens and walked quickly past pools filled with relaxing guests. A couple of women peeked over dark sunglasses and smiled at him.

Wyatt just kept walking. Any other day, he would have stopped and winked. Today, his thoughts were on Cassie. The way her dark hair caught the sunlight. The slight flush her cheeks took when she was excited.

He hoped to see her excited again soon.

The front lobby was empty. Wyatt walked up to the main desk and looked around, not seeing any employees. He frowned, checked his watch, and looked around again. The workers were probably helping a guest. He peered over the desk, looking for a note about his scheduling change.

That's when the hair on the back of his neck stood up. This was how a rabbit felt when a hawk circled overhead.

"They're getting me some champagne," a woman's voice said from behind him.

Wyatt slowly turned to see an attractive woman lick her lips at him. She was too perfect to be real. Her boobs were too big, her waist too narrow, her nose too perfect, and her hair too big. She was beautiful in a plastic kind of way. It made him appreciate Cassie's natural beauty even more.

"Ah," he said, glancing at his watch again.

The woman took a step closer. "The chocolate covered strawberries are already up in my room."

Wyatt swallowed hard. "That's nice."

The woman ran a finger down his chest. "That's a great shirt. You must work out," she murmured, sidling in close to him. She bit her lower lip and looked up at him through fake eyelashes.

Wyatt took a step back.

"Ma'am, I just work here." Usually, he called customers "miss" rather than "ma'am." The older women appreciated the gesture that he thought they were younger than they were. Here, he used ma'am intentionally.

"Oh, don't ma'am me. You can call me Lorna. And you definitely don't look like you work here. Not with that shirt," Lorna replied, fluttering her eyelashes. She flattened her palm against his chest and started to head south. She grinned at him like she was about to give him a tremendous gift.

He grabbed her wrist as she passed his naval. "Ma'am, this is inappropriate. I work here," he repeated, gently pulling her hand from his waist.

Where was that front desk staff?

Lorna giggled, throaty and sexual. "I'm supposed to go to a stupid bachelorette party, but for you..." She ran her eyes up and down his body and grinned. "Want to go up to my room and have some of that champagne?"

"Ma'am, I have to work," Wyatt told her firmly, taking a step away from her. She looked like a cat hunting a mouse. Him moving away was just part of the challenge.

"Wyatt? What are you doing here?"

Wyatt turned to see Annette come up to the desk. She was an older woman that worked the front desk during the week instead of going into retirement. She liked Wyatt, and he was glad she was the one working the front desk. She was a no-nonsense kind of woman.

"There was a schedule change," he said, grateful that there was now a witness to this guest pawing at him.

"I don't have anything up here," Annette said, looking around. "James is in the break room, though."

"He was supposed to leave me a scheduling change,"

Wyatt replied. He took three quick steps away from the feral woman next to him. "There's nothing up here?"

Annette rummaged around the desk as Wyatt attempted to put a little more space between the overly-sexual guest and himself.

"Huh. You really do work here. The shirt threw me. I thought it was designer," the woman said, looking over his shirt. She pouted her overly puffed-up lips. "Darn. That's no fun."

She crossed her arms and walked off, shaking her hips with every step.

"What did you say to her?" Annette asked, watching the woman saunter away.

"I told her no," Wyatt replied, straightening out his shirt.

"She doesn't look like she gets told that very often," Annette said. "Be careful with that one. She's trouble."

"Trouble?" Wyatt asked.

"She's one of those problem guests," Annette told him. "She insisted she had champagne ordered and paid for, but there was no record or receipt of it. She threw a big hissy fit about it, threatening to tell my manager and write up a bad review. She wanted me to just give up and give her free champagne to make her happy."

"Did you give her the champagne?" Wyatt asked.

"Nope. Why do you think she was so eager to walk off? I came back without the bottle," Annette replied with a proud grin. "She's worse than my two-year-old grandson. I don't give into him either, and he's much cuter."

Wyatt chuckled and glanced at the door as if the woman might return and try to capture him again.

"I'm going to go find James before I'm late," Wyatt told Annette. "If you see that lady again, do not give her my number."

Annette chuckled. "No problem. Have a good shift!"

Wyatt waved and hurried to the break room. He was going to have to run so he wouldn't be tardy for his shift. It wouldn't be his fault, but James would still make him pay for it. James loved to use his power over his employees as much as possible. James didn't know who Wyatt actually was and that was a good thing. The man was petty enough as it was. He seemed to enjoy making Wyatt's life difficult.

If James knew that Wyatt was a billionaire, the man would either make Wyatt's schedule far too easy in order to suck up to Wyatt, or too hard to make Wyatt pay for working when he didn't have to. Neither sounded pleasant. It was better just to keep it a secret as he did with everyone.

Wyatt hurried into the break room. It wasn't much of a room, just a couple of couches and an ancient cracked TV, but it was away from guests. James sat on the couch watching a rerun of an old game show when Wyatt walked in.

"What are you doing here?" James asked in crisp Queen's English. "You're going to be late."

"I don't know where I'm supposed to be," Wyatt replied, doing his best to keep a calm voice. Lorna had definitely rattled him. "There wasn't anything at the front desk about the schedule change."

James sighed. "Miranda called in sick. You're taking her spot," James told him. His eyes went back to the TV.

"And what was Miranda supposed to be doing?" Wyatt asked. He couldn't believe this man was a manager some days. If this were his company, James wouldn't be a manager. Not with this kind of attitude.

He had a feeling that Cassie would be much better. Everything about Cassie was better.

"Private party at the Oceanside Bar," James said, his eyes on the TV. "You're the private bartender for a bachelorette party. Don't be late."

"Bachelorette party?" Hope sprang up in Wyatt's chest.

"Yes. Get going." James glanced over at him. "And nice shirt. Looks expensive."

Wyatt glanced down at his shirt and realized it was one of his good ones. No wonder Lorna hadn't believed he was a lowly hotel employee. He was wearing a shirt that cost more than a hotel worker made in a week. He had wanted to look good for Cassie, so he'd worn one of his nicer shirts. Unfortunately, it was one of his shirts from his billionaire days.

Lorna had seen that shirt and thought he had money. That was why she'd come onto him so hard. It used to happen all the time when he was known as the billionaire playboy. Women used to hear the name Wyatt Landers, of Land, Inc., and suddenly give him all their attention.

It was something that he didn't miss from his old life. Being targeted for his wealth had always made him question every relationship in his life. Until he came to the islands, he wasn't sure who was his friend and who was his *money's* friend.

Life as a bartender was so much simpler. So much more fun.

James was already back into his TV show and didn't see Wyatt grin and hurry to the locker room area to quickly change before heading to the bar.

Was he going to be the bartender for Cassie's party? He hoped so. That would make his night so much better. It wouldn't be work if it were with her. He couldn't wipe the goofy smile off his face as he stripped and changed into his hotel approved khaki slacks and a black polo.

He couldn't wait to see Cassie. Just thinking of her put a smile on his face. He put his nice shirt in the locker and wondered for a moment what Cassie would think if she knew who he really was. Would she be interested in his money? Or him?

Would he want her if she was interested in his money? He

loved that she liked him just the way he was. She didn't look at him like a meal ticket. She looked at him like a person.

He'd never even asked himself if he wanted to tell a woman before. Every guest he'd been with had been a quick vacation fling. There was no way he would ever reveal his true nature to those women. Yet, he was thinking about it with Cassie.

Wyatt shook his head and slammed the locker shut. He was getting ahead of himself. They'd just met and had a great afternoon on the beach. That didn't mean they were ready to get married and share a bank account.

However, he hoped they were ready to share a drink because, with a little bit of luck, he was going to be her bartender for the evening.

9

Cassie

"Not bad," Brianna said, looking around the bar. "Not bad at all."

Cassie had to agree. The Oceanside bar was nice. They had a private table off to the side of the room with the bar to themselves. There was a window with seating looking out over the ocean and a small dance floor off to the side. It wasn't much, but it would be a fun place to dance later. There was a karaoke machine as well, but Cassie was hoping they didn't bring it out tonight.

"I wish we could have gotten the private table at the Platinum Club, but they were all booked," Janessa said, looking around with just a hint of disappointment. "This will work though. This will be fun."

"Damn straight," Brianna replied. "We're going to have a blast."

Cassie nodded in agreement, raising her glass of water to

clink with Janessa's fruity cocktail. It was then that Brianna crowned Janessa with a crown made of penises.

"Is it 'penises' or 'pensisi'? Or maybe 'penii'?" Janessa wondered, sipping on her second drink. She had a straw and was sucking it down. "Like octopus and octopi."

"Penises," Cassie replied, putting a hot pink sash over Janessa's head. "Definitely penises."

Janessa nodded and took another sip of her drink. She adjusted her crown, giggling as she touched the erect penis in the center.

"Speaking of pensisisis," Janessa stumbled over the word. "You are positively glowing, Cassie."

"Am I?" Cassie tried to sound nonchalant, but she knew why she was glowing. It was because she'd had the best orgasm in her life just a mere hour ago.

"It's that guy," Brianna said, a big grin filling her face. "The bartender."

"You did look glow-y coming off the jet-ski, but I thought it was just sunshine and sea air." Janessa stepped closer to Cassie, squinting her eyes and peering hard. "You got some. On a jet-ski?"

"Spill," Brianna advised. "Before everyone else gets here. Otherwise, you'll have to tell the whole crowd. I'm sure Katy would love to hear all about this."

Cassie wrinkled her nose at both her friends, but she knew they would be relentless. Better to get it out now.

"He took me on a jet-ski out to a private island," she told them. "We made out."

"You did more than that, happy-face girl," Janessa informed her. She finished off her drink.

"He might have felt me up a little," Cassie said, feeling her face start to heat. "We would have done more, but *someone* interrupted us." She gave a pointed look to Janessa.

"Me?" Janessa's eyes went wide, and her mouth opened. "You were going to get some?"

Cassie nodded solemnly.

"Well, damn it. I didn't know that. I would never have interrupted if I had known." Janessa frowned and her crown tilted forward. "You were late. You're *never* late. I was fairly sure sharks had eaten you or you'd drowned. If I'd known you were getting some, I'd have paid the jet-ski guy off myself."

Cassie sipped on her water, grateful for the dim lighting of the bar. She was blushing. She wasn't big on kissing and telling. Corporate Rule 4: Keep guests lives as confidential as your own. And there was Corporate Rule 9: Be personable but not personal.

"It was pretty hot," Cassie admitted. "I haven't felt like this in years."

Screw the rules, she thought to herself with a smile.

"I think I like this new Cassie," Brianna said.

"Me too," Janessa agreed with a nod that nearly knocked her penis crown off her head. She pushed it back up and then looked at her empty glass. "I need another drink."

"You're going to have some water," Cassie told her. "Then you can have another drink. It's a marathon, not a sprint."

Janessa narrowed her eyes. "I want fun, Cassie. Not rule Cassie. More drinks!"

"She's right," Brianna told her, taking the empty glass. "We have all night. You need to pace yourself. I don't want you passed out in an hour."

Janessa sighed. "Fine. But I *am* getting drunk tonight. It's a rite of passage."

"Yes, you are." Cassie reached over and straightened out the penises on Janessa's head. "And we're going to have a blast."

"Good." Janessa's smile faltered. "Guys, don't let me do anything stupid. I love my Kyle. I just want to have a crazy fun night. Don't let me flirt too much or do anything I'll regret later."

"You got it," Cassie assured her. "A little bit of flirting, but nothing that you can't tell Kyle about in the morning."

"We'll just have to live vicariously through Cassie," Brianna teased. "She's already gotten more action than either of us on this trip."

Cassie rolled her eyes, but it was true. Janessa and Kyle were staying apart until their wedding night, and Brianna was recovering from leaving her last relationship. She was still in the "men are scum" phase.

"You need a drink," Janessa told Cassie. "I want more details about this guy, and you'll be all prim and proper until you have a drink. Something about Corporate rule-thirty seven."

"Thirty-seven has to do with laundry," Cassie informed her. Janessa rolled her eyes.

"I'll get her one," Brianna said. She glanced around. "Aren't we supposed to have a private bartender for this party?"

Janessa nodded, sucking on her empty drink straw like she might manage to get more alcohol to magically appear.

And that's when Wyatt walked through the door.

Cassie heated instantly at seeing him, and her girl-parts remembered just how he'd felt touching her. An echo of her orgasm shivered through her just being near him.

"Oh, hell yes," Janessa whispered, glancing from Wyatt back to Cassie. "Not only do I get a hot bartender, but he's totally going to bang a bridesmaid later. That's a thing, right? Like in a movie?"

"You need more water," Cassie said, taking the empty drink away from Janessa.

Janessa grinned at her. "Go get a drink, Cassie."

"Grab me one too," Brianna chimed in sweetly.

Cassie looked at the two of them and shook her head. They watched her like she was some sort of fascinating soap opera as she walked to the bar.

"I need two sex on the beaches and a glass of water," Cassie said, standing demurely at the bar.

"Today wasn't enough sex on the beach for you?" Wyatt asked, a grin filling his face as he pulled out two glasses and began prepping her drinks.

Cassie tingled in all the right places. "I could go for more."

"Me too," Wyatt replied, his green eyes settling on her and making it hard to breathe. He was so damn sexy. All she could think about was how good he'd felt underneath her on the beach.

"So, are you following me?" she asked him, watching his hands make the drinks. He was quick and sure in his movements, just like on the beach. "When you said you had to work later, I assumed it would be at the tiki bar. Not as my own personal bartender."

"Well, first of all, I'm *her* personal bartender," Wyatt explained, pointing his head toward Janessa. She giggled and gave a little wave. "And secondly, I was supposed to be at the tiki bar, but the schedule changed."

"So you're not following me?" Cassie put on a big fake pout.

"I can if you want me to," he replied, setting the two drinks out for her. He poured the water and added a wedge of lime to it.

"Maybe a little," Cassie admitted, taking one of the alcoholic drinks and sipping it up through a straw.

"Are you two going to be flirting the whole time?" Janessa asked, coming up and putting an arm over Cassie's shoulder. "I need my alcohol."

"The water's for her," Cassie told Wyatt, giving Janessa a grumpy side-eye.

Wyatt pushed the water with lime across the bar. "Well, I'm not really supposed to flirt too much with the brides. Boss says I broke one too many bride's hearts this year. But for you, I might make an exception."

He gave her a sexy wink that had Cassie feeling just a tiny bit jealous.

"I like him." Janessa chuckled and nudged Cassie. "Carry on."

With her water in hand, Janessa went to greet her guests. Various women were starting to arrive. Katy, Janessa's daughter came in wearing a tiny black dress. Everyone was dressed in short shorts and sexy tank tops or short skirts and sexy tank tops.

Cassie was glad Brianna had talked her into wearing her new shorts and the low cut top they'd purchased at the store. She also wore an oversized necklace that sparkled every time Cassie moved, also from Brianna. She was glad Brianna was there to dress her, make her look good, and fit in with the crowd. This was much better than the short sleeved, very conservative maxi dress she'd been planning on wearing.

Especially since Wyatt was checking her out when he thought she wasn't looking. That was a better confidence booster than three shots of tequila. For the first time since her divorce, she felt sexy, and there was someone in the room that agreed with her.

"Hey, you know it's my job to flirt with the guests, right?" Wyatt caught her wrist as she reached for Brianna's drink. His touch was gentle and she looked up into worried eyes.

"It's how you make tips," she replied. "I get it."

His serious eyes stayed on her. "Yes. But, I want you to know, it's all an act for them. Not for you."

Warm heat surged through Cassie's stomach and she felt

like giggling. He liked her. The little twinge of jealousy vanished like smoke in the wind. The way he looked at her right now told her that she was the center of his attention.

Wyatt released her hand and she missed his warmth immediately. She wondered if Janessa really needed a bartender for tonight, or if she could just steal him away for a few hours to finish what they'd started on the island...

"You coming, Cassie?" Brianna called from across the room. "You said you were getting me a drink, not making the rum yourself!"

Cassie decided to let the party keep the bartender for now. She was already planning on having him after the party anyway. She could wait.

Cassie gave Wyatt a wink as she picked up Brianna's drink and headed to mingle with the other bachelorette party goers. Other than Brianna, Katy, and Janessa, she didn't really know any of the women here, but they were all pleasant and excited to be on the island for the wedding.

It looked like it was going to be a great night.

"Cassie, we have a small emergency," Brianna whispered, motioning her over. Cassie handed Brianna her drink.

"What's wrong?"

"I got the wrong batteries," Brianna explained. "For the games. I need AA batteries and I brought AAA batteries."

"I saw a little shop near the lobby," Cassie said, checking her watch. "I'll go grab some. AA batteries, right?"

"Yes. Thanks," Brianna replied. "I'll keep setting up the games. Don't worry. I'll tell your bartender you're coming back."

"You better," Cassie told her with a smile. She glanced over at Wyatt, hoping to get his attention, but he was busy making drinks for the new guests. She thought about saying something, but the store was about to close. She had to hurry.

Cassie jogged across the lush gardens of the resort to the main lobby. The sun was already dipping behind the ocean and tiki torches burned against the starry sky above. Everything was warm and humid, but the gentle sea breeze made it comfortable.

Cassie made it to the small store just in time. She found a stack of overpriced AA batteries and headed back to the register. Along the way, she saw a condom selection.

She grabbed a box. Just because she was being fun-loving, risky Cassie didn't mean she had to be *that* risky. She could still be her prepared self and have fun. She made sure to grab the extra thin for her pleasure variety.

Luckily, the attendant didn't even blink an eye at her purchases. At least she wasn't wearing Janessa's penis crown while buying batteries and condoms. That might have at least made the clerk look up.

The party was in full swing by the time Cassie returned. She tucked the condoms deep in her purse, not wanting Janessa or Brianna to see them. She didn't mind their gentle teasing, but she also didn't want to give them ammunition either.

Music filled the room, and dance lights flickered around the dance floor. Cassie looked for Wyatt and found him behind the bar.

Unfortunately, Lorna had discovered him as well.

She wore a sexy little black dress that showed off more cleavage than Cassie could ever hope to achieve. The skirt was nearly nonexistent, and everything was skin-tight. Her blonde hair was piled up in a sexy, careless style on her head that Cassie suspected took a serious amount of time.

For the first time all night, Cassie felt plain. Her sparkly necklace felt gaudy. The shorts were too short and her low-cut tank top not low-cut enough. She didn't stand out against Lorna.

She was boring. Like usual. She wasn't worth attention. *Corporate Rule Five: Remain inconspicuous. Guests are here for the hotel, not the staff.*

Cassie hung toward the back of the room, hiding in the dark. This party and outfit weren't her. She didn't take risks. She wasn't the kind of girl to walk around with a box of condoms in her purse. She didn't sleep with men until at least the sixth or seventh date, and not until she was absolutely sure they weren't married and that they had a healthy 401K plan.

She didn't want to make the same mistakes she'd made with her ex-husband. She didn't need to be forgotten and unwanted again. She was the kind of person that worked in the background, getting things done. She didn't draw attention to herself. That's who Cassie was. She wasn't the kind of girl to take a chance like this. Stealing the bartender away from Lorna wasn't her style. She thought about leaving. Janessa would understand.

But then Wyatt looked at her. He looked up and across the room and found her. Relief filled his features that she was still there. He smiled at her. He ignored Lorna and her overflowing cleavage. In fact, Lorna looked downright annoyed that he wasn't giving her the time of day.

He was giving Cassie the time of day. He was giving her the whole damn clock.

Maybe the risk was worth it. There were things in life she regretted because she didn't take the chance. She'd always played it safe. That's why she was so good at her job. She liked being safe and her company rewarded that. No innovation, no mistakes, but no growth. She was stagnant.

She needed to be a little risky.

She needed to take a chance. And Wyatt looked like the best chance she had.

10

Cassie

Aunt Suzette sang in a key generally reserved for cats in heat.

The bar sang along, belting out the warbles and key changes along with Whitney Houston. Cassie would never hear "I Will Always Love You" the same way ever again. The song would forever be about tonight.

Cassie was having a blast.

The music was loud, the drinks strong, and the people fun. Everyone was singing and dancing under the glittering disco lights of the karaoke bar. Color and laughter filled the room.

"Time for blow-jobs!" Wyatt yelled from the bar. The women all turned and grinned.

Wyatt had eight shot glasses filled with liquor and topped with a healthy dose of whipped cream. He'd been calling out dirty shots all night. So far they'd had sex on the beach, banana "dick"uiri, buttery nipples, and a pink climax.

Every one of them had been delicious, but Cassie was

careful only to take half the shot. She was still embarrassed by the last time she'd had too much to drink.

"So, the rule here is no hands," Wyatt explained as women lined up at the bar. "You have to take the shot using just your mouth."

All the women giggled and grinned at Wyatt as he added a little more whipped cream to Janessa's shot glass.

"Show me how you do it," he told the women, winking at Aunt Suzette. Aunt Suzette was well over sixty and happily married, but she still blushed like a love-struck school girl.

"Oh, you," Aunt Suzette giggled. She snuggled up to the bar, wrapped her lips around the shot glass, tipped her head back, and took it like a champ. She carefully set the glass down and then licked her lips. "Yum. Better than the real thing."

Janessa howled with laughter. Katy stared, stunned. Aunt Suzette looked like the perfect church lady in a pale blue knit set and conservative skirt. She even had a pair of reading glasses hanging from a sparkly chain around her neck for reading the karaoke lyrics.

Wyatt cracked up from behind the bar as Aunt Suzette sashayed back to the karaoke stage.

"Bride's turn," Brianna announced, pushing Janessa forward. "Gotta get your practice in."

"Oh, I have plenty of practice," Janessa assured her. Katy made a disgusted face and shook her head.

Janessa squared her body to the bar, took a deep breath, and bent forward. Whipped cream covered her face when she stood back up.

"Looks accurate to me," Cassie quipped.

"That's how you know it was good." Janessa managed a dignified blink before taking a napkin from the bar. She dabbed politely at the whipped cream near her eyebrow. "How about you show us how it's done, Cassie."

Cassie looked up at Wyatt in time to see his pupils dilate and then constrict. He grinned at her, leaning against the bar with an interested look on his face.

Butterflies fluttered in Cassie's stomach. Everyone was waiting on her. She could do this. She'd never done this shot before, but if Aunt Suzette could manage to make it look easy, then Cassie could do a decent job.

Lorna elbowed in, pushing Cassie out of the way. "I'll show you how it's done."

Lorna made eye contact with Wyatt the entire time as she bent over, showing him her displayed cleavage. She wrapped her ruby-red lips around the shot glass, moaning slightly as she tipped her head back and swallowed.

Lorna set the glass back down, licked the rim of the glass suggestively, and stood back up. She adjusted her strapless corset-top and ran a pink tongue over her red lips.

"I still have those strawberries," she said to Wyatt, looking him up and down.

"I think it's Cassie's turn," he replied, turning his body away from her and sliding a glass toward Cassie. He looked at Cassie and grinned. "I want to see how she takes it."

The preference for Cassie was obvious. One of the drunker aunts snickered. "Oh man, he turned her down hard."

Lorna's cheeks flamed even in the dim lights of the bar. Her chin rose, and her seductive look turned petulant. She glanced around the bar at the other bachelorette party guests and then turned and flounced off.

Inwardly, Cassie winced. This wasn't something Lorna was going to forgive or forget. Lorna did not do well with humiliation, especially when it came from someone she believed was beneath her.

But at that moment, Cassie didn't care. Wyatt was looking at her with green eyes that made her heart flutter and her thighs tremble. Her body remembered the orgasm. She hummed with the way his skin felt against hers.

It was time for a blow-job.

Cassie carefully situated herself in front of the shot glass. Now that she'd seen several people take the shot, she had an idea of how it would work. She was careful. She had a plan.

She lowered her head, wrapped her lips around the top of the shot glass, and lifted her head. The shot was delicious. Amaretto and Irish cream mixed with the creamy sweetness of the whipped cream as it slid down her throat. She swallowed and carefully returned the shot glass to the bar top.

"You missed a little," Wyatt told her, reaching across the bar and wiping some whipped cream from the edge of her mouth. He then sucked that whipped cream from his fingers. Cassie flashed with heat.

Apparently, so did half the bar. Cassie could hear heavy breathing and appreciative murmurs from behind her. She glanced back to see Janessa and Brianna looking like proud parents. Lorna was glaring at her from a table.

"My turn," one of Kyle's attractive aunts shouted. "And I know I'm going to get whipped cream on my face if that means the bartender will lick it off."

The bar laughed, and the party resumed. Wyatt did not lick off the whipped cream from Kyle's aunt's cheek, but he did reach out and gently dabbed her face with a napkin. He was playing the part of a flirt, but it was obvious who he was actually interested in.

It was Cassie. Her knees trembled with the thought. He wanted her. He could have his pick of women in the room, and he chose her.

It was enough to make her want to sing.

"Brianna, come sing with me!" Janessa said with a laugh, tugging Brianna to the stage. "It's our turn!"

Brianna grabbed Cassie's hand. "You get to come too!"

The three of them giggled as they stepped up on the small stage. A screen with the words glowed brightly in front of them. Janessa handed everyone a microphone.

"What are we singing?" Cassie hissed to Brianna. The words hadn't come up on the screen yet.

"Dirty by Christina Aguilera," Brianna told her.

The music started, and dark words appeared on the bright screen. Cassie didn't need the lyrics. She already knew them. This was something she liked to belt in the shower when she pretended that she had a future as a rock star.

Cassie threw her hair around like she was a pop singer. Brianna and Janessa moved their hips, and all three of them undulated on the stage.

It was fun. And then Cassie made eye contact with Wyatt. It changed from fun to sexy as hell. Heat rushed through her core at the way he looked at her. He looked positively hungry. He liked what he saw up on that stage, and it wasn't Brianna or Janessa.

It was her.

He licked his lips, and his eyes watched her like she was the hottest thing he'd seen in months.

She winked at him and flipped her hair back over her shoulder before finishing up the song. She hadn't felt this way in a very long time.

Sexy. Desired. Wanted.

Wyatt, the sexy bartender who could have anyone, wanted her.

It was intoxicating and powerful. She finished the song with a flourish of her hips. The crowd clapped and cheered, and the next group of singers came on stage.

Cassie felt like a rock star. She sidled up to the bar, grinning from ear to ear.

"Hot damn," Wyatt said, handing her a drink.

She sipped and found it was just water. She grinned. He wasn't taking chances with her being drunk again either.

"You liked it?" she said, feeling coy as she sipped on the straw.

His eyes darkened, and for a moment, Cassie wished they were the only two people in the bar. She was tempted to jump over the bar and kiss him right there. She wanted him as much as he wanted her. She felt like the wooden bar stool should have caught fire with the heat their gazes were generating.

"When do you get off work?" she asked, continuing to sip on her water. She'd only had a couple of half shots, so she was in complete control. There was no way she was messing tonight up.

"As soon as your party's done," he replied, his gaze still focused entirely on her.

Cassie suddenly wished that the party was over and done. She didn't want to wait.

But she was here to celebrate her friend. She winked at Wyatt and took her water to the table where the girls all sat. Different kinds of party games decorated with versions of male genitalia filled the tables, all of them using Cassie's recently purchased batteries. The music hummed and throbbed through the room as various people got up to sing.

At the third bad rendition of "Love Shack," Janessa announced that it was time to go to the club. She was ready to dance the night away, and she wanted real music. Cassie checked her watch and saw that it was nearly one in the morning.

"I love you sweetie, but this old lady is done for the night," Aunt Suzette told Janessa. "I've got to get to bed before your uncle worries that I'm having too much fun without him."

"I'm to bed as well," Aunt Harriet added. "You youngsters are just too much."

Several other members of the bachelorette party announced that they were heading to bed as well. It was the perfect escape.

"I don't really feel like dancing..." Cassie told Janessa. "I think I'm going to head back to the room."

Janessa chuckled. "You just don't feel like dancing at a club," Janessa told her. "You want to do the horizontal tango."

Cassie spluttered, trying to sound innocent.

"No, no, it's good," Janessa quickly told her. "I like him. He's been wonderful, and he obviously is super into you. You deserve some fun in your life."

"I—" Cassie wasn't sure what to say.

"I want you to be happy." Janessa hugged Cassie close to her. "If you really are going back to the room, that's fine. I'm not trying to be pushy. You just have been so smiley since you met him. You don't seem as stressed around him. It's the version of you I love."

Cassie hugged her friend back. "He does make me happy."

Janessa pulled back and smiled. "Then go for it. Be happy. And don't worry about what any of us think."

"Honestly, we're all just jealous," Brianna told her. "The way he looks at you is hot."

Cassie felt the blush heat her cheeks. "Thanks, guys."

"Go have fun with the sexy man," Janessa said. "I'm going to dance with Brianna until our feet hurt. And then sleep until the rehearsal dinner."

Brianna hugged Cassie. "Go get 'em, tiger," Brianna whispered.

Brianna and Janessa gave Cassie thumbs up, making Cassie grin.

Cassie turned to see Lorna at the bar, trying once again to seduce Wyatt. She was practically laying across the bar, her breasts about to spill out everywhere. She reached for Wyatt, and he stepped away. He said something to her, his face serious and firm.

It was too loud to hear anything they were saying, but Lorna's cheeks pinked, and she slid off the bar. She turned and saw the three of them looking at her. Humiliation burned in her eyes for a moment before she sneered at them and huffed past them.

"He must have a thing for ugly chicks," Lorna said as she passed, just loud enough for Cassie to hear.

"Don't mind her," Brianna said. "She's just mad that he picked you over her. The room's all yours tonight. I'll be with Janessa and Katy."

With that, Brianna and Janessa waved and hurried out of the bar with the rest of the bachelorette party heading to the dance club. Cassie watched them go with butterflies starting to dance around in her stomach.

She was going to be alone with him. Was she ready for this?

She turned and saw Wyatt saying goodnight to one of the older ladies. It was one of Janessa's grandmothers who he'd flirted with throughout the night.

"Thank you, dear," the grandmother told him. "I haven't felt this young in years. Thanks for flirting with a woman old enough to be your grandmother."

"The pleasure is all mine, miss," he replied with a smile. "I meant every flirt."

She patted his cheek and smiled. "There you go again," she said, her face lighting up.

"Do you need someone to walk you back?" he asked. "I can get security to come."

"Oh, I'm fine," she assured him. "But, thank you."

She turned and left, her face bright with happiness. She

walked like a young woman, full of confidence and pride. He'd made that woman's night.

He smiled after the grandmother, his eyes soft as he watched her go. There was no false pride or ego in the smile, just pleased that he'd made someone happy.

It was that smile that took away any indecision Cassie might have had.

Not only was he sexy and super attractive, but he was also good. He was kind. He cared about people. That was sexier than his muscles and beach-blond hair.

"So, are there any rules about helping you clean up?" Cassie asked, leaning against the bar.

"What?" He frowned slightly as he looked at her.

"I don't have a work visa for the Caribbean. I don't want to violate any labor laws," Cassie replied.

"You want to help me clean up?" His smile was slow but warm.

"Yup."

He handed her a bar cloth. "You can wipe down the tables," he told her. He leaned forward. "I won't tell the labor board."

She grinned, taking the bar cloth. Her stomach was quickly turning into excited knots, and her feet danced without her meaning to. She sang along to the music still pumping through the speakers, full to bursting with excitement.

She was going to have a wonderful rest of the night.

Music throbbed through the speakers as guests slowly filtered out of the bar leaving Wyatt and Cassie alone. It seemed that once the bride left, everyone else decided to leave as well.

And that was just fine with Cassie.

She wiped at a table, her eyes on Wyatt. He was putting bottles of liquor back up on shelves. He stretched up to reach the top shelves, his long limbs showing muscle. His shirt rode up giving her a hint of tanned skin on his lower back.

Cassie's entire body heated. She licked her lips in anticipation.

Her table was clean. The bar was empty.

She looked over at Wyatt, all lean lines and sexy angles. His shoulders were broad, and she could see the hint of muscle definition under his shirt. Just looking at him filled her mind with impure and delicious thoughts as he came around to wipe the bar off.

She was here to have a good time. She was here to be herself and let herself have a little bit of freedom. She was here to have what she wanted.

And right now, she wanted Wyatt.

She'd been waiting for this since they'd left the beach. She wasn't waiting any longer.

She took a deep breath and crossed the room. Her hand hesitated for a half second as she reached to put it on the back of his neck, but she didn't stop. Her stomach twisted with nerves, but she gently pulled him down to her as she went up on her toes to kiss him.

She pulled back after a short kiss, her stomach in knots. Was she doing this right?

"Too forward?" she asked, keeping her eyes closed.

She felt him smile, his lips close to hers but no longer touching. "No. It's perfect."

And then he kissed her back. One hand tangled in her hair while the other went to her hip, pulling her into him. She relaxed into him, focusing on the kiss.

His lips were soft, but the stubble of his beard scratched at her lips and cheeks. She didn't care though. His tongue swept across her as she shivered with a sudden wave of hot desire. Again, he smiled as he kissed her, pleased with her reaction.

Corporate Rule Number Eleven: Work areas are not to be used for private business. They shouldn't be here. They shouldn't be doing this.

But she didn't want to stop. For once in her life, she didn't want to follow the rules. She wanted to just live her life the way she wanted. She wanted to be happy and not worry about rules and regulations.

She wanted to live her life the way that made her happy.

"Let's go to your room," Wyatt whispered. "This place is clean enough."

She knew it wasn't, but she didn't care. She thought about just continuing here and using one of the tables, but there were probably cameras and there was the possibility of someone walking in. Besides, a bar table wasn't exactly the best place for after-sex cuddling.

She grabbed his hand and pulled him out of the bar. They giggled and laughed as they sprinted through the gardens and past the pools. She couldn't get him upstairs fast enough...

11

Cassie

Wyatt pinned her in the elevator and kissed her hard enough to make her dizzy with lust. The bell dinged her floor and they staggered out into the empty hallway. He kissed her as they stumbled down the hallway to her room and it was pure skill that she opened her hotel room door without needing to look.

The room was dark as they tumbled inside, mouths pressed together. She wanted to rip his shirt off and if there were a way to be instantly naked, she would have done it.

"Here's my room," she whispered, feeling like she should say something now that they were here.

Wyatt just chuckled, the sound low and throaty, before kissing her again.

The back of the bed bumped against her legs and Cassie looked up into Wyatt's green eyes, her breathing coming hard and fast. He looked back at her with lust and desire. He wanted her. It was the biggest ego boost Cassie had ever felt.

This stud muffin of a man, with his beachy hair and beautiful body, wanted *her*.

She swallowed hard, and the corners of his mouth twitched up into a smirk of a smile. His eyes left her face, going to her shoulders. He kissed the bare skin of one and then slid the strap of her tank top off her shoulder.

She shivered, and he did it again.

With his eyes back on her face, he tugged on her shorts. She undid the button, and they fell to the ground.

Wyatt's playful smirk vanished and was replaced with awe. His eyes darted up and down her body as she tried not to cover herself. She'd chosen her nicest underwear and strapless bra, but she still felt like it wasn't enough. It was beige and practical, even though it was decent quality. She wished she had something lacy and sexier. At least she still had the sparkly necklace on.

"You are gorgeous," he whispered, his voice close to reverent.

Cassie flushed at the compliment, feeling heat spread from her cheeks down her chest.

"So beautiful." He kissed her bare shoulder again, reverent and delicate. His hands traced her arms, sending goosebumps across her skin. With his gentle touch and soft kisses, she felt beautiful. Even her simple underwear didn't matter anymore. She merely closed her eyes and focused on his touch.

With her eyes closed, she reached her hands under the hem of his shirt. His stomach muscles tensed under her fingertips, turning into hard rocks of muscle and hot skin. A low, primal moan escaped her throat.

Her eyes opened as she lifted the shirt. He helped pull the fabric up and over his head. His skin was sun-kissed and hot. The muscles were defined in his chest and stomach, but not overly so. It was just enough to show that he spent time on his body.

He grinned at her. She bit her lower lip and grinned back. His body was excellent, but good lord that smile was what did her in. That confident little grin matched with sparkling green eyes was what made the heat in her belly ratchet up to a million degrees.

His hands went to her hips, his fingertips rough against the smooth skin of her waist. With careful strength, he pushed her onto the bed so that she was sitting with her feet on the floor. That sexy, confident smirk filled his face as he dropped to his knees and shouldered his body between her legs.

Cassie's breath caught in her throat. Was this really happening?

Don't think. Just do, she told herself, closing her eyes and trying to relax.

Relaxing was hard when he looked at her with that cocky grin. Slowly, she lay back as he kissed her knees and then worked his way up her thighs with his mouth.

His fingers hooked the edges of her underwear, and he pulled down. A low, male growl escaped his lips as he nibbled on her inner thigh.

He leaned forward and kissed her sweet spot. The unexpected touch shot electric desire straight up Cassie's spine and short-circuited her brain. It didn't help that then he started to use his mouth and fingers to keep the electricity going.

She lost herself to the pleasure, her hips arching to match the beat of his tongue. Every lick, every caress sent waves of heat up and down her spine until she was sure she would burst into flames at any moment. Her fingers white-knuckled the bed sheets as she crested over a mountain of pleasure.

She lay gasping on the bed, lost in pleasure and sensation. Her whole body shook and yet felt like jello at the same time. The necklace felt cold against her hot skin.

She opened one eye to look down and see Wyatt smiling up at her. He seemed pleased with himself.

"I think that was even better than the beach," he told her.

"We never finished what we started there," Cassie replied, slowly sitting up. "I think you need fewer clothes."

Wyatt grinned, rocking back on his heels and then standing. Cassie watched, her eyes hungry for his body as he undid his pants and kicked them to the side. He wore boxer-briefs, and they made his ass look amazing. Wyatt winked at her before pulling them down.

"Wow," Cassie murmured. She couldn't pull her eyes away from him. He was a glorious specimen of a man. She swallowed hard. "There's condoms in my purse."

She quickly stood and rushed to her purse, pulling out the small box. Her hands shook with excitement as she tore open the package and handed him one.

"You still have more clothes on than me," he teased gently, motioning to her bra as he slipped the condom on. As fast as she could manage it, Cassie had her bra and panties off and was back in the middle of the bed.

"Come here." Cassie beckoned him forward with a finger and was rewarded with a grin. He put one knee on the bed and bent his head to her chest. His mouth found her breast, and Cassie moaned as he flicked his clever tongue against it.

His chest pressed against her stomach, his mouth on a nipple, and his skin radiated heat better than the tropical sun. Cassie's head lolled back as her eyes rolled up.

Wyatt's erection throbbed against her thigh, a physical indication of his desire for her. Her entire body ached to feel him inside of her. Needed to feel him inside of her. It was more than just a simple wish; it was every fiber of her being screaming to join with him.

She had a feeling she would never feel complete if they didn't finish here in this bed.

She reached down, cupping his jaw with her hand and having him look up at her. The green of his eyes was intense, matching the need she knew must shine in her eyes as well.

"Please?" she whispered. He moved, dipping his head and kissing her as he positioned his body over hers. He smelled so good, looked even better, and felt like heaven.

She held her breath as he completed her, and then gasped in amazement at the pure pleasure of feeling him with her.

He groaned, burying himself deep inside of her. She writhed, trying to take ever more of him into her. If this much felt good, she wanted more. His hips worked a languid loop, taking his time as he explored and filled her.

Nothing in her life had ever felt this good. This right. She gasped and moaned, her mouth searching for his skin as he filled her with pleasure over and over again.

Her breaths came short and fast as he found a rhythm that suited them both. She looked up at him, eyes wide as she took in the most beautiful sight of her life. His arms were flexed, and his chest was broad and strong. A strand of blond hair fell across his forehead, but his green eyes stayed fixed on her.

Frantic need began to stir. Her body needed his in a primal, almost spiritual way. This was good, but she needed more. She needed all of him.

She wrapped her legs around his waist, drawing him deeper into her. The low, masculine groan as he filled her to the hilt drove her wild. His hips sped up, driven by increasing need. He felt it too — the urge for more.

He looked down at her, his eyes wide with pleasure. "Cassie."

Hearing her name like that undid her. She shattered beneath him and with her shattering, brought him to breaking with her. His breath came hard and fast and then suddenly stilled. His body tightened as hers squeezed around him.

She'd never had this before. This kind of sex was something that she'd only seen on late-night TV or read in books. It didn't happen in real life. There was always something in real life to distract her. The bunching of the sheets, an itch on her ear, the sound of a siren outside.

Only this time, this was perfect. Wyatt was perfect. There were no distractions or things to take away from focusing only on the perfection of his body joining with hers. He filled her so completely that she could think of nothing else.

He tucked his head into her shoulder, his breath coming in panting gasps. Her own breathing was short and fast, her arms and legs locked around him, keeping him with her. His weight was comforting and warm. The pounding of his heart matched her own. She didn't want to move from this spot.

Slowly, their breathing came back down. He kissed her shoulder, his mouth sweet against her skin. She hated when he shifted off of her, freeing her from his body. Yet, he wrapped his arm around her, snuggling her into him and she found that it was almost as good.

"Worth the wait?" she asked him, looking up at his face.

He grinned. "If I had known, I never would have given you a drink that first night. We would have just come straight up here. There would have been only one small problem."

"What problem?" Cassie asked, frowning slightly.

Wyatt grinned. "We never would have left this room."

Cassie giggled and kissed him. "Who says we need to leave?"

It was Wyatt's turn to grin. "Then I guess I'll just have to stay here in heaven with you forever."

And although this was supposed to be just a vacation fling, that sounded like an excellent plan to Cassie.

12

Wyatt

Wyatt woke with the morning sun like he usually did. The early morning light flickered through the windows and stopped his dreams. Just like every morning, he wished he'd closed the curtains better. He sat up and glared at the offending light.

Except, he wasn't in his bungalow. He wasn't home. He was in bed with Cassie.

He blinked twice, looking around the room and remembering where he was. He'd slept so well he'd assumed he was home. The sleep had been deep and restful. Even though it was just after dawn, he felt ready to take on the day.

Cassie shifted in her sleep beside him. She was so beautiful in the morning light. Her dark hair splashed against the crisp white linen, and she looked utterly kissable. He knew she was still completely naked under the sheet, and despite the fact they'd gone twice last night, he already felt like he could go for a third.

She was just that attractive to him. She made him feel twenty years younger.

But, he didn't want to wake her either. She looked so peaceful. He stared at her in the morning light, memorizing the curves of her face and the soft sound of her breathing. In this moment, she was perfect. She was his. Time held still while he watched her.

Wyatt knew he should leave her room. As a hotel employee, he wasn't supposed to be here. If he were found, it would mean his job. Since he wasn't working for the money, this wasn't a huge problem, but it would mean he would have to find another hotel to work at. It would be incredibly annoying.

It had taken a fair amount of effort to hide who he really was. Getting hired somewhere new took effort. Plus, he liked bar-tending here. He had friends on the staff, and he'd found all his favorite places to go in the area. He had a life here. A life he liked.

He knew he should go, but he wasn't about to leave Cassie. Not willingly, anyway. The "Do Not Disturb" sign was out on the door, so he didn't have to worry about one of the maids finding them. He was probably safer hiding out in her room until it was time for his next shift anyway. There wasn't a good reason for him to be on hotel grounds right now.

Wyatt carefully eased out of bed and tugged on the curtains. As much as he loved the way the sunlight warmed Cassie's face, he didn't want it to wake her as well. She needed the sleep. This was her vacation after all.

The room darkened, but he could still make out the curves of her hips under the thin sheet. He crawled back into bed, and she rolled into him, snuggling into his shoulder.

"Don't leave," she whispered, her eyes still shut. "I don't want this to be a dream."

He smoothed a strand of hair away from her face and caressed her cheek with his fingertips. "I'll stay," he promised.

She sighed with contentment and fell back asleep. He watched her, wondering how she could have this kind of effect on him. She mesmerized him. She made him laugh and smile. He found himself feeling alive when she was around. She filled him with energy and excitement, yet at the same time made him feel calm and safe.

He found himself wishing that she never had to leave. He never wanted her vacation to end.

It was the first time he'd ever wished that for a guest.

For a moment, he let himself imagine what life would be like if Cassie stayed. They would have to rent a place together, but that wouldn't be a problem. Wyatt could provide her with any kind of house she wanted.

She worked in the hotel business, so it wouldn't be hard to get her a job here if she wanted.

Or maybe they could just get on a sailboat and drift on the ocean from island to island. They didn't have to work. Wyatt worked the bar because he liked talking with people. He loved working and having something to do, plus it gave him a great way to meet women.

If Cassie were here, he didn't need to meet women. They could find other things to occupy their time. The idea of all the things they could do "filling time" made Wyatt's body start to respond. It didn't help that Cassie's breast pressed against his chest, teasing him with her every breath.

"You are thinking so loud I can hear it," Cassie murmured. Her eyes were still closed, and her hand rested on his chest. She peeked one eye open and looked at him. "You aren't having second thoughts, are you?"

"Second thoughts?" Wyatt asked.

"About being here." Her voice was steady, but he could hear a tremble of emotion run through it.

"If I didn't want to be here, I wouldn't be," he assured her. He smiled softly. "And the only second thoughts I'm having are the plans I'm coming up with to get you back into bed again tonight."

Her smile stretched across her face as if he'd given her the best compliment of her life.

"I think I can arrange that," she told him. "You don't even have to do anything fancy."

"Well, there go all my plans then." He shrugged and did a fake sigh. Cassie chuckled, pressing her cheek into his chest.

"What were you thinking about, though?" she asked. "You were all tense."

"Was I?"

"Yeah. Like you were worried about something," she explained. She looked up at him and pressed her fingertip gently at the center of his forehead. "Plus, your brows were all thoughtful."

He took a deep breath, then asked the question on the tip of his mind. "Would you ever leave your job?" he asked her.

She shifted her body so that she could see him better but still have her head on his shoulder.

"Possibly. I like my job, but I don't like how corporate it all is. I would like more freedom," she answered. "Are you thinking of leaving your job? Is that what you were thinking about?"

"If you could do anything, what would you do?" he asked, not answering her questions.

"I'd open my own hotel," she answered without hesitation. "It's a pipe dream, but if I could do anything, that's what I'd do. I'd run it how I want to run things. Why? What would you do?"

"I'm doing it," Wyatt replied. "I live in one of the most beautiful places in the world. I have a job where beautiful women take body shots off of me."

"That does sound fun," Cassie said with a grin. "It's definitely not corporate."

Wyatt had to agree.

"Why are you working here?" Cassie asked him. "I mean, other than for the beautiful people and the body shots. You are smarter than just a bartender."

He raised his eyebrows at the backhanded compliment. "Thank you?"

"You're not just a bartender," she clarified. Her eyes went to his face. "There's more to you than that."

"It's what I want to be right now," he replied. "It's the carefree life. I worked all my youth, teenage years and early adulthood for my father. All I ever did was work. There were no spring break parties or summers abroad. It was always about the work. I wanted something that I chose. Something I wanted but could never have."

"So you picked an endless spring break after years of not having any." Cassie nodded thoughtfully. "I can see the appeal."

"You'd be one of the first," Wyatt replied. "My father must be rolling in his grave."

Cassie rolled up on to her elbow. "Are you happy?"

The question caught him by surprise. "What?"

"Are you happy?" she repeated. She motioned to the room. "With what you've chosen. This life you've made here on the island."

He thought for a moment before nodding. "Mostly."

"Then who cares what your father would think?" Cassie asked. "What matters is that you're happy. It's your life. You should do with it what you want."

"You know, you're gorgeous when you get passionate," Wyatt told her. He loved how bright her eyes were. The slight pink in her cheeks and the way she seemed to vibrate with energy was absolutely stunning.

She blushed at his words.

"And you're right," he continued. "Maybe you should join me."

He hadn't meant to say it so bluntly. He hadn't meant to say it all. It had just slipped out.

"Here?" Her eyebrows raised, but at least she didn't give him an immediate no. He could see she was at least considering it. Slowly, she started to shake her head. "I can't."

"Why?"

"Why? Because I have a life back in Arizona," she replied. "Because I'm not a risk taker. I'm a planner. I'm responsible and boring most of the time."

"So?"

"It's not me. It's not who I am." She shrugged and sighed. "I couldn't just leave everything I've worked for on a whim."

Wyatt knew that they'd only known each other for a few days. They weren't really a couple. There were no promises, no real dates, and she didn't even know who he really was. Yet, her words stung. She wouldn't stay.

It was a fantasy anyway.

"If you change your mind, I know a great guy looking to share rent on a bungalow," he told her, covering up his feelings with humor. "He'll give you a great rate."

She chuckled. "Yeah? You'd be my roommate?"

"Me? No." He shook his head. "The guy who rents the jet-skis is the one looking."

Cassie chucked a pillow at his head. He caught it and tossed it to the side, looking over at her. She'd sat up, and the sheet no longer covered her body.

"How much time do you have before your friends come looking for you again?" he asked, his eyes glued to her chest. He was definitely ready to go again.

She grinned at him, her eyes dark and lustful. "Long

enough to make you jealous of the jet-ski guy being my room-mate," she replied.

And then she pressed her body against him and kissed him.

13

Cassie

For the second time this week, Cassie was late to an event.

This time, Brianna just stood there grinning at her as Cassie jogged up to the meeting place five minutes late and out of breath. Luckily, Cassie wasn't the last one to arrive.

"Wyatt?" Brianna asked as Cassie joined them on the edge of the beach and the resort. "You're never late."

"Maybe." Cassie tried an indifferent shrug.

"Right. That's why your positively glowing and can't stop smiling," Brianna said with a chuckle. "And you have sex hair."

Cassie's hands flew to her head, and Brianna laughed again. Her hair was fine. It was still smoothed neatly back into a ponytail. Brianna was messing with her. Cassie glared at her, but Brianna just grinned.

"Is Julia here?" Cassie asked Brianna. "I haven't seen her yet."

"That's because you haven't left your room all day," Brianna teased. She grinned at Cassie. "Julia just got here a little while ago. She should be here soon. She wanted to change out of her airplane clothes."

"I'm glad she was able to make it," Cassie replied. "She's been putting in a lot of overtime."

Brianna turned and looked back toward the hotel, shading her face with her hand. "There she is," Brianna said, with a smile. Then, the smile quickly faded. "Oh no. Lorna's right behind her. Why is Lorna here?"

"That's because Lorna's a bridesmaid," Janessa informed them, coming up behind the two of them and joining the conversation.

"What?" Cassie turned and stared at Janessa.

"I didn't get much say in it. She went to Kyle's dad." Janessa sighed and shrugged as they watched the two women walk down to the beach. "It was easier to just say yes than cause a family fight."

Cassie's eyebrows raised. "You're okay with Lorna being in your wedding?"

Janessa shrugged. "It's just a wedding. I'm not inviting her into my marriage," Janessa explained. "Besides, it keeps the peace. I want my day to be happy and fun, not full of sullen glares and Lorna sabotaging things because she didn't get to wear a blue dress too."

Cassie kept it to herself that she didn't think it was about the blue dress. It was just Lorna's style to sabotage things. She hoped that being in the wedding was enough to keep Lorna satisfied and protect Janessa's special day. It felt like sacrificing a virgin in hopes it would satiate the dragon's hunger long enough to escape. Only, you never really knew how hungry the dragon was.

"I made it!" Julia announced with smiles and hugs as she arrived at the beach. "It was close, but I'm here!"

"I'm so glad," Cassie told her, wrapping her friend up in a hug. "It wouldn't be the same without you."

Lorna sniffed as she passed, making a disgusted face at Cassie.

"Where are we supposed to be?" Lorna asked Janessa, pointedly ignoring Cassie and Brianna. "I have plans this afternoon."

Janessa put on a neutral smile. "Katy and Kyle are just down there talking with the minister. I'm sure they could use some help."

Lorna tossed her shiny blonde hair over her shoulder and flounced down the beach.

"Wow. Who peed in her cheerios?" Julia asked.

"Cassie did," Brianna replied. "She stole the sexy bartender."

Julia's eyes went wide, and she grinned. "Seriously? That's fantastic." She wrapped Cassie up in another hug.

"Is it seriously that impressive that I went out with a guy?" Cassie asked her three friends.

The three of them glanced at one another and Janessa nervously shifted her feet.

"I'm going to be straight with you," Brianna said, putting her hands on Cassie's shoulders. "Yes it is."

Cassie's mouth opened, but no words came out.

"What Brianna means is..." Julia paused and thought for a moment. "She means yes. But, it's just because you've been working so hard. Your job is important to you, but you do let it dictate a lot of your life."

"I think you needed this vacation," Janessa said gently. "And we're all just glad that you took the chance. You look so happy today."

As much as Cassie wished they were wrong, she knew they weren't. She'd been so focused on her career and work that she'd let her personal life slide. She couldn't remember the last time she'd gone on a date that wasn't work related.

She was glad she was letting herself take this chance. The way that Wyatt made her feel was worth it.

"If everyone could come over here, we'll start going over how this is going to work," Kyle called out, motioning the groups of people waiting to step forward. "The sooner we have this figured out, the sooner we can go eat."

"Time to practice getting married," Janessa told them. She grinned and did a little happy dance. "I'm so excited."

Together, the four of them headed down the beach to where the ceremony was going to be held.

"I am not walking with him."

Lorna stood in the center of the what was going to be the aisle and crossed her arms. She shot a disgusted look at the poor groomsman she was humiliating.

"Lorna..." Janessa pressed her fingers into the bridge of her nose.

"I don't look good with him," Lorna explained. "He's too short for me. And fat. And do you not know how to shave your face or brush your hair?"

Lorna gave the poor man an eye roll.

The man was around five feet four inches and was stout, not fat. His hair was messy, but that's because it was windy on the beach and everyone's hair was a little messy. No one was dressed up except Lorna. Even the groom had a two-day stubble beard going. All the groomsmen did.

It was utterly shallow and incredibly unfair of Lorna to say anything.

"That's the way we have this planned," Janessa tried to explain. "You come down the aisle with Chad. Then Cassie and Ben. Then Julia and Steve. Then Brianna and John. Then

Katy with Max. Then me. It's been planned this way for weeks."

"Well, I don't care. I won't do it." Lorna crossed her arms and looked stubborn. Everyone in the bridal party glanced around, unsure of what to do next. The bridal planner just stared at Lorna, her mouth working like a fish but nothing coming out.

Cassie sighed. "I'll switch."

Janessa looked relieved. "You will?"

"Of course." Cassie smiled at Chad. "We'll have fun."

"Okay. Cassie, change places with Lorna, and we can continue," the bridal planner announced. Janessa mouthed a thank you to Cassie behind Lorna's back.

Lorna fluttered her eyelashes at Cassie's escort and puffed out her chest, obviously proud of her new arm candy.

Cassie and Chad took their spots at the back of the beach as everyone reset. The 'aisle' was marked with stones and tomorrow there would be rows of chairs leading to the spot on the beach where Janessa and Kyle would say their vows.

"I'm sorry about Lorna," Cassie said as they waited for the planner to motion them forward.

"Eh, it's okay," Chad told her. "My girlfriend told me all about her. I'm trying not to take it personally. Thanks for doing what you did."

"It's no problem," Cassie told him. "This way I'll get a better view of the bride and Kyle's face when he sees her."

Chad offered her his arm, and together they walked down the sandy aisle. Cassie's foot slipped on a pile of loose sand, and she nearly went down, but Chad caught her arm and kept her upright.

"Thanks," she told him with a chuckle. "See? I knew I was smart to switch."

Chad laughed and together they went down the aisle with smiles on their faces. Lorna came after looking pissed. She'd switched for Cassie's date, a tall and handsome young man, who as Lorna probably just found out from her expression, had a negative net worth.

Luckily, the rest of the rehearsal went smoothly. Lorna didn't make any more fusses, and everyone understood what they were supposed to do the next day.

"Thanks for coming and practicing, everyone," Kyle announced, standing where he would be married tomorrow. "We have reservations for everyone at the Beach House for dinner. Just in case we don't remind you again, be sure you're here early tomorrow. Thank you!"

Chad clapped Kyle on the back, and the two of them laughed.

"So, you have to tell me everything," Janessa said, coming up alongside Cassie.

"Yup. I need details," Brianna agreed.

"I have no idea what we're talking about, but I want in," Julia added, joining the group.

"Cassie is going to tell us all about her hottie bartender," Janessa said. "Because lord knows I need something to tide me over until tomorrow."

The four of them began to stroll along the beach toward the restaurant.

Cassie sighed. "You guys don't want to hear about it."

"Girl, I haven't had sex in two weeks because Kyle wants it to be 'special,'" Janessa informed them. "I went from getting some every day to cold turkey. I'm dying. I need to live vicariously through you."

"Two weeks? That's it?" Brianna scoffed.

"Yeah. How ever do you survive?" Julia added sarcastically.

Janessa glared at them. "Do you guys want the details from her or not?"

"Oh, I want the details," Brianna replied. "She gives me

hope. If Cassie can find a sexy man than there is a possibility that I can too."

"Even I want to know how things went last night," Julia said. She bumped Cassie with her hip. "Tell us it was glorious. Give hope to us mere mortals."

Cassie couldn't help but chuckle. "He is definitely Greek God material," she admitted.

Brianna whistled. "I knew it!"

"Tell me what he looks like," Julia asked. She blushed when she realized how she'd phrased it. "I mean, his face. I don't need to know other parts."

"If his other parts are as nice as his face..." Janessa kissed her fingers like an Italian chef praising the food.

"Beach body, beachy hair, strong jaw, pretty eyes," Brianna listed off. "He's handsome."

"And everything matches," Cassie added.

Brianna clapped, and Janessa squealed with delight.

"I'm going to have to see this guy," Julia announced. She grinned at Cassie. "Way to go."

Cassie grinned. "He's sweet, too. He's good, and then he's *good*." She shivered with the memory of just how *good* Wyatt had been last night.

"You should bring him to the wedding," Janessa said. "He can be your date. We've got more than enough space."

"You totally should," Brianna agreed. "There's a couple of guests that couldn't make it, so you don't have to worry about food or anything."

Cassie liked the idea of him coming to the wedding. She liked the idea of having Wyatt as her wedding date and getting to spend more time with him.

She just wasn't sure if it was such a great idea since he wasn't going to be a permanent presence in her life. This was a vacation fling, right? This was just something for the week she was here. In just a couple of days, she'd go home and back to her real life far from the warmth of the Caribbean.

"Ask him," Janessa counseled as if reading her thoughts. "I'm fine with him coming. If he says no, then that's fine, but you'll never know unless you ask."

"It might be against hotel rules," Cassie said, looking down at the sand as they walked.

Julia shrugged. "So? You'd have to ask to find out."

"Okay, I'll ask him." Cassie felt nervous and excited about it at the same time. It felt like a relationship step. It felt like a real date and not just a vacation hook-up.

It had a feeling of seriousness to it.

Which Cassie found both thrilling and terrifying.

14

Cassie

Dinner was just like old times. Cassie, Janessa, Julia, and Brianna all sat around the table making jokes and laughing as they reminisced and told stories. They remembered their late nights and early mornings, the boys and the heartaches, the adventures and the support they gave one another. They'd helped raise Janessa and Brianna's children as surrogate aunts. They were family, not just friends.

Cassie loved being able to spend time with her college roommates. Time had changed them, but it hadn't changed their friendship.

Brianna was still full of fire and quick sass. She was always ready with a sarcastic comment. Even though her last relationship had gone down in fiery chaos, she still believed in love. It helped that Janessa and Kyle had a great relationship showing her that love was still possible.

Julia was softer, but still just as energetic. She was passionate about her job and seemed to be putting in even more hours than Cassie. Cassie suspected it had something to do with a very attractive boss, but Julia wasn't giving any hints.

Janessa grinned the entire dinner. She was getting married to the love of her life tomorrow. She kept glancing over at Kyle and smiling without realizing she was doing it. Cassie caught her several times, and it made Cassie's heart warm.

True love existed. Love was real. Janessa and Kyle had it. They'd been high school sweethearts, but it had ended in college. Janessa got pregnant with Katy while still in school. She'd been a single mom for a long time. It was only when Katy wanted to purchase a new car that Kyle and Janessa had reconnected. It had all fallen into place from there.

"I'm going to bed early," Janessa announced as they finished dessert. "I want to get lots of rest for my big day tomorrow."

"You're still hung over, aren't you?" Brianna asked, popping a piece of fruit into her mouth,

"Yup." Janessa nodded.

"At least it means you'll sleep tonight," Julia told her. "Instead of being all nervous energy and staying awake all night."

"As long as Brianna doesn't snore again," Janessa teased.

"I do not snore!" Brianna crossed her arms and glared at Janessa.

"Right. Tell that to my poor busted eardrums," Janessa replied.

"Do you need to come back to our room?" Cassie asked Brianna.

"No!" Brianna and Janessa both told her in unison.

"No. You get another night to yourself," Brianna said. "Or, mostly by yourself."

Julia and Janessa snickered, and Cassie rolled her eyes but thanked her friend.

They all stood and said goodnight to the other dinner guests. Janessa and Brianna waved, heading off to their room and leaving Julia and Cassie at the table.

"I want to see this guy," Julia said, turning to face Cassie.

"He's probably working right now," Cassie told her.

"Even better," Julia replied with a grin. "He can't hide."

Cassie chuckled. "I'll introduce you," she promised. Together, the two friends stood up and headed out of the restaurant.

"Oh, Cassie?" Lorna called out after them. "Can I talk to you for a second?"

Cassie paused. She debated just sprinting for the front door and pretending that she hadn't heard Lorna at all, but that would make tomorrow awkward.

She put on her manager smile and turned. "Sure. What do you need?"

"Well, Julia can keep walking," Lorna said, giving Julia a pointed look.

Julia made eye contact with Cassie. She wasn't about to abandon her friend.

"I'll be right there," Cassie told her. It was better to get this over with quickly.

"Okay. I'll be in the chairs right in front of the restaurant," Julia said. "Remember, we have that thing we're doing. I don't want you to be late, so be fast."

She gave Cassie's arm a gentle squeeze before brushing past Lorna. Cassie sent her mental thanks for giving her a great reason to keep the conversation short.

"What's up?" Cassie asked Lorna.

"I just wanted to thank you for switching with me," Lorna said with a smile. "I always worry about the pictures at these kinds of things, you know?"

"I get it," Cassie replied noncommittally.

"Are you interested in him?" Lorna asked.

"Who? With Chad? No. He's got a girlfriend," Cassie said, shaking her head. Lorna had about two more questions before Cassie used Julia's appointment excuse to get out of this conversation.

"Oh, no. He's so not your type," Lorna said with a laugh. She put her hand on Cassie's arm like she was an old friend. "I meant the bartender. You two seemed to know one another."

"That's not really your business," Cassie said, pulling away.

"I'm sorry, I don't mean to be rude or anything," Lorna said with a soft laugh. "I just thought you might be into him. But, I'll warn you, he's not going anywhere. And I've heard that he just picks a different woman every week and has them fall in love with him and then..." She shrugged. "I just don't want you getting hurt."

Cassie's cheeks blazed with heat. "Thanks for your concern. I think I can handle it."

"I'm just looking out for you," Lorna said, her expression innocent. "It's what girlfriends do for one another. If I were you, I'd dump him now before he breaks your heart."

Right, Cassie thought to herself. *And that way you can pick him up right after.*

"There's something familiar about him. I don't think he's giving you the full story." Lorna looked thoughtful. "I can't place where I know him, but I swear I've seen his face before. I never forget an attractive face."

"I need to go," Cassie said, taking a step away.

"If you ever want to talk about him, or any of your male friends or hotel guests, I'm here for you." Lorna smiled sweetly. "I'd like us to be friends."

"Sure." Cassie needed friends like Lorna like she needed holes in her head.

"But seriously, you can do better than that guy." Lorna's smug look gave her true motive away. She had struck out this trip to find rich husband number four and wanted the hot bartender as a consolation prize.

"I'll keep that in mind. Thanks, Lorna. I'll see you tomorrow." Cassie flashed her manager smile again and hurried out of the restaurant. Julia stood by the front doors, checking her watch.

"Thirty more seconds and I was coming back in for you," Julia told her. "What did she want?"

"She thinks I can do better than Wyatt and that I should totally not talk to him the rest of the trip," Cassie explained. "She's determined to try and snag him for herself."

Julia blinked twice. "Wow. That's low, even for her. Now I really want to meet this guy. If Lorna's falling all over him and he's not worth millions, he's got to be insanely hot. Does he have a brother?"

Cassie chuckled. She thought back to their conversation on the beach. "I think he said he was an only child."

"Darn," Julia responded, and Cassie giggled at the way she said it.

Cassie thought she'd check the tiki bar where she'd had too much to drink that first night and then the lobby bar if he wasn't there. They had plans to meet up after his shift, but she didn't want to bring Julia up to her room and wait until then.

Luckily, he was working at the tiki bar.

"Is that him?" Julia asked as they got closer. Wyatt was busy laughing with some patrons as he poured drinks.

"Yup."

He looked up and flashed them both a smile. Cassie's knees went a little wobbly.

"Holy crap. No wonder Lorna wants to steal him away," Julia said. She grinned at Cassie. "Way to go."

Cassie flushed, a smile filling her face. "Thanks."

Together, they sat down on tall bar stools and rested their arms on the bar.

"Hello, ladies," Wyatt greeted them, putting down napkins. "What can I get you?"

"The usual," Cassie replied.

"I'll have what she's having," Julia said.

"Sex on the beach it is." Wyatt reached for two glasses and began mixing the cocktail.

"Oh my," Julia whispered under her breath. She leaned over to Cassie. "Please tell me you misremembered, and he has a twin brother. Or any brother. Or a cousin. I'll take a second cousin twice removed, even."

Wyatt set down their drinks with a flourish before Cassie could say anything.

"Here you go," Wyatt announced, adding tiny umbrellas to each drink.

"Thank you," Julia said, reaching for her glass.

"Wyatt, this is my friend Julia." Cassie motioned toward her friend. "She just got in today."

"Hi." Julia flashed a smile at Wyatt. "It's nice to meet you."

"Likewise," Wyatt replied with a warm smile. "I hope you're enjoying your stay?"

"So far," Julia replied. She glanced down the empty bar and then at Cassie before picking up her drink and standing. "I should be getting back to my room. Have a good night, Cassie." She grinned at Wyatt. "It was nice to meet you."

Julia squeezed Cassie's shoulder and then politely left the two of them alone at the bar. She hummed softly as she walked away.

"How's your day going?" Cassie asked, sipping on her drink.

"Good," Wyatt replied. He grinned. "I get off in ten minutes."

Cassie grinned at him. "Then maybe I can make it into a great day."

She loved the way his smile widened, and his eyes sparkled. "It's certainly heading in that direction."

Heat fluttered up in her stomach, and she could feel the smile on her face turn stupid with joy.

It was definitely going to get even better.

15

Wyatt

Wyatt hummed the theme song to *Mission Impossible* as he carefully snuck out of Cassie's room and headed down to the lobby. He'd managed to extricate himself from her bed safely and was now on a mission of utmost importance: breakfast.

The hotel had a small selection of breakfast food set up in the lobby. There was one restaurant on the property that also served breakfast, but that was on the far side from Cassie's room. Luckily, the lobby's continental breakfast was more than enough.

Wyatt glanced around as he grabbed a plate and began filling it with food. Several hotel guests lounged in chairs while sipping coffee and reading newspapers. Annette was at the front desk, and she just shook her head and sighed when she saw him.

He wasn't supposed to take the guests' food. He wasn't supposed to be filling up a plate, let alone bringing a plate back upstairs to a guest he was sleeping with. It was very, very against hotel policies. But, Annette liked him, and he knew she would turn a blind eye to his doings.

He gave Annette a wink as he passed the desk with a plate full of fruits and pastries. She sighed and rolled her eyes, but the hint of a smile crossed her face.

The spy-based theme song continued to play in Wyatt's head as he carefully made his way back upstairs. He'd snagged Cassie's room key on the way out so that he could get back in, but he didn't want to come across another employee in the hallway accidentally. Not all of them were as fond of Wyatt as Annette was.

Luckily, the elevator and hallways back to her room were blissfully empty. He let out a sigh of relief once he was safely back in her room with the door firmly shut behind him. He set her key card back on the table where she'd left it and headed into the bedroom.

Cassie came out of the bathroom, toothbrush in her mouth and hair still mussed from sleep. Her frown quickly shifted into a smile as soon as she saw him.

"I thght oo eft," she mumbled around her toothbrush. She quickly ducked into the bathroom and spat. "I thought you left."

The edge of pain in her voice at the idea of him leaving pulled on his heart. He held up the plate of food. "Just to get breakfast."

She grinned at him. "That kind of leaving I can get behind," she told him. "Let me finish brushing my teeth."

She hurried back into the bathroom, and when she emerged a few moments later, her dark hair was neatly pulled back into a ponytail and her face clean of sleep. Wyatt pulled back the curtains, and they both sat on the bed, looking out the windows at the ocean.

Cassie leaned her head against his shoulder and let out a happy sigh. For a moment, Wyatt let himself pretend this might continue, and that she didn't have her airplane ticket poking out the back of her suitcase. That she wasn't leaving in a day.

But, that would mean telling her who he was and that he'd been lying to her this whole time. Well, not really lying, but definitely omitting some significant facts. He was a billionaire. He wasn't just some beach bum with nothing to offer. He could give her a good life here.

"I still have a few hours before the wedding," Cassie said softly, her eyes still out on the water.

"I don't know if I can go again," he answered honestly. He was used to a lot of sex, but this much amazing sex was something he had to pace himself with. He wasn't eighteen and unstoppable anymore.

She chuckled, the sound low and sexy. "I was thinking we could go lay out by the water. I haven't just laid on the beach yet, and it sounds like a wonderful calm thing to do before a wedding."

He smiled softly. "That sounds like the perfect thing to do today."

He didn't tell her that he wasn't supposed to do that. That he could potentially get fired for lounging on the beach with her. He didn't tell her because he wanted to lay on the beach with her. He wanted to have a quiet moment of just the two of them enjoying the beauty of the Caribbean.

They both stood up and brushed the crumbs from the bed before heading out. She put on her adorable bikini, and for a moment he nearly forgot about the beach. He wasn't sure how her swimsuit that covered everything and wasn't skimpy turned him on so thoroughly. It was like her cute and yet somehow sexy at the same time without meaning to be. The fact that she wasn't trying only made her hotter.

He took her to the row of lounge chairs settled in the soft white sand. Seagulls cried above in the pale blue sky as the ocean waves made a melody with iridescent blue below. They selected two lounge chairs that stood side by side. She scooted hers so that they touched and became one giant lounger rather than two separate ones.

She lay on his right, their hands entwined as they looked out at the blue water. For a moment in time, Wyatt's world was perfect. For the first time in years, he felt perfectly content. There was no need for words or action. Just laying on the beach with Cassie made his heart feel full to bursting. This was something he could do every day and never tire of.

He had come to the Caribbean to live the life he'd never had. He'd worked from the moment he could hold a calculator, and never got to experience any of the wild teenage or college years he'd heard so many stories about. He'd always been working and building his business.

He'd come here to have his heydays. To feel what it was like to take time off and just play- to have no responsibilities or deadlines. He enjoyed bartending because it was simple, yet took skill. He liked talking with people and learning their stories. No one ever opened up to Billionaire Businessman Wyatt the way they did when Bartender Wyatt poured them a drink.

Yet, something had still been missing from his life. He'd had more women than he could ever want, both as a billionaire and a bartender, yet they didn't matter. They didn't make him feel the way he did when he was with Cassie.

Cassie was the missing piece, he realized. She was what was missing all this time. It wasn't the job or the responsibilities; it wasn't the island or the relaxation, it was the friend and companion that he needed. He could see himself still working if he could have come home to Cassie every night.

But she was leaving in less than twenty-four hours. This would all be just a memory in a day's time.

"Well, well, well. Look what we have here."

Beside him, Wyatt felt Cassie stiffen.

"Lorna. How nice to see you," Cassie said rigidly, rising to a more seated position.

Lorna stood in a teeny tiny bikini with just a sheer scarf tied around her waist. The bikini was more string than fabric. It was meant to be sexy, but somehow Wyatt found Cassie's swimsuit far more appealing.

"I see you're still slumming it with the help," Lorna said, pointedly ignoring Wyatt.

"It's actually none of your business," Cassie told her.

"I thought there was a rule that the staff wasn't to be with guests," Lorna said, tapping a finger against her chin. "At least that's what James said."

Wyatt's blood ran cold for a moment. If James heard about this, Wyatt would be fired in an instant. While he didn't need the job for money, he liked working here. He didn't want to have to find a new resort and start over again. Hiding his identity and getting hired was tedious and something he didn't want to have to do again. Short of finding out his true identity, this was the worst thing that could happen.

Lorna saw him react and she smiled. She knew his weakness now.

"It really is none of your business," Cassie repeated. "Keep walking, and I'll see you at the wedding."

Cassie lay back down, pushing her sunglasses firmly onto her face, and forcing herself to relax. Wyatt could feel the tension radiating off of her, but he tried to do the same.

Lorna scoffed, flipping her hair over her shoulder and walking away. She looked back once and smiled when she saw Wyatt looking. It made Wyatt blush and tense at the same time. She kept walking, but she swung her hips so much Wyatt was half afraid she was going to pop her femurs out of her hip sockets.

The woman had an attractive body, but that was where the beauty ended. Lorna was walking trouble and strife.

"You okay?" Wyatt asked Cassie once Lorna was out of earshot.

Cassie glanced down the beach and sighed. "Yeah."

"She sure knows how to kill the mood," Wyatt remarked.

Cassie chuckled and then turned and smiled at him. "I should probably go get ready anyway. It's just about time."

He leaned over and surprised her with a kiss.

When he pulled back, her eyes fluttered, and she drew her lower lip into her mouth. "Wow."

It was a nice boost to his ego that he could do that to her with just a kiss.

She looked up at him, her big brown eyes swallowing him whole. "You're still coming to the wedding, right? As my guest?"

He nodded. "Of course."

She grinned. "Okay. I'll see you in two hours."

She got up and started walking away before turning to look at him one last time. She grinned and winked, then sashayed her hips like Lorna had done. Only, Cassie made it look sexy as hell.

He watched her go until he couldn't see her anymore. Then he sighed and left the chair. It wasn't a good idea for him to just lounge on company property. He walked along the beach, thinking about what he should wear to the wedding.

He was hesitating on what to wear. Lorna had noticed his designer shirt. He didn't want a repeat of that or really anything that would out him as someone more than a simple man. Unfortunately, that meant he needed to purchase a new shirt. He only had work shirts, beach shirts, and expensive shirts.

The gift shop near the beach sold clothing. He knew there were shirts that the resort sold to tourists who had forgotten or lost their clothing. It had bright Hawaiian style prints as well as subdued linen shirts appropriate for a wedding. He'd sent many a guest with lost luggage to buy their shirts there.

Now it was his turn. He wandered into the shop and began to browse. He skipped the colorful prints and decided on a simple light gray linen shirt. It would look nice with a pair of his work slacks. He would fit in with the wedding crowd.

"Do you want to use your employee discount?" the shop clerk asked him. He looked up in surprise and realized that it was Bree, the store manager. Someone must have called in sick for her to have to work the checkout line. She usually worked in an office near the lobby bar.

"Um, sure." He fumbled with his wallet, wondering when the last time he'd ever used an employee discount was. He could have bought the whole store without even hurting one of his bank accounts, but it didn't hurt to keep up appearances.

"Have a nice day," Bree said, handing him a bag. She looked behind him, and her face soured. "Look out. Here comes the boss."

Wyatt looked over in time to see James heading for the front door. Wyatt didn't particularly feel like talking with the man today, so he ducked behind a row of sunscreen. He couldn't make it to the door from here, but at least he wouldn't be seen.

"Bree, did you do as I asked?" James sauntered through the door, his nose held high and proud.

"Yes. I fired her," Bree replied. "I still don't think that–"

"It is against the rules," James cut her off. "We can't have sales clerks ending up in guest's rooms. It's unseemly."

"It was her first offense," Bree told him, crossing her arms angrily.

"It sends a message," James replied. "I will not have hotel staff interacting inappropriately with guests. If I see it happening, the offender will be fired. There are no exceptions."

Bree sighed. Technically, James was her supervisor, so she had to do as he said. It was evident that she didn't like firing her employee, though.

"I'm glad to hear you did what was necessary," James said. He glanced around and sniffed. "You really should organize better in here."

And then he turned on his heel and walked back out into the tropical sunshine.

"I wish I could fire that man," Bree mumbled as Wyatt came out from behind the sunscreen aisle.

"What happened?" Wyatt asked as they both watched James' figure slowly disappear.

Bree sighed. "One of my cashiers. She got a little friendly with a guest and ended up in his room. They were both single, consenting adults. James found out about it and made me fire her."

Wyatt's mouth dried. He'd done more than just end up in a guest's room, and he was about to go to a guest's wedding.

But it was for Cassie. He wasn't about to back out now. He'd take the risk because making Cassie happy was worth it. She wanted him there, so he was going to be there, even if it cost him his favorite job.

"You fired her?" Wyatt repeated.

Bree shrugged. "James has a stick up his butt about looking proper," she explained. "He's overzealous, but there's not much I can do about it."

Wyatt nodded slowly.

He had a feeling this wedding was going to cost him his job, but he was willing to risk it. Sure, he could ask James for permission, but he had a feeling it would be better to beg for forgiveness than ask permission in this situation. There was a chance he could keep his job if he begged. Asking would only get him fired faster.

"You okay?" Bree asked. "You look like you swallowed something bitter."

Wyatt forced a smile. "I'm fine. Just thinking about changing things up."

Bree nodded and smiled as if she understood.

Wyatt thanked her and left, his thoughts on Cassie. He was actually rather excited to see her. Now that he'd made the decision, he wasn't nervous about it anymore. It was just a job. But Cassie- she was something worth keeping.

Now, it was a game to see if he could dodge his boss long enough to keep his job.

16

Cassie

Cassie didn't see Wyatt as she walked down the aisle. She looked for him, but she couldn't find him amid the crowd. Her heart sunk. What if he hadn't come? What if he'd changed his mind? What if his boss had found out and he was fired? What if he hadn't attended in order to save his job?

She couldn't blame him if he did stay away, but she still felt a little sick. She'd been looking forward to spending time with him.

She turned at the end of the aisle and split from Chad to take her position lining the altar. That's when she saw him.

Wyatt sat toward the back, but he was looking at her like she was the most beautiful thing he'd ever seen. The small, impressed smile as he looked her over made her feel more stunning than any compliment ever could. He didn't even look away when the bride walked past him.

He was looking only at her.

Her heart sped to a million miles per hour, and her smile turned into something that glowed. He had come. He was risking his job to be with her. He was here.

The ceremony went by in a blur. Janessa was stunning in her white gown, and Kyle looked like the happiest man in the world. Katy cried tears of joy. Cassie had a hard time paying attention at times since she kept sneaking glances at Wyatt in the audience. It wasn't that the wedding wasn't beautiful or love-filled, it was just that he filled her thoughts.

For a moment, Cassie let herself imagine her and Wyatt up on this beach altar. Would Wyatt smile like Kyle did when he slid the ring onto a finger? Would she cry tears of joy like Janessa did reading her vows?

It was a beautiful fantasy. Even though it felt right to imagine him with her, Cassie knew that it was just pretend. He was a bartender on a Caribbean island. She managed a hotel in Arizona. They were two very different worlds that just happened to collide for a short time. The collision was beautiful, but it couldn't last.

She blinked away surprise tears at the thought of leaving. She was going to miss Wyatt terribly when she left tomorrow. Cassie dabbed at her eyes, hoping that everyone would just think she was happy for her friend. This had been the best week of her life, and after tonight, she'd have to go back to her old life.

She decided that instead of being bitter about it ending, she was going to enjoy every moment. She couldn't stop time, but she could focus on remembering every second of it. She glanced over at Wyatt again, determined to have the best night ever.

The wedding ended, and everyone cheered. Chad held Cassie's arm as they walked back down the sandy aisle and headed toward the picture area for photos. Cassie wished she could just head straight to the reception area to see Wyatt, but her duties were to the bride and her new husband.

Cassie and the other bridesmaids dutifully took the wedding photos that would soon grace Janessa and Kyle's walls. Lorna managed to mostly behave herself, and only pushed to the front of the picture once or twice. Cassie genuinely smiled for her friend but was glad when the photographer released the rest of the wedding party to the reception while she finished taking portraits of just the happy couple.

Once free, Cassie and the other bridesmaids hurried to the reception area. Fairy lights twinkled in the eaves of the gazebo over the tables and chairs. Guests mingled on the outdoor dance floor and walked through the garden area as they waited for dinner to be served. A small band played soft jazz.

Cassie chewed on her lower lip as she looked for Wyatt. She wanted to find him before Lorna did. Her eyes darted around the guests, looking for his tall frame and easy smile.

"You look beautiful," a deep voice said from her side. She grinned as she turned to face him.

He wore his work slacks and a nice button up shirt. He could make a brown paper bag look good, so the dressy shirt looked terrific on him. He'd brushed his hair back with just a touch of gel, and he had shaved. He looked movie-star handsome.

"Thank you," she told him. "You look pretty nice yourself."

He grinned in return, his eyes soft and sparkling.

"I found our table," he told her, offering his arm. She took it with a smile as he led her to a large table adjacent to the bride and groom's center seats.

Two glasses of wine sat waiting for them. She grinned at Wyatt and together they sat, sipping on the wine. Cassie glanced around the reception, taking it all in. Everything was outdoors in the Caribbean evening breeze. Fairy lights lent a magical glow to every structure, and beautiful people chatted and laughed as they waited for the bride and groom to arrive.

Lorna glared at Cassie. The slim woman sat at the opposite table and luckily nowhere near Cassie and Wyatt. Cassie sent a silent thank you to Janessa for the seating arrangement. The look on Lorna's face was sour as she crossed her arms. Cassie tried not to worry about it. She wasn't about to let Lorna ruin her evening.

She turned to face Wyatt, pushing Lorna from her mind.

"Cheers," she said, lifting her glass to his.

"Cheers," he repeated, clinking their glasses. "This is a very nice wedding."

"I think so too," Cassie agreed. She smiled softly at him. "Thank you for coming."

"I wouldn't miss it," he replied taking a sip of his wine. He took a deep breath and relaxed into his chair as he looked out at the wedding guests. "Do you have any more trips planned when you get home?"

Cassie wondered if it was a sneaky way of asking if she could come back to the island. "Unfortunately, this used up most of my time off," she said, only a little bitterness creeping into her voice. "I don't get very many vacation days."

Wyatt nodded, smiling softly as he looked over at her. "That's too bad."

"What about you?" she asked, setting her glass down. "Any big plans coming up?"

He looked out at the crowd for a moment before answering. "I might be changing islands," he said after a moment. "I feel a change in the wind."

"Where will you go?" The idea of him not being here scared her. Even though she had no real way of getting back to the island, she liked the idea that she could find him here again. She had this fantasy in her mind that she would come back, and he would run across the beach to meet her, sweeping her up in his arms. She knew it wasn't really a possibility, but the loss of the fantasy hurt.

Wyatt shrugged. "There are a few islands nearby that have resorts I can work at," he said. "I have contacts in other places. Maybe I'll teach surfing or help run a booze cruise."

She tried to smile like he'd made a funny joke, but she had a hard time. She knew it didn't really matter. She was going home tomorrow. He wasn't a part of her life. Yet, the idea of him not being here or knowing where he was, bothered her greatly.

Before she could say anything, the bride and groom arrived. Janessa and Kyle were greeted to applause and whistles as they made their way to the head table under the gazebo. Then, there were speeches, food, and toasts.

Cassie sat next to Wyatt and just enjoyed his presence. They didn't need to speak. Just having him near her was a balm to her soul. They clapped and cheered at the various speeches and toasts, raising their glasses with smiles.

"And now, we welcome all couples to the dance floor," the emcee announced when Janessa and Kyle finished their traditional dances. "All couples come to the floor."

Cassie glanced over at Wyatt, unsure as to what to do. Were they a couple?

He didn't pause. He just stood and offered her his hand with a smile.

Cassie's heart fluttered, and she felt a blush cross her cheeks. Even though it was all ending tomorrow, he was going to dance with her as a couple. They walked out onto the dance floor with all the other matches. They joined couples that had been together for years, mingling among them as if they belonged.

The music started, and Wyatt swept Cassie into his arms

and began to dance. His hands were strong and confident on her hips, telling her body where to go and what to do without words. Her body followed his without fail, finding the rhythm together. They dipped and swung, sweeping across the dance floor with grace.

"Where did you learn to dance like that?" Cassie was breathless at the end of the song, but grinning from ear to ear.

"My mother taught me," Wyatt explained as they walked back to the table. "She felt it was important that I know how to dance at a wedding."

"She did an excellent job teaching you," Cassie replied. "I'd like to dance more with you if I can."

Wyatt pretended to take something out of his back pocket. "Hmm... it looks like my dance card is all yours for tonight."

Cassie giggled and grinned at him. Her heart was light, and she couldn't remember the last time she'd smiled quite this much. She was happy. Pure and simple. She didn't feel the weight of the world pressing down on her when Wyatt was near.

They danced the night away. It was something out of a dream. Dancing and laughing under the sparkling lights and glittering stars while the ocean sang nearby. Cassie pinched herself at least twice when she thought Wyatt wasn't looking because she couldn't imagine a way for this night to get better.

But somehow it did. The night simply continued to amaze her the longer they stayed together. Slowly the crowd began to thin around midnight, and just after one in the morning, Janessa and Kyle disappeared off to their room to enjoy their wedding night.

"Walk with me?" Cassie asked Wyatt, motioning to the beach.

He took her hand and smiled. They left their shoes by the gate to the resort and went to walk along the water.

As they walked along the moonlit beach, she could almost imagine she was leaving her own wedding, with her own new husband. Everything felt right and like nothing bad could happen.

17

Cassie

Moonlight made the ocean glow as they strolled on the sand. The soft sounds of music and the last bits of laughter floated up through the warm darkness as their feet splashed the edges of the waves.

They were in their own magical world. Nothing could touch them here. For a moment, Cassie let herself live only in this moment. She was falling hard for the sexy bartender even though she knew it could never be, so for this moment, she let herself fall. She let herself have this night with him, even though she knew it risked breaking her heart.

She stopped, stepping in front of him. Moonlight glistened in his light hair and reflected in his eyes. He stole her breath away with his beauty.

She reached up and caressed his cheek, her heart thrilling at the small smile he gave her as he pressed his cheek into her touch. His eyes held hers, wrapping her up in warmth.

She wasn't sure if he kissed her or she kissed him, yet somehow his mouth was on hers. He tasted sweet and smelled like wedding cake and aftershave. She moaned slightly, her eyes closing as she focused on the kiss.

His lips were soft, but his five-o'clock shadow was starting to poke through. She could feel his scruff, and she brought her fingers to his cheek to caress it. Wyatt's body pressed into hers, his arms wrapped around her and his fingers in her hair.

She could have lived in that kiss forever and been happy. She could have spent the rest of her life in that moment, feeling his mouth take hers, and his body call out her name.

But, she had to breathe eventually. They both did. Time didn't stop.

Reluctantly, they pulled back, pressing their foreheads together to keep the closeness of the moment. All she could smell was his delicious scent. All she could hear was his breathing and ocean waves. Her own heart pounded in her chest, and her body ached to feel him everywhere all at once. She burned with passion for him.

"Stay with me," he whispered, his voice barely above the ocean. "Stay with me."

"What?" She pulled back slightly and looked into his green eyes. They were dark and full of desire as he looked at her.

"Stay with me," he repeated. "Stay here, on the island. Don't leave tomorrow."

Cassie didn't know what to say. Her mind blanked, and she stumbled for words. "Stay? I can't..."

"We have something," Wyatt continued, his word speed picking up. His hands gripped her shoulders. "It's special. I feel it. You feel it. I want to see where this can go. I don't want you to leave."

Cassie couldn't remember how to breathe correctly. Her lungs wanted to take deep breaths to steady herself, yet all she managed were short shallow gasps. Her mind whirled with the possibility.

What if she did stay? She wanted to. She wanted to stay here forever with Wyatt. Her body ached for him, and her mind wanted to be with him always.

Yet, that would mean leaving her life. Leaving everything she'd ever known and everything she'd worked so hard to achieve. As stressful as her job was, she was proud of it. She'd put in years of her life to be where she was. It was all that had saved her when her marriage fell apart.

Staying would be throwing it all away.

"What if you came back with me?" she asked. "My apartment's big enough. There are tons of bars nearby."

He pulled back. "I can't."

"What do you mean you can't?" Cassie's brow furrowed.

Wyatt's face hardened. "I can't. I won't."

Cassie stepped back, shrugging his hands from her shoulders. "So, you expect me to drop everything. To leave the job I've worked at for years, the job that pays me well and that I'm proud of to come here? Where I have nothing. I don't have a job. I don't have a place to live. I don't even have clothes here."

"We can get them," Wyatt replied like it was nothing. Like leaving behind all her things was simple.

"Why don't you come with me? I have a better job, and we can pack your things and bring them with us. It's actually easier if you come with me," Cassie said, trying to sound logical.

"I can't go back there," Wyatt said, his face darkening. "You don't understand."

The magical moment was breaking. Cassie could feel the magic shattering and draining away. The moonlight was still there, but the warm, happy feelings were quickly fading.

"No, I don't," Cassie told him. "I don't understand. I can't stay here, and you won't come with me, but you won't give me a good reason why."

"I'm telling you, I can't. That has to be enough," Wyatt snapped. He paused and took a steadying breath. "I can take care of you. I swear it."

Cassie stared at him, dumbfounded. "Why can't you go back? Are you a criminal? Or... what?"

"Please," Wyatt said softly, his eyes big. "I don't want to go back to that world. If I go back..." He sighed and ran a hand through his hair, messing it up. "Please just stay here."

Despite the craziness of it, Cassie was tempted. She was tempted to throw her career away for this man she'd only known a few days. She was tempted to lose her apartment, her things, her job. Everything. For him.

The fact that she was tempted scared her. The fact that she would give up everything she'd worked so hard for because of a couple of amazing days on the beach terrified her. What if it was all just an illusion? What if those things Lorna had said about him were true? What if he found the next cute vacationer at his bar and left her? She'd have nothing.

"No." The word came out unbidden. She watched it fly through the air and hit him like she'd thrown a punch. He took a step back.

"Cassie..."

"No, Wyatt." She shook her head, feeling her heart start to crack. "I can't stay."

"Cassie..." His voice held so much desire and emotion that she nearly gave in. She almost promised to stay.

"No." She shook her head. Overwhelming feelings of panic, despair, heartache, and fear all lurched up from the pit of her stomach.

Corporate Rule Number Two: When faced with a confrontation, it is better to take a breath and step back than make a rash decision.

She ran away, leaving him on the beach with his hand stretched out to her.

18

Wyatt

Wyatt stared after the woman he loved running from him and out into the darkness. He knew he should chase after her, but his feet refused to move. It was like they were stuck in the sand, held by invisible magnets that wouldn't let him go.

"Stupid, stupid." He dropped his head in shame. He'd been overzealous. He hadn't sold it well. He'd messed up the timing, and now it was all screwed up. He always waited for the right moment, but this time he hadn't. This time, he'd screwed things up because he hadn't read the situation correctly.

He wouldn't do that again. Wyatt sat down in the sand and looked out at the dark water, trying to figure out what to do next.

He needed to go up to her room and apologize. She was only here for one more night, and he didn't want to spend it apart.

He also needed to tell her who he was. He couldn't blame

her for running. By all appearances, he was a beach bum with barely a job. It wasn't exactly an exciting prospect to leave her life and career to go live out of a shack on the beach.

He sighed. She was right to ask him to go to Arizona. But he knew that if he stepped foot in any major city, there would be reporters on him. He was the missing billionaire. Even now, he'd see the occasional news story on him and how he'd disappeared. If anyone saw him, he was a headline story just because he was trying to stay hidden. He'd tried once before to sneak back to New York to sign some papers, and he'd been mobbed at the airport.

He shuddered with the memory. He'd left the life of lights and money behind for a reason. He loved his new, simple life. There was no pressure to perform here. No threats, no body-guards, no worries, because on this island, he was the same as everyone else.

Back on the mainland, he was billionaire Wyatt Landers. He couldn't just go back and live in Cassie's apartment. If he returned, he would thrust her into the blinding world of money that he'd worked so hard to escape.

Watt threw a small pebble into the ocean waves, quickly losing sight of it in the foam and turbulence of the water. He was that pebble when he was a billionaire. Unusual and unique in the water, but surrounded and lost.

He laughed bitterly. Being a billionaire wasn't all he'd thought it would be. He much preferred the simple life he had here. He was happy here.

But Cassie wasn't going to be here anymore. He needed to convince her to stay.

He stood up and dusted the sand from his pants. He would go to her room. He would tell her who he was. He would sweep her off her feet, and they would live happily ever after. He knew it.

With determined steps, he ran to his beach house. He

fixed his hair and put on an expensive shirt. He wore the expensive watch. He wore the expensive shoes that were almost as comfortable as his sandals. He fixed his appearance and made sure he looked like a billionaire.

He needed to prove to her that she could stay here without losing everything she'd worked so hard to achieve.

An hour later, Wyatt walked across the marble lobby, his shoes clicking softly with each step. He should have brought flowers. Or chocolates. Something.

Annette was working the front desk. Maybe she had some flowers he could take with him.

"Hello, sir. How may I help you?" Annette asked pleasantly as he approached.

Wyatt frowned. "It's me, Annette. Wyatt."

Annette's eyebrows went into her graying hair, and her mouth went wide. "Oh, my word. You don't look like you."

"Do I really look that bad?" Wyatt asked, checking his clothing.

"Oh, no. You look like a million bucks," Annette quickly replied. "You just don't look like usual. Your hair, your clothes. Even the way you're walking is different."

"Is that good or bad?"

"It's fine. Just different. Like an actor playing two different people in the same movie." She stared a little at him. "You look like you should be a guest here."

He could probably afford to buy the whole hotel, let alone just a room for the night.

"I need some flowers," he said.

Annette glanced around the front desk, and her eyes settled on a tropical bouquet on the edge of the counter. "Here, take these. We always get new ones in the morning. They're pretty, and no one will miss them."

"Thanks, Annette," Wyatt said, carefully picking out the flowers and arranging the prettiest ones in his hand.

"Good luck, Wyatt," Annette replied. She smiled at him. "And you should dress up more often. It looks nice."

He flashed her a smile before heading up the elevator and up to Cassie's room.

He knocked with confidence, even though his chest was so tight he was sure his heart would be crushed any moment. "Please, Cassie. I need to tell you something."

The door cracked open, and his chest relaxed slightly.

"She's not here," Brianna told him, standing defiantly in the door with arms crossed. "You should leave."

"Please, I just want to talk to her," Wyatt replied, trying to look past her and into the room. Brianna blocked his view.

"I told you, she's not here." She glared at him.

"Can you get a message to her?" Wyatt asked, deciding to try a new tactic. "I need to apologize before she leaves."

"Well, that's going to be rather difficult," Brianna informed him. She checked her watch. "Her flight leaves in ten minutes and the airport's twenty minutes away."

Wyatt took a step back in surprise. "What? Her flight's not until tomorrow."

"Well, it was. We switched flights," a voice from inside the room informed him, coming to the door. It was one of the other bridesmaids. He was fairly sure her name was Julia. "My flight was for tonight. Hers was tomorrow. She took my flight, and I'm taking hers."

"Whatever you told her had her in a panic," Brianna told him, her eyes still hard. "She paid the transfer fees and everything. She's gone. You scared her off."

Wyatt's shoulders slumped. His heart went through his expensive shoes. He shouldn't have changed. If he'd come straight here, he could have caught her and explained. Instead, he'd decided to show off his wealth and wasted precious time.

Yet another example of why money isn't everything, he thought to himself.

He held out the flowers. "Here. Someone might as well enjoy them."

Julia took the flowers and held them to her nose. "Sorry, you missed her."

He nodded. "Tell her I'm sorry," he said, his voice wooden in his ears. He turned and walked down the hallway, every step feeling hollow.

He was too late. He'd missed his chance, and she was now gone.

He moved robotically into the elevator and hit the button for the lobby. This wasn't how he'd seen the evening going.

"Thanks, Annette," he said, passing the front desk.

Annette's eyes went wide again. "Get out of here. James is looking for you, and he's pissed!"

"What?"

"He's on the warpath," she hissed. She shooed him with her hands. "Get going."

Wyatt nodded. He hurried his steps through the side door of the lobby and ran directly into James.

"All dressed up for the wedding, I see." James' eyes went up and down over Wyatt's fancy clothing.

Wyatt didn't have any excuse prepared. He was still reeling from finding out Cassie had left and his brain couldn't come up with anything to say.

"You realize you're fired, right?" James crossed his arms and looked down his nose at Wyatt.

"Sir, I can explain," Wyatt replied, hoping he could come up with something.

"A concerned guest notified me of your attendance at the Frankson wedding," James said. He held up his phone to show a picture of Wyatt and Cassie dancing. They both looked so happy it took Wyatt's breath away.

"Cassie..." She was so beautiful with her dark hair and eyes. He could nearly feel her fingers still on his shoulders as they danced.

"You've been warned before," James continued. "This was the final straw. You're fired, Wyatt. Get your things and get off the hotel property immediately, or I'll have security throw you out. Your last paycheck will be mailed to you."

Wyatt stood there for a moment. He'd been deliriously happy just hours ago. Now, it was all crumbling around him.

"Did you hear me, Wyatt?" James pressed, getting up into Wyatt's face.

"Yeah. I heard you. I'm fired." Wyatt took a step away from the man. He glanced over to see Annette's concerned face. He looked back to James and shook his head. "Your loss."

He stepped around James and continued to walk out of the hotel. Wyatt kept his shoulders back and his steps even and measured. His head stayed up as he walked out of the hotel, despite the horrible ache in his heart.

Wyatt slept until noon. He usually woke with the sun, but today, he just wanted to sleep. He wanted to wake up and find that it was all just a terrible dream. That Cassie was still asleep beside him. That he hadn't lost his favorite job. That he wasn't going to have to leave the island.

That he hadn't screwed everything up.

But, his bed was empty.

He sighed and swung his feet onto the floor. Usually, the sound of the ocean waves outside soothed him. Today, it sounded noisy. He considered going back to bed, but he knew it wouldn't solve anything.

He looked at the map of the Caribbean hanging on his

bedroom wall. There were still dozens of islands for him to explore. He was a good bartender. Life could go on. But, he found it difficult to pick the next island.

The truth was, he didn't want the next island. He wanted Cassie.

He wanted her more than he'd wanted anything in his entire life.

He wanted her enough to go get her.

He wanted her enough to be a billionaire again.

He picked up his phone and called his assistant in New York. He needed to book a hotel room at the StarTree hotel in Phoenix, Arizona.

19

Cassie

The first day back at work felt surreal. Home didn't feel like home anymore after her trip to the Caribbean. The sky was the wrong color, the air too dry, and the heat different. Despite living the majority of her life in the desert, she now felt out of place without the sound of the ocean.

Or maybe, it was that she felt out of place without Wyatt.

She shook her head, trying to remove the thought as she looked over the previous week's sales reports. The hotel had survived her trip. There was a lot of things that she had to make up for, but there wasn't anything out of the ordinary.

Cassie walked out to the main lobby and looked around at her hotel. It was clean and spacious. She tugged on her suit jacket and felt a little bit of pride. She'd worked hard to become the manager. There were a lot of things she wished she could change policy on, but overall she was happy to do the work here.

She heard her email ping on her phone. The message said

that a StarTree executive would be coming by for a surprise inspection today. Lenny Patton, a StarTree regional executive, would be arriving this afternoon to look over the hotel and make sure it was up to corporate standards.

Cassie frowned but wasn't worried. Even with her recent absence, she knew the hotel could pass any inspection. She tucked her phone back into her pocket, mentally making lists of things that needed to be checked before Lenny arrived. The timing could have been better, but she could handle it. She just needed to get some lunch first.

The front doors opened, and Cassie couldn't help but grin.

Brianna walked in with a brown bag full of fast food. She still had on her traveling clothes, but Cassie knew the hotel was on the way to Brianna's apartment from the airport.

"Lunch?" Brianna asked, holding up the bag as she crossed the lobby.

"Yes, please," Cassie told her. "We can eat in my office."

Cassie led the way to her office in the back. She cleared off a stack of paperwork and files from her desk, trying her best to keep the stacks somewhat organized. Brianna set the bag down and then flopped into her chair.

"How was your flight this morning?" Cassie asked, settling more delicately into her own chair.

Brianna shrugged. "Totally normal," she replied. "I'll be glad to be back in my own bed, though. Janessa snores."

"You didn't sleep with Janessa last night," Cassie replied, opening up the paper bag. The scent of greasy cheeseburgers and fries hit her nose, and she smiled. Brianna always got the good stuff.

"Julia snores even louder," Brianna informed her. She held out a hand for a cheeseburger from the bag. Cassie handed her one and took one for herself. She wasn't on a bridesmaid dress diet anymore.

"Sorry to hear that," Cassie replied. "It's probably the pillows. They had the super fluffy ones, but they aren't good for neck support. They really should put firmer pillows in for their guests."

Brianna chewed on her burger but raised a single eyebrow at Cassie. "Thanks, Ms. Hotel."

Cassie ignored her and bit into her cheeseburger. The greasy goodness combined with the sweetness of the bread and the sour of the pickles perfectly. She let out a happy little moan.

"How was your flight?" Brianna asked. "I thought you had today off since you were supposed to be on my flight."

Cassie shrugged. "The flight was fine. I couldn't sleep this morning, so I came in to work on things."

Brianna nodded, chewing carefully.

"What?" Cassie asked.

"You doing okay? I mean, with Wyatt and everything?"

Cassie carefully set her burger down on the wax paper. "I'm fine."

"He came by after you left. He even brought flowers."

Cassie stared at her food. Her heart ached for Wyatt. She'd cried nearly the entire trip home, which she hated. She never cried. She actually came into work this morning just to have something to distract her. She didn't want to be alone in her apartment with thoughts of Wyatt and the life she could have had.

Better to stick to the life she knew. The life she liked.

"Well, it wouldn't have worked out anyway," Cassie said, picking up her food again. "He was a bartender on a tropical island. What about kids? What about a house?" She shook her head. "There was no future there."

"You're right." Brianna nodded. A wistful smile crossed her face. "He was hot, though."

Cassie grinned. "He sure was. And sweet. And smart.

And..." The smile faded. "And totally not what I need in my life right now. I did the right thing coming back early."

"Are you trying to convince you or me of that?" Brianna asked.

"Neither. We both know it was the right thing to do."

Brianna crumpled up the wrapper from her burger and leaned back in her chair. She glanced around the office, looking at the stacks of paper and piled up extra uniforms.

"You going to be okay?" Brianna asked after a moment.

Cassie took a breath. "Yeah. I'll be fine. Just have to get used to being back in real life again."

"I get that. I needed that vacation. The ocean was good for my soul," Brianna told her. She checked her watch and stood up. "Well, I have to get home. Ian will be home in a few hours and I want a shower before he gets there."

"Say hi to him for me," Cassie told her. She knew Brianna was ready to see her son. "And thank you for lunch. This is way better than the PB&J sandwich I had planned."

"PB&J?" Brianna frowned. "Seriously? I didn't know you were taking culinary tips from Ian."

"I don't have any groceries yet." Cassie shrugged as she stood up to walk Brianna out to the lobby.

Brianna gave Cassie a hug and a wave before leaving Cassie back at the front desk. Cassie glanced around. Nothing had changed in the past twenty minutes. Nothing ever seemed to change here. The hotel was constant.

Corporate Rule Twelve: All StarTree hotels shall have the same consistency. Guests should feel as though they are always staying in the same place, every time, at every location.

Cassie sighed, feeling the lack of sleep from the night before starting to catch up with her. She was seriously considering leaving a little early. No one would mind since she'd come in on her day off anyway.

"Cassie, there you are. I've been looking all over for you,"

Lenny Patton said, crossing the lobby and coming to her side. He fussed with his suit jacket, barely stretching it over his ample belly.

Cassie kept the snide reply in check. She'd literally been in her office. He hadn't looked at all. She kept quiet, though as she wanted to stay on her boss's good side.

"It's good to see you, Lenny." Cassie held out her hand for a handshake.

"Do you have the penthouse suite made up?" Lenny asked, ignoring her hand.

"Of course. Housekeeping did a double check on it the morning after Mr. Gustav left," Cassie explained. "Everything is at corporate standards."

Lenny swallowed hard. "It needs to be better than corporate standards," he informed her. "I don't know how you did it, but you have a huge guest arriving. He should be here any minute."

Cassie frowned, shaking her head. "A huge guest? What are you talking about?"

Lenny patted nervously at his gray comb-over, making sure it was in place. "Landers. Landers is staying with you. Did you not read the email?"

"What email?" Cassie asked, frustration rising. If an important guest was arriving, she needed to know about it. "I haven't gotten any notifications."

"You probably just missed it while you were gallivanting around the beach," Lenny scolded her. "You have Wyatt Landers coming to stay at your hotel."

Wyatt... it couldn't possibly be him, though. He was a beach bum bartender, not a penthouse suite who made hotel executives nervous. Wyatt was a common enough name.

"Who is Wyatt Landers?" Cassie asked, straightening up the pens on the check-in desk. "And why is he so important?"

"You seriously don't know?" Lenny scoffed. He shook his

head and rolled his eyes. "The Landers family owns the 'Lands INC,' you know, the biggest home goods store in the world. Wyatt Landers is the current owner. He's a multi-billionaire."

"Wow. A real-life billionaire is staying here?" Cassie's brain started doubling up on the needed lists.

"Oh, not just any billionaire." Lenny shook his head. "Wyatt hasn't been seen in years. He just up and vanished one day. Said he didn't want to run the business anymore. He kept his money but left the company to board of directors. How have you not heard about this?"

"I don't read gossip columns?" Cassie suggested.

Lenny's mouth pursed. "Anyway, he's the prodigal son returned. And we're hosting him."

"Why is a billionaire staying here?" Cassie asked. "I mean, I know it's a nice hotel, but it's not billionaire nice. The majority of our guests are business travelers or conference attendees. Not billionaires. He should be staying at the Ritz or something."

"Don't look a gift horse in the mouth," Lenny advised her. "Maybe his fortunes have fallen. Maybe he wants to try and stay under the radar."

"It's still weird," Cassie told him, crossing her arms.

Lenny was about to say something when his eyes went to the door. He swallowed hard and went just a little more pasty than usual.

"Here he comes," Lenny said, straightening up and tugging on his tight jacket.

Cassie followed his gaze to see two big black SUVs parked outside. She smoothed her skirt and put on a pleasant smile. This wasn't exactly what she'd expected when she came to work today. It was a good thing she'd left the island early. What if she'd not been at work today?

The SUV doors opened, and Cassie's heart faltered and then failed.

Wyatt Landers walked into her hotel with a security team.

Only, it was her Wyatt. From the island.

Apparently, he was a lot more than just a bartender.

20

Cassie

Cassie stared in absolute shock at the handsome billionaire standing in front of her.

It was Wyatt. Her Wyatt, only in a suit that cost more than her car and with two bodyguards that probably competed in WWE wrestling competitions.

He smiled as he came in, his body language calm and collected. He looked at absolute ease walking into her hotel. He wore a dark suit that highlighted the soft golds in his slicked-back hair and made the green of his eyes stand out.

Cassie, on the other hand, felt like having a panic attack. Not only was the man she'd fallen in love with at her hotel, but he was also a freaking billionaire. Half of her wanted to run into his arms and kiss him, and the other half wanted to run screaming out to the parking lot.

She did neither as her boss was standing beside her. That, and she wasn't sure she was going to be able to make her legs work. They seemed rooted to the floor in shock. Her mouth hung open, but no words seemed to be coming out.

"Mr. Patton. Ms. Turner," Wyatt greeted them. His smile was warm for Cassie, and his eyes sparkled.

She wanted to smack him. He was enjoying this.

"Mr. Landers, we'd like to thank you for choosing Phoenix StarTree as your hotel," Lenny said, stepping forward. "We have your room ready for you."

"If you'll lead the way, Ms. Turner," Wyatt said, motioning toward the elevator.

"Ms. Turner can stay here." Lenny let out a nervous laugh, purposefully stepping in front of Cassie.

"No. I'd like her to show me the room. That's not a problem, is it Mr. Patton?" Wyatt's smile was cold and calculated as he looked at Lenny.

"No, no, of course not," Lenny stammered. "Cassie, if you will."

Cassie gave herself a small shake. "Right. Follow me, please."

She tried to walk confidently to the elevator, but her knees were shaking. She was having a hard time breathing, and her palms were drenched with sweat. She missed the elevator button on the first attempt but managed to hit it on the second.

"We have a pool and gym on the third floor. There is a free continental breakfast from six to ten in the lobby. Checkout is noon," she said, using her usual script to give her something to say. The words were a habit ingrained her after years of practice, yet she still stumbled over them as she tried and failed not to stare at Wyatt. She knew he didn't care about the continental breakfast, but she wasn't sure what else to say.

"Thank you, Ms. Turner," Wyatt said. He leaned against the back of the elevator, looking cool as a cucumber as the doors shut and the elevator brought them to the top floor. "I'll be sure to check the pool out."

Cassie stumbled out of the elevator with Lenny right behind her. Wyatt and his two massive bodyguards followed.

"You have our penthouse suite," Cassie said, fumbling with the key card. She nearly dropped it but managed to get it into the door without looking like a complete idiot. She pushed open the heavy hotel room door and motioned inside. "If there's anything we can do to make your stay more comfortable, please let us know."

"Oh, I will." Wyatt smiled at her, his green eyes sparkling.

She had so many questions. They all bounced around in her chest, fighting to come out yet staying trapped. She didn't want to ask them with Lenny standing right there.

"Thank you for choosing the StarTree line, Mr. Landers," Lenny said, giving Cassie a slight glare. It was the last line of the corporate script when renting out the penthouse suite. Cassie had forgotten to say it.

"Yes, thank you, Mr. Landers," Cassie quickly added. It felt strange to call him that after shouting out his name in bed just days earlier.

"Ms. Turner, let's leave Mr. Landers to settle into his room." Lenny took Cassie's arm and practically dragged her into the hallway. They both waited until the firm click of the hotel door was heard.

"I can't believe he's here," Cassie whispered.

"I can't believe you almost screwed that up," Lenny hissed. "You didn't tell him about the laundry service or the rewards program."

Cassie blinked twice.

"It's fine," Lenny assured her. "I'm not angry about it."

"Okay." Cassie wasn't sure what to do now. Usually, she'd just go back down to her office and finish up paperwork, but it was Wyatt. She wanted Lenny to leave so that she could talk to him in private.

Instead, Lenny took her arm and guided her to the elevator. "I can't tell you how big this is for StarTree," he said, jamming his finger against the button. "Don't screw this up. Corporate is very impressed that he chose your hotel, but don't let it go to your head. Just keep doing what you're supposed to. Don't improvise."

Cassie crossed her arms and bit her tongue. Don't improvise? She had a freaking billionaire with bodyguards staying at her hotel. There was no corporate policy for this. There was no script or manual for how to do this. No Corporate Rule number worked here.

Especially when the billionaire was here to seduce the general manager of the hotel.

The elevator chimed, and they both got out. Lenny made a big show of smiling at the various employees before talking loudly about his expensive dinner reservations. Cassie left him and went to her office, her brain and heart scrambled.

"What is he doing here?" she asked to the empty room, collapsing into her chair. She leaned the back of her head on the backrest of the chair, staring at the ceiling. "And what am I going to do about it?"

She had no idea. She wasn't even sure who he was anymore. She lifted her head and typed his name into her computer. Dozens of pictures and articles came up. She scanned them all, trying to get a grip on the situation.

He had taken over his father's company at a young age. Every article said that he was a hard worker and had helped make the company into the billion-dollar corporation that it was. Then suddenly, not long after the death of his father, he vanished. He went from being at all the fancy rich-people events to dropping off the face of the earth.

Of course, the media loved him for this. There were

hundreds of articles and people that thought they'd seen him in Paris or Amsterdam. No one mentioned the handsome bartender in the Caribbean. Everyone was sure he was living it up in Ibiza or London, spending ridiculous amounts of money, not slinging drinks to tourists.

Already, news of his arrival was spreading. In just the past hour there were three new reports on the appearance of Wyatt back in the States. Speculation as to where he'd been and why he was back was rampant. So far, no one had connected him to the StarTree hotel, or to her.

It was days like these she wished she had whiskey in her desk drawer. But that was against corporate policy number twenty-two.

Her phone buzzed, and she picked it up. "This is Cassie Turner."

"Cassie, the guest in the penthouse wants to speak with you. Personally. In the penthouse." The front desk girl's voice quivered slightly. "Do you want me to call Mr. Patton?"

"No, don't call Lenny," Cassie quickly said. "I'll be right up. Thank you."

She hung up the phone and felt her heart skip a beat. What was she going to say to him? What was he going to say to her?

She didn't have any good answers. This was too far out of the norm. For once, she wished there was a corporate slogan or script to follow, but she was on her own.

She quickly smoothed her hair, put on some lipgloss, and headed up the elevator. She was trembling, but she was also determined to put on a good face. She was a professional. She could handle this. She knocked smartly on his door, trying not to think about what she was doing. If she thought too much, she knew she'd panic.

"Come in."

She took a deep breath and opened the door.

Wyatt stood by the small bar, the sunlight streaming in through the big open windows. His bodyguards were nowhere to be seen, but she had a feeling they were nearby.

She froze, once again frozen by his handsome looks. He had taken off his suit jacket but still wore the dress shirt and tie. It looked good on him. It didn't match his easy-going smile as well as the t-shirt and swim trunks did, but it still looked absolutely amazing on him.

"Hi." She wished she had something smarter to say, but at least "hi" was better than telling him about the credit card rewards club.

"Hi, Cassie." He smiled as he said her name, his lips caressing the sound of her. The back of her neck went hot, and her knees threatened to give out. "And here's my room."

She remembered saying something similar the night he'd come to her hotel room.

"What are you doing here?" She didn't mean to be so blunt, but she didn't have any other ideas.

"I came to see you."

Her heart sang, and her chest tightened at the same time. He set down his drink and walked across the room, standing before her. He was close enough to touch, yet he made sure to give her some space.

"I hated the way we left things on the island," he continued. His voice was low and soothing. His green eyes watched her face like she was a work of art. "I couldn't leave it like that. You said to come to Arizona, so I did."

"I didn't mean quite like this," she said without thinking. "I mean, this isn't what I expected."

"I'm sorry if I've made things difficult for you," he said. "I can find another hotel if you'd like."

"My boss is thrilled. You've gotten me some serious brownie points," she replied. "I just... I'm not sure what your plan is."

He reached out to touch her, but she stepped back. She wasn't sure enough of her emotions to be touched. Part of her wanted to tackle him into the bed and show him how much she ached for him, but another part was angry.

"You lied to me," she said softly, her eyes on his outstretched hands. "You didn't tell me this was who you really are."

He dropped his hand. "This isn't who I really am. The bartender on a tropical island who is happy with his life is who I really am. This is what I left behind. This isn't me."

"You could have told me."

"Would you have believed me?" he asked her. "Would you have done things differently? I don't tell people who I am for exactly that reason. People change when they know you have money."

Cassie wasn't sure she could honestly say he wasn't right. She probably would have dismissed him telling her he was rich as little lies to impress her.

"Would you have stayed if you had known?" His eyes went to hers, and she felt her core tighten. When he looked at her, she was the only thing in the world that existed.

"I don't know," she said honestly. "Maybe. It would have been a very different conversation."

He nodded and looked away.

"What do you want?" she asked. "Why are you here?"

His eyes came back to her. "I'm here for you, Cassie."

"You shouldn't be," she told him. Her thoughts were so jumbled, and she could smell his aftershave. She wanted to kiss him so badly it hurt. She needed to take a step back. She needed to be careful and cautious. She needed to evaluate and plan. Jumping into things too quickly was what got her into this mess. "I should go."

"Please, don't." He reached out and grabbed her arm.

When she froze, he released it. "At least get dinner with me. I did travel all the way here to see you."

Cassie chewed on her lower lip. It had all the markings of a bad idea. He'd lied to her about who he was. What else was he lying about? What other secrets and surprises were in store?

She couldn't trust him.

Yet, she couldn't say no to him either. Her heart and her body wouldn't let her brain form the words.

"Fine," she mumbled. "Dinner. I'll make a reservation."

He smiled, and her heart leaped with joy. His smile brightened the room better than the sun. "Anywhere you want. My treat."

She made a noncommittal noise and turned from the room.

Cassie made it back to her office and locked the door. Then she collapsed on the floor and forced herself to remember how to breathe.

21

Wyatt

Wyatt expected Cassie to pick a safe location. He thought she'd pick the hotel restaurant or perhaps even the sandwich shop across the street. He was sure she would want something with lots of people and plenty of easy exits. So he was a bit surprised when he walked into Mangia Ristorante to find that it was an intimate and cozy Italian restaurant. For the first time since arriving on the mainland, he felt hope spring up in his chest again.

He made his way to the back of the restaurant to a small booth. It would be intimate, but still public enough to make her feel comfortable. He ordered two glasses of wine and sat watching the front door. She arrived right on time.

His tongue felt thick, and his heart sped up. She hadn't seen him yet, but just watching her made his whole body tingle with anticipation. She was so beautiful.

The simple burgundy dress she wore was classy and elegant. But, just like with her bikini, it looked sexy as hell without meaning too. It was just the way Cassie wore it. She was sexy and anything she wore looked good to him.

She wore her dark hair pulled back into a low bun at the nape of her neck, and he thought she was wearing lipstick. It was hard to see by the candlelight of the restaurant, but if she was, it definitely boded well for him.

"Mind if I join you?" she asked, catching his eye as he approached. She smiled, but it felt formal instead of playful.

He quickly stood, motioning her to the seat opposite of him.

"Thank you for coming," he said, settling back into his chair once she was seated. "I was worried you would change your mind."

"I almost did," she informed him. Her voice was cool, and she kept her posture perfect as she sat. "But I figured I might as well give you a chance. You did travel thousands of miles just to see me."

She crossed her arms, and her chin rose as if she was appraising him and not liking what she saw.

"You're angry," he said. The hope from earlier flickered like a candle in a strong wind.

"Yes." Her mouth tightened, her eyes and face serious. "You lied to me."

"I didn't lie," he quickly countered. "I never said I *wasn't* a billionaire."

She snorted a laugh. "Right. Because that makes this all better." She narrowed her eyes. "You lied by omission."

She was beautiful when she was angry, but there was no way Wyatt was going to tell her that right now.

"I didn't mean to hurt you," he said honestly.

She leaned back in her seat, arms still crossed. "When you said you couldn't come back to Arizona with me, I thought maybe you were running from the law. Or that you had a wife and three kids waiting for child support. Every reason not to come back was negative. It made me doubt who you were and my choice of being with you in the first place."

"I was afraid," he told her, guilt weighing heavily on his shoulders. "But I don't want to lose you."

"You kept a huge part of who you are a secret." She glared at him. "Yet you expected me just to drop my life and everything I know to be with you. To be with someone who doesn't feel the need to tell me the truth."

He sighed. Where was that wine?

"I should have told you," he admitted. "But, I was afraid of what would happen. Would you have stayed for me? Or for the money?"

She fidgeted slightly. "You should have told me."

"You're right. I should have." He looked up at her, his heart pounding in his chest. "I made a mistake. I'm asking you to give me a second chance. Let me make things right."

Her mouth pursed and he felt like he might be sick. He needed her in his life. Just these past few days had made him miss her terribly. It didn't feel right to be in a world without her.

"Fine. But no more secrets. No more lies of omission," she told him. "You tell me everything, and I'll do the same."

He sighed with relief. The world no longer felt like it was going to spin out of control. He had a chance to make things right with the most amazing woman he'd ever met, and he wasn't going to screw it up again.

"What do you want to know?" he asked. "I'll tell you anything. Everything."

A flicker of a smile crossed her face. "Start with why you were bar-tending. You're a billionaire. You don't need to work."

"But I like to work," he told her. "I like to feel useful."

"So, why not work for a charity or something?" she asked.

"I have a charity. It's through the company. But I wanted

something for myself. All my life, I've just been my father's heir. The company has dominated everything I do. I never had a real childhood. I never got to be a rebellious teen, and my wild twenties, and thirties, were all spent making sure the company was taken care of," he explained. "I wanted some of my life to be just for me. To have something, a job, that was purely my own. Not my father's, or my company, or even a friend's. Something that was only mine."

The wine arrived, and he gratefully took a sip. Cassie sipped gingerly on hers.

"I tried just doing nothing for a while," he told her. "But it was boring. I was so used to doing something all the time; I couldn't relax. I fell into tending bar by accident and ended up loving it. It felt enough like work to keep me busy but fun enough that it wasn't work. Plus, no one ever suspected who I was. It would be absurd for a billionaire to sling drinks."

"That's definitely true," she agreed. Again, there was almost a hint of a smile. "I certainly never guessed."

He ignored the jab, spinning the wine glass slowly in his fingers.

"After working for the company all my life, I was burned out. I needed a break." He took another sip of wine, the memories floating past him like ships on a river. "The freedom was intoxicating. I could be anyone. Do anything. For the first time in my life, no one bothered me for a business opportunity. No one asked for a raise. I didn't have to wonder if people liked me, or if they just liked my bank account."

He looked up at her. Her dark eyes were focused on him. The candlelight danced across her face, making her neutral expression hard to read. He wasn't sure if she was still angry or if she were warming to him.

"I loved my life on the island," he told her. "I loved the freedom I had there. I loved the structure of my simple job. I was happy there. Or, at least I thought I was. And then I met you."

Her eyes flickered up to his.

"And suddenly, I needed you to be happy," he said, his voice soft and full of emotion. His palms were sweating with nerves. He felt a little sick to his stomach.

If she left him now, he'd be heartbroken.

"Me?"

"Yes. You make me feel complete. You make me happy," he answered simply. "I want you to be in my life. If I can't be a bartender anymore, then so be it. I'll be anything you want, just as long as it's *me* you want. Not what I have."

Cassie took a slow sip of her wine. "I think we can try again. We have to take things slow. I'm not jumping into something this big without some planning." She set her glass down, and a slow smile crept across her face. "But, you make me happy, too."

Wyatt thought his heart might burst. The anxiety, joy, worry, and relief of this conversation were rough on a man. Now that he knew where they stood, he could start to relax and enjoy the evening.

"I hope I'm not causing you too much trouble at the hotel," he told her. "I know my presence at places can cause problems."

"Oh, no. You're fine." She grinned. "Actually, I'm probably going to get a raise or a promotion because of you. My boss is super pleased. But, if Lenny asks, tell him I really sold you on the rewards credit card."

Wyatt laughed, feeling the tension leak out of him. With her smiling at him, it felt like they were back on the island.

"You won't get in trouble for dating a guest?" he asked, thinking of how he didn't have a job anymore for that very reason.

"Well, we aren't dating. We're taking it slow, remember?"

She played with the stem of her wine glass. "It's frowned upon by corporate, but there's no official policy against it. It's one of the very few things corporate *doesn't* have specific rules about."

"At least that means I've got a chance," he told her.

She smiled and then quickly hid it again. "So, what are your plans while you're in town?" she asked him, changing the subject. "I hope you're not just going to hang out at the hotel all day. The bar isn't nearly as nice as the one at the resort, and we aren't hiring."

He chuckled. "I have some business to attend to since I'm stateside," he told her. "There's always paperwork and charity fundraising. I have plenty to do, although I'd rather work for you."

The waitress arrived then to take their order. He had the lobster ravioli. She ordered eggplant parmigiana. He had half expected her to choose the most expensive item on the menu, as most people did when dining with a billionaire. Yet, she didn't.

Their conversation flowed comfortably. Wyatt could almost pretend they'd never left the island or been apart. If not for the occasional glance, he would have thought that nothing had changed.

She told him of her family, how her father was out of the picture, and her mother currently between men.

"If you ever meet my parents, don't tell them how much you're worth," she told him. "They'd just take it to the casino and blow it all. Luckily, they don't live here. It's one of the reason's I moved to Arizona."

She told him about her first marriage. She told him about how her ex-husband had changed when she'd had a pregnancy scare. She'd been excited, her ex had been terrified. After that, he changed and started blaming her for everything wrong in his life.

"I started just staying at work," she explained. "I didn't want to go home. I didn't want to be yelled at for things I couldn't control. I didn't want the blame anymore. He didn't want me. I guess it was good that we didn't have any kids."

She kept things vague, yet there was a hurt to her words that cut him to the core. The people she had trusted most had hurt her. Her parents had gambled everything away. Her ex-husband had broken her joy.

It made him regret not being honest with her even more. He could see how her parents' bad decisions guided her current ones. Her ex had marked her even more. She was cautious now. She didn't let surprises change her decisions. She wasn't going to take a risk that she wasn't sure was going to pay off.

He loved watching her talk. She used her hands, and she smiled when she spoke. She would ask him questions and wait with an interested look for him to answer. The conversation flowed into the night.

Dinner was good and the dessert excellent. Wyatt ate slowly, trying to make the meal last. He was afraid that if they left this restaurant, the magic of being together would vanish. He knew she was still unsure of him, and to be honest, he was slightly unsure of her now as well.

He was a billionaire again. People wanted money and power from him. He hoped she wasn't one of those people. He thought she wasn't back on the island, but now...

She'd turned him down when he was a broke bartender. What was different about him being a billionaire now?

"I should head back to the hotel," he said long after they finished dessert and the bottle of wine emptied. The restaurant was nearly deserted, and he had a feeling the manager would be coming soon to kick them out for closing time.

"I'll head over there with you," she said, reaching for her purse. "I have to grab a couple of things from the office. I have an important guest, you know. Corporate needs things to be perfect."

He smiled, knowing that he'd at least get a few more minutes with her.

He typed a command into his phone, and thirty seconds later, the SUV with his bodyguards was at the front door.

"Well, that's certainly convenient," Cassie said, looking impressed. "Way better than a cab."

He chuckled. "I have to get used to having someone watch me all the time. I'd gotten used to being alone. It's strange to know men in suits are following my every move."

She chuckled, and he helped her into the comfortable SUV. She didn't say much on the short drive over. He didn't blame her. Thor and Odin were somewhat intimidating, and he wasn't sure what to say in front of them either.

The SUV came to a stop at the front of the hotel. Thor hopped out, scouted, and then motioned for Wyatt and Cassie to exit the vehicle. Wyatt sighed. He missed the days of just driving himself to the beach. He missed not worrying about being kidnapped and held for ransom. Being anonymous had been nice.

Flashbulbs went off around them. Two men with cameras ran off after taking a picture of Wyatt and Cassie getting out of the car. Wyatt sighed. He'd known it was only a matter of time before news of his return to the states would come out, but he'd hoped to avoid a lot of publicity.

Thor and Odin escorted Cassie and Wyatt up to the penthouse suite. Cassie tried to break away in the lobby, but the bodyguards shepherded her into the elevator with them. She kept a smile on her face, although her body language became tenser the closer they came to the penthouse door.

Once at the suite door, Odin and Thor vanished inside. They came out a moment later, and suddenly Wyatt and

Cassie were alone in the hallway. The room was secure. The floor was secure. For now, Wyatt was safe to be on his own.

"Sorry about that," Wyatt said, running a hand through his hair. "They can be a little overzealous."

"It's okay. I get it." She shrugged like it was nothing. Her eyes went to the hotel room door, and she took a small step away from it.

Part of being a businessman was reading people. Wyatt was good at it and being a bartender had only enhanced that skill. He knew what people sometimes thought before they themselves did.

She wasn't ready to be alone with him, and she was nervous. He decided not to invite her in. She would just say no, and he didn't want to push things.

"I had a really nice time tonight," he said, leaning casually against the corridor wall. "I was hoping we could do it again. There's a charity ball coming up. My company sponsors it. Would you be my date?"

Her eyes went wide for a moment. "A charity *ball*?"

He nodded with a smile. "I know it sounds fancy, but it's a lot of fun. I'd like to take you."

"Um, sure." She shrugged. "I've never been to a ball before. Sounds fun."

"Excellent. I'll have my assistant call you with all the details." He pushed off the wall and kissed her cheek. He was glad to see she didn't shy away from him. "Thank you for a wonderful evening."

With that, he turned and went into his hotel room, leaving her out in the hallway. He caught a glance of her surprised face just before the door closed. It made him remember the business adage of "always leave them wanting more."

He certainly wanted more of Cassie.

22

Cassie

Cassie stared at the picture on her phone in total horror. It was her. Getting out of Wyatt's car. The headline read, *"Prodigal billionaire returns! Who is the new mystery woman?"*

There were well over a thousand comments on the one site alone. Cassie didn't want to read any of them. The first had been that she was too old. She didn't want to know what the world thought of her or her looks. She didn't want to know what they thought of her being with Wyatt. She had a feeling that it would all be negative.

"What have I gotten myself into?" she wondered out loud as she sat down at her kitchen table with her morning coffee. She felt like banging her head against the table.

She still wasn't entirely sure how she felt about Wyatt being here. She was still reeling from finding out that he was actually a billionaire and that he'd lied to her, but at the same time, he was Wyatt. She had fallen in love with him on the island.

The big question was whether or not Billionaire Wyatt was the same as Island Wyatt. The smaller question was whether Island Wyatt really was who she thought he was? What kind of man gave up the billionaire lifestyle to work as a bartender?

Last night had been great. She was surprised at how annoyed she was that all she got was a good night kiss on the cheek. It had felt like they were connecting again. She'd almost been ready to forgive him. But, then seeing the picture in the morning news, she was glad she'd stayed out of his room.

Everything around Wyatt felt like a big mess. She was better off staying away from him.

He wasn't the safe choice. He wasn't the smart choice right now. Not if she wanted to keep her life simple and under control.

Knock, knock, knock.

Cassie went to the door and squinted out the peephole to see Brianna holding up a bag marked with the bakery across the street. Cassie quickly opened up the front door and let her in.

Brianna went straight to the table and sat down, opening up the bag and putting bagel sandwiches out for each of them.

"I'm liking this Brianna food delivery service," Cassie said, closing the door and joining Brianna at the table.

"Apparently, it's the only way for you to tell me anything," Brianna replied, unwrapping her sandwich. Cassie ignored the hint of guilt tugging at her chest.

"What do you want to know?" Cassie opened up her wrapper to find an egg and bacon bagel sandwich. Her favorite. Brianna knew her well.

Brianna slid her phone across the table. Up on the screen was the news article Cassie had just been reading. The one about Wyatt returning to civilization. Again, she cringed at herself in the photo.

"Oh. Right. That." Cassie pushed the phone back to Brianna. "So, apparently, Wyatt the bartender was actually Wyatt, the billionaire. Surprise."

"Surprise? Why didn't you tell me?" The hurt in Brianna's voice made Cassie feel bad even though she hadn't done anything wrong.

"I only just found out myself when he showed up at the hotel last night," Cassie replied. "I'm still trying to figure it out."

"Wait, he didn't tell you?" Brianna's brow furrowed.

Cassie shook her head. "Nope. Complete surprise."

"Huh." Brianna looked thoughtful. "I guess I can understand that."

"You can? Because I'm struggling with the fact that he lied to me all week." Cassie bit angrily into her sandwich. "He didn't even tell me on the last day when he was asking me to stay with him."

"Wait, he asked you to stay? On the island? And you didn't? The guy probably has the best beach house in the world!" Brianna exclaimed.

"But I didn't know that at the time," Cassie reminded her. "All I knew was that he was a bartender. I didn't know he had enough money to actually make moving to the island feasible for me. I thought I was going to be the sugar mama in the relationship, and I didn't know if I had enough sugar."

Brianna nodded thoughtfully. "That's why he came all dressed up to the room after you left. I bet he was going to tell you then."

"You're probably right," Cassie sighed. "If I'd taken my original flight, I'd be sipping daiquiris in the Caribbean right now."

"You didn't know," Brianna said, reaching across the table

to pat her hand. "And who knows? Maybe this will work out better."

"I still wish he would have told me sooner." Cassie slumped in her seat as she took another bite of sandwich.

"I can get why he didn't tell you." Brianna took another bite of her sandwich.

"Seriously? You can get why he lied to me?" Cassie stared at her, dumbfounded.

"You know how when people win the lottery, 'family' members come out of the wood-works? If you win, you're supposed to change your phone number and stop being on any social media because all your random relatives and long-lost friends suddenly want some of your money?" Brianna shrugged. "It would be like that, only all the time. He basically wins the lottery every day. People must ask him for stuff all the time. Can you imagine not knowing if someone is your friend because they like you, or because they want your money? Or a job at your company? Or a free ride on your jet?"

Cassie swallowed her bite of sandwich. "I guess that would be hard to know how people really feel about you."

"And dating? That would be a mess. Is that really attractive woman into you, or just into your bank account?" Brianna shook her head. "It would be a King Midas kind of curse."

"When he said he moved to the Caribbean to have some freedom, he wasn't just talking about his work," Cassie realized. "At least when he's the hot bartender, he knows exactly why those women are into him."

"I would bet he never tells them who he is," Brianna replied. "But he told you. That means you're special."

Cassie stared into her coffee, her stomach twisting inside of her. She was special. He liked her enough to reveal his true self to her. That had to mean something.

Slowly, the anger and betrayal faded. With that gone, the feelings of love and desire came rushing back.

"I need to get to work," Cassie said, shaking herself from her thoughts. "Thank you so much for breakfast."

"My pleasure. It gave me an excuse to have bagels instead of a protein bar for breakfast. Just don't tell Ian. I made him have a Pop-tart in the car on the way to school. He'd kill me if he knew I'd had breakfast sandwiches without him," Brianna replied with a laugh. She crumpled up her sandwich wrapper and dropped it into the bag. "I'll walk out with you."

Together Brianna and Cassie cleaned up their breakfast and headed out the door. Cassie waved goodbye to Brianna as they each got into their cars. As she turned on the engine, a smile started to bloom on her face.

She was going to see Wyatt.

23

Cassie

Cassie had to struggle to get past the reporters crowding the lobby. Men and women with phones and cameras of various sizes were all camped out and waiting for Wyatt to come downstairs. One of Wyatt's bodyguards from yesterday currently guarded the elevator and was checking key-cards.

That was definitely against Corporate Rule Twenty-Five: *No guarding the elevator and checking key-cards unless there is a specific event in progress. Guests and their guests must feel welcome at all time.* Cassie didn't even care, though.

The hotel was in chaos.

The poor girl running the front desk looked like she was ready to cry and two bellhops were cowering in the storage closet, occasionally peeking out and gawking at the reporters.

"Thank god you're here," Lenny announced as soon as he saw her. He grabbed her arm and nearly hauled her into Cassie's office. He shut the door and then sagged against it, like the escape from the lobby had exhausted him.

"What's going on?" She looked around, trying to get her bearings.

"Your big guest," Lenny replied tersely. "Apparently, it's bigger news than we thought. The lost billionaire returned. And, of course, the fact that he has a mystery woman."

Lenny fixed her with his stare. He knew it was her, and he wasn't happy about it.

"Lenny, I can explain—"

"You don't have to. At least I know why he chose this hotel now." Lenny crossed his arms.

"I'm sorry. I promise that it won't affect my work and—"

"I don't care," Lenny cut her off. "What I do care about is that other guests can't get into the hotel right now. There have been six cancellations this morning alone. Corporate has called three times. We're in violation of at least seven policies."

"We need to ask the reporters to leave." Cassie started a mental list of all the ways to fix the problem.

"Corporate policy says we can't since they haven't technically done anything wrong," Lenny informed her. "Rule number twenty-three. Also, some of them are also members of our Rewards program and are asking for access to the lounge. I've got it currently closed for cleaning, but policy states they must have access."

Cassie didn't even bother asking if they could go against policy. Lenny worshiped corporate policy like it was his religion. Most of the upper members of the StarTree Hotel group did. To even suggest it was heresy.

"Unfortunately, as much as we appreciate Mr. Landers choosing the Phoenix StarTree Hotel for his travel needs, he needs to leave," Lenny informed her.

Cassie nodded. He was right. If they couldn't go against corporate policy to make things work, then the hotel wasn't a good place for Wyatt to stay. "Of course, sir. I'll tell him right away."

"We just aren't equipped to handle this kind of publicity," Lenny told her. He tried to give her a gentle smile like he was doing her a favor for telling her this. "Next time you have a gentleman caller like this, have him pick a hotel that can handle this kind of attention."

"Of course, sir," Cassie promised. She had no intention of ever dating another billionaire again.

"Oh, and one more thing." Lenny stepped closer, leaning forward so that only Cassie would hear him if there had been anyone else in the room. "I've kept the extent of broken rules quiet from corporate for now. You've been a good employee. I don't want to see you get fired for breaking policy."

Cassie's mouth hung open for a moment. She shook herself at the absurdity of it. She was the one who *always* followed the rules. This was none of her doing.

"Of course," she managed to stutter after a moment. "Thank you, sir."

Lenny patted her shoulder and left the office. She peeked out the door and watched him go back to the check-in desk. Several reporters came to speak to him, and he beamed at them. It was obvious he was enjoying the attention, even if he wanted Wyatt out of the hotel.

She heard him start the spiel to offer the StarTree credit card membership.

Cassie sighed and shut her office door. This was not the day she'd been expecting. She went to her desk and saw four urgent emails in her inbox. All of them were from corporate, and none of them were happy.

She sighed again, leaning back in her chair and trying not to feel overwhelmed. She loved managing the hotel, but she hated the way corporate breathed down her neck on every little thing. This was just another example. If she had a little more leeway on hotel policies, she was sure she could have accommodated Wyatt and the reporters outside better.

But, that wasn't her problem for the day. Today, she needed to kick out her semi-boyfriend.

She stood up, checked her hair and makeup, smoothed her work jacket, and headed up the back elevator to Wyatt's room.

The guard standing at the elevator entrance was definitely against corporate policy twenty-three and thirty-six, but Cassie wasn't about to say anything about it. The guard let her pass with a stiff nod. She hit the elevator button and rode up to the top floor alone.

Cassie knocked with her manager knock. She wore her manager's face and had her manager mindset. This wasn't personal. This was business. Wyatt would have to understand.

"Cassie." Wyatt grinned as he opened the door. "Please come in."

She stepped inside the room. She could see a messy bed through an open door, and the TV was on low. Other than that, it barely looked like Wyatt had even set foot in the place. Wyatt stood beside her in comfortable looking slacks and a polo. It was similar to his bartender uniform, but this set looked much more expensive.

"I'm afraid I have some bad news, Mr. Landers." Cassie felt it was best to keep this professional. She stood up straight and clasped her hands behind her back.

Wyatt frowned. "Mr. Landers? Cassie, what's wrong?"

"We're afraid that the hotel can no longer accommodate your needs," she replied, quoting the handbook precisely. "We appreciate you choosing StarTree Hotels, but feel that it is not a good fit for you to stay with us at this time."

Wyatt looked at her and then chuckled. "So you're kicking me out?"

"The StarTree requests that you find alternate lodging," Cassie replied.

Wyatt took a step toward her, his smile cocky. "You're kicking me out."

Cassie fidgeted, struggling to maintain the expected Star-Tree image. "We're not kicking you out, as we do not kick out guests, but we are diplomatically asking you to go somewhere else due to the disruption of other hotel guests. We are happy to help accommodate you in this process."

He laughed this time. "I already have alternate lodgings," he told her. "I've rented an apartment downtown that can, how did you say it, 'better accommodate my needs.'"

"Oh, thank heavens." Cassie let out a sigh of relief before catching herself. "I mean, thank you. We appreciate your business."

Wyatt chuckled and shook his head. "Does the hotel really have you say it like that?"

Cassie nodded.

Wyatt put his hand on her shoulders and gave her a warm smile. "Then I shall tell them you did an exemplary job kicking me out."

She narrowed her eyes at him. "I didn't kick you out. I suggested you find alternate lodgings."

"Right. You did an excellent job of kicking me out to find alternate lodgings." He grinned, knowing that he was pushing her buttons.

At least it made her smile, even if it was because he was being a goofball.

"There's the smile," he said softly. He gave her shoulders a gentle squeeze before letting go. She could tell he wanted to do more but held back. "It suits you better than the frown."

"Well, just get out of my hotel, and I'll smile more," she teased, throwing all the corporate policies out the window.

Employees were not to make sarcastic remarks to guests. The goal was polite and sincere at all times. Rule Ten.

"I'll be out in an hour," he told her. "We're still on for this weekend though, right? The ball?"

There was just a hint of concern in his voice that she might choose not to go, and it made her heart tighten. She didn't want to let him down.

"I'm looking forward to it," she answered honestly.

His smile warmed his whole face and made Cassie's stomach fill with excited butterflies. She felt like a teenage girl getting smiled at from her crush.

"Will you come to dinner with me tonight?" he asked, green eyes hopeful.

She spoke before thinking. "Sure." Though, with him smiling at her like that, she would have said yes to just about anything he asked of her.

He grinned wider, and the butterflies increased their dancing in her stomach.

"I'll text you the address to my apartment," he replied. "We can go from there."

"Okay."

There was an awkward silence for a moment as they both just stood there and smiled. Cassie wasn't sure what she was supposed to say next. Should she apologize or kiss him? The bed was right there, and her body said that it was a good idea, but she was at work.

"I should let you pack," she said, going with the safest option for her job. "Thank you again for your understanding about alternate lodging."

Wyatt nodded. "Of course. Thank you for kicking me out."

Cassie rolled her eyes and laughed. She looked up at him and his beautiful green eyes. Her chest tightened, and she bit her lower lip without meaning to. She didn't stop to think.

She just went over and kissed his cheek. He smelled like fresh soap, and his face was smooth from a recent shave. It made goosebumps flow down her arms.

"Thank you," she said, and quickly darted out the door.

She'd gone against at least three different policies in the last five minutes.

Everything about Wyatt was against corporate policy.

24

Cassie

The rest of the day was a nightmare.

The press kept the lobby filled and nearly caused a car accident when they saw Wyatt's SUVs leaving the parking lot. Even after they learned he was no longer staying at the hotel, many of them refused to leave.

They'd figured out that Cassie was the mystery woman from the night before. The press figured out why Wyatt Landers would be staying in a regular business hotel faster than Lenny did. It wasn't long before they were trying to sneak into her office and were calling her work phone non-stop.

She couldn't leave her office. Every time she stepped out to check the linen supplies or go to the employee areas to post the schedule, some reporter was hounding her for information.

Where had Wyatt Landers been hiding? How did she know him? Were they in a relationship? What was he doing back in the states? Was he going to disappear again? What did this mean for his company?

She didn't have answers for any of them. She didn't even have answers for herself.

"No comment" and "You should ask him yourself" were repeated until she grew hoarse.

It wasn't even lunchtime, and she was exhausted. It was easy to see now why Wyatt had chosen to hide out on a tropical island. A deserted one sounded even better at this point. She wished the reporters would just leave her alone.

There was a knock on her office door.

"Please go away," she shouted at it. "I'm not interested in any interviews."

The doorknob rattled, and she picked up her stapler, ready to chuck it at whoever decided it was a good idea to open the door. The door opened, and she let the stapler fly.

The stapler crashed against the wall, luckily avoiding Lenny's head by inches.

He jumped in the air and looked at her completely startled. "Misuse of company materials is not allowed, Miss Turner."

Cassie blushed a deep crimson and hurried over to the fallen stapler. It was luckily unbroken and still in perfect working condition. "I am so sorry, sir. It's been a rough day."

"Indeed it has," he agreed. He cleared his throat. "That's actually why I'm here."

"Sir, I'm doing everything I can to remedy this situation. Mr. Landers checked out hours ago. I'm sure the photographers will leave soon." She hurried back to her desk, carefully putting the stapler back where it belonged.

"Unfortunately, Corporate doesn't agree." His frown deepened as he looked at her. "They've asked me to tell you to take some personal days until this is settled."

"What?" Cassie had to steady herself on the chair.

"In light of the current situation, Corporate feels it would be better for the hotel if you were not here causing a disruption," he explained. "I'm sure this will all be over in a few days, but we need to think of what's best for the hotel."

"What's best for the hotel..." Cassie sat down hard in her chair. There was still so much that needed to be caught up on from her vacation. The schedules needed to be posted. There were repairs that needed to be ordered, the kitchen required new staffing, and a multitude of other small issues that only a manager could deal with.

"Please, Cassie, I'm sure you understand. Corporate doesn't feel this meets their policy guidelines." Lenny's mouth thinned. "Take a couple of days. You have vacation days still saved up."

Cassie nodded slowly. "Of course. I'll take some time and let this all blow over."

"I'll look after the hotel," Lenny assured her. "I can manage. As long as you've been following corporate policies, everything will be fine."

"Right." Cassie didn't feel like everything would be fine. She felt betrayed by the company. She'd worked here for years, and at the first sign of trouble, they were forcing her to go home.

She stood slowly and grabbed her purse from the shelf on her desk.

"The manager's binder is in the front drawer of my desk," she told Lenny. "It's up to date through yesterday. I'm afraid I haven't had time to update it for today."

Lenny sighed. "It's supposed to be at the front desk. And it really should be updated for today. You know the policy, Cassie."

Cassie just shook her head. There wasn't a place for it at the front desk, and she'd been busy all morning. It was a stupid policy. "Good luck, sir."

She managed to sneak out through the back kitchen exit without the press seeing her. Luckily, they didn't know her car, so she just kept her head down, wore big sunglasses, and went the back way out of the hotel parking lot.

All she wanted to do was go home and relax. She planned on taking a nice shower and putting on a clean outfit before heading over to the address on her phone for dinner with Wyatt. At least that part of the day would hopefully be better.

Despite it all, she knew seeing him would make her feel good. Just thinking about him made her smile.

She turned into the street of her apartment building and stared in shock. There were cars everywhere. People filled every square inch of open space leading to her apartment. At first, she thought there must be a party for a neighbor, but then she saw the cameras.

They were all there for her. They wanted her photograph, and they were going to wait in front of her house to get it.

She parked on a side street and tried to come up with a plan.

Her phone rang with the apartment complex's name and number on the screen.

"Hello?"

"Ms. Turner, it's apartment procedure to notify you when someone wants into your apartment. I have your mother here, and she says she left something inside. May we let her in?"

Cassie hadn't spoken to her mother in months. The last she'd heard, she was at some casino in Florida and was going to "win big" any day. Her mother hadn't called since Cassie stopped sending her money.

"Whoever it is in your office is not my mother," Cassie informed the office staff. "No one is allowed in my apartment. Not even if they're my long lost twin."

"Of course. Is everything okay?"

"It's fine." She sighed. "Actually, I'm going to be out of town for a few days. Will you tell whoever is pretending to be my mother that I'm going to visit her in Florida? And have security keep an eye on my place while I'm gone?"

"Of course. Thank you for letting us know."

Cassie clicked off the phone and tried to come up with a plan. She couldn't go to her apartment. They were watching. She looked at the address on her phone. At least she could go there.

Her stomach felt sick. She wasn't safe. There were people trying to break into her house. They were trying to find her secrets, and while her secrets were arguably mild, they were hers. The idea of someone going through her underwear drawer had her sweating and ready to throw up.

She didn't know how to handle this. Two days ago, she'd felt safe in her home city. Now, it felt like everyone might turn on her. She needed someone to show her how to live this kind of public-eye life.

The only person she could think of that could help her feel safe again was Wyatt.

25

Wyatt

"You can stay here as long as you need," Wyatt promised Cassie.

She sat on the couch with her feet curled up underneath her like a cat. He handed her a cup of iced tea that she carefully sipped on. Cold drinks seemed to be favored in Arizona, no matter the season.

"Thank you," she told him with a small smile.

"Do you need anything?" Wyatt asked, taking a seat next to her on the couch. He made sure to give her an appropriate amount of room. "I can send someone out to get you a toothbrush and anything else you might need."

She smiled up at him. "I stopped and picked up some essentials on my way here. Luckily, the paparazzi don't know where I shop yet. I still had my suitcase from the trip in my car, so I have some clothes if I can use your laundry machine."

"Of course. Maria will be happy to clean them for you."

"Maria?" A hint of jealousy crossed her face, and it gave hope to Wyatt's heart.

"My housekeeper," he quickly explained. "She makes sure everything is taken care of for me. Food, laundry, errands, that kind of thing. I will admit, I did miss having someone do that for me on the island."

The jealousy faded into a comfortable smile. She startled as her phone rang. She reached into her purse and frowned at the screen.

"Another unknown number," she said, silencing the call without answering. "The reporters found my phone number."

"I'm so sorry, Cassie." His stomach felt like ice. The last thing he'd wanted to do was make her life harder. He wished there had been another way to win her back, rather than coming back to the states. The media frenzy was because of him. If he had simply let her be, she wouldn't have to deal with this. She could have just continued in her life.

She reached out and touched his hand. "It's okay." She waited until he looked up at her. "You didn't tell them to all call me. You couldn't have known this was going to happen."

"I suspected," he admitted. "I just hoped that I could fly under the radar a little bit longer. I didn't mean to make your life more difficult."

She shifted on the couch, turning her body to face him better. "The way I see it, there were two options. The first is that you didn't come and find me. We both would have lived out our lives wondering what would have happened between us."

He nodded, wondering if that was what she would have preferred at this point.

"The second is this." She motioned to the world around them. "That you gave up your peaceful life to find me. To give us a chance." She reached up and touched his face. "Just so you know, I'm glad you went with option two."

His heart sped up. She wasn't angry. He looked into her eyes, seeing all the melted chocolates and hints of warm gold in their depths. She was so beautiful it made it hard to breathe sometimes.

"You would choose this?"

"I choose this." Her voice was husky as she leaned in and kissed him. Her lips were so soft against his. Everything about her was wonderfully sweet and sensual. Her skin, her lips, her scent, even her laugh. They all pulled at him with a primal need to feel her.

Time froze as he kissed her back. It started gentle, their lips simply pressed together, but then she sighed, and her mouth opened. He tasted her tongue, and she tasted his. The floodgates of their passion opened once again. The physical connection between them couldn't be denied.

Her fingers went to Wyatt's shirt. He could feel them press against the fabric as she undid buttons and then pushed the material away from him. Without breaking the kiss, he shrugged out of his shirt. Her hands sent heat surging south as she pressed her palms into the skin of his chest. He was surprised she didn't feel his chest pounding under her fingertips. Maybe she did, but she didn't say anything.

She pulled back slightly from the kiss, looking up at him with big brown eyes. Once again, he was caught off guard by her beauty. It shone out of her like the sun. She grinned before biting her lower lip between her teeth as she looked up at him.

He could feel his pants getting uncomfortably tight.

Her hands went to his waist, and with that seductive grin still filling her face, she undid the button and zipper. Her eyes came back up to his as she pulled down on the pants. She looked a little nervous, but excited.

"Are you sure?" His voice came out husky and thick with desire.

She nodded. "I've been sure since last night."

"So I didn't have to wait?" he teased, putting his palm to her neck. He stroked her jawline with his thumb, marveling at her beauty.

She chuckled. "Good things come to those who wait," she replied. "And I seem to recall *you're* the one always turning me down."

She leaned back and began undressing. It was a good thing that his underwear was made with elastic because anything else would have torn at the seams as he watched her.

She slid out of her silk blouse, tossing the shirt to the floor. She shimmied out of her very work appropriate skirt, but the motion showed off her curves to the point where Wyatt was panting. Her body was curves and softness. Her bra was simple, as were her panties, but they held the same simple elegance that made everything she wore look good.

When she reached behind her and undid her bra, Wyatt nearly lost himself.

She grinned, noting the effect she was having on him. She kicked her skirt out of her way and kissed him, pressing her naked breasts against his chest.

"Cassie..." He loved the way her name felt in his mouth. He loved the way her eyes sparkled when he called to her.

His hand went to her side, feeling the swell of her breast pressed against him. She had such lovely breasts. Firm and smooth, small but sensual. They were perfect in his eyes.

"I need you," she whispered, her lips barely breaking the kiss to speak. "Please don't make me wait any more."

He grabbed her hand, leading her to the bedroom. The grand tour of the apartment could wait. Right now, a primal, urgent need filled him. It stole his thoughts and made his body hard. He didn't just want her. He needed her like a man dying of thirst required water.

He couldn't survive without her.

The bedroom shades were drawn, so the room was a comfortable shade of darkness. Light filtered in through cracks in the curtains, giving him just enough light to find the nightstand with the condoms. His hands shook with need.

"Let me," she whispered, coming up beside him.

She took the foil packet from his hands and dropped to her knees. The sight of her looking up at him from that position was quite possibly the hottest thing he'd ever seen. She tugged on his underwear, freeing him from its confines.

He loved the little whimper she let out when she saw him. He loved the way she unconsciously licked her lips as she wrapped the condom around him. Her touch was light and soft, but it sent spirals of heat and pleasure up his spine.

She stood up slowly, wrapping her arms around his shoulders. She was so warm against his skin as she pressed her body into him, kissing him with her delicious mouth.

He grabbed her thigh, raising it up and hooking her leg over his forearm. Her arms tightened around his shoulders as she looked into his eyes and nodded.

With his free hand, he guided himself into her and found heaven.

Her smile faded into a moan of pleasure as he filled her. She tightened around him, her body calling for more as she whimpered her pleasure.

Wyatt thrust deep, filling her. The motion satisfied and yet made him hunger for more. It felt so good, yet it wasn't enough. He needed more of her. He needed to fill her.

The motions were primal and raw, yet gentle and sensual. Every thrust urged for another, and her little moans of delight spurred him on. He loved the way her body responded to his, wrapping and tightening around him. She was so warm and wet, sweet and sexy.

He needed more. He dropped her leg, and she whimpered like she'd lost something precious. But, then she saw the bed behind him and grinned, giving a gentle push to his shoulder. He lay down, and she was on him in a second, legs straddling his hips and poised with heaven over him yet again.

His hands tightened on her hips as she slowly lowered herself onto him. A fresh wave of unbearable pleasure rolled through him. Wyatt's head fell back, and he groaned. He let her lead for a moment, watching her undulate and dance on his length. She rose and fell, her mouth and face twisted in the exquisite pleasure she found riding him.

Wyatt could no longer control himself. His hips began to thrust upward as she came down. Every motion was powerful and primal as he lost control. He needed her. He was lost to the pleasure that she gave him. It was unlike anything he'd ever experienced with a woman.

"Wyatt..." She moaned his name like a prayer of need.

His entire body vibrated with desire. There was no stopping him now. She turned him on and sent his body to the edge without even trying.

She looked down at him, her brown eyes shining in the dark. The sensations weren't heaven. She was. Cassie was heaven. She was worth coming here for. She was worth leaving his life and coming back to the world he hated.

Because with her here, it really was heaven.

Her palms splayed on the smooth skin of his chest, her eyes fluttering as she too found the apex of pleasure. Other than her name, his mind went gloriously blank. Other than the essence of Cassie, he didn't exist. Her body tightened and clenched around his as she lost her soul to him the way he'd lost his to her.

She collapsed onto him, her breaths coming fast and hard. His heart beat out of control. His body twitched with the release she'd given him. Her skin stuck to his, but he loved it. He never wanted her to leave.

Wyatt reached up and touched her cheek. She was an

angel. He couldn't believe how good it felt to have her back with him. The world was right when she was near.

"Stay with me. Here. Until this, all blows over. It'll be like we're back on the island, only without the ocean nearby."

Cassie sighed with contentment. "Okay."

He couldn't believe it was that easy, but if something was meant to be, maybe it could be.

26

Wyatt

Wyatt hated being back in the public eye.

He hated knowing that if he looked out the window, someone might photograph him. He hated that he couldn't just go to the grocery store without bodyguards. Heck, he couldn't even go get the mail without Thor or Odin watching his back.

He missed his simple life on the island. He missed the freedom of anonymity. He missed talking to strangers without them knowing his entire life because they'd read his Wikipedia entry.

But he loved having Cassie.

Cassie made it all worth it. To wake up and find her sleeping in his bed or sitting at the kitchen table drinking coffee, was like living in a dream. Time didn't matter when they were together. He would suddenly find that the sun had set and the only thing they'd done all day was snuggle and talk about their favorite jobs growing up.

He found that they really could just talk for hours, or that they could simply sit in comfortable silence. Just being near her felt right, like a missing part of him had been found. She completed him just by being near.

However, he knew he couldn't stay here indefinitely. City life wore at him. He chafed at the constant leash of security. The sounds of the city outside grated on him and he found himself missing the serenity of the beach more and more.

If he could have gone outside like an average person, he might have felt differently. But, his face was on every phone screen. The appeal of a long-lost billionaire bachelor with a possible love interest that was an ordinary woman from their town had Phoenix in a frenzy. Everyone wanted a piece of them.

After two horrible failures to go eat out, they stayed in their apartment and just sent Maria out for food. Despite the circumstances, Wyatt found that the three days they were stuck in his apartment, trapped by the paparazzi, were three of the best days of his life.

He loved her. He was sure of it now. You couldn't spend three days alone with someone and not know how you felt about them. Even though it was fast, he knew he wanted to spend the rest of his life with her.

He didn't mean to propose anytime soon. They could take the actual steps slowly and comfortably, but he knew the outcome. He could feel it in his bones that this was the woman he was supposed to spend the rest of his life with. She was someone who could be his friend, his partner, his confidant, and lover.

Tonight was the charity ball. He'd already arranged for her to have an amazing day of pampering, hair and makeup, and a dress that would make Cinderella jealous. He planned to ask her to move back with him to the islands after the ball.

She knew who he was now. She knew he could provide for

her. That they could live a life of luxury and spend every day like they'd spent the last three. He knew she'd be leaving behind her life here, but he hoped she would take the chance to be with him, just as he'd taken the chance to be with her.

He sat at the breakfast table, sipping his coffee and going over his plans. The ball would be elegant. It would be romantic. They could then slip away on a private jet and disappear back into obscurity in the safety of a small island.

"Good morning," Cassie greeted him, coming out of the bedroom.

Her dark hair hung loosely around her shoulders, and the thin white men's t-shirt did nothing to hide her curves. She stretched, and the shirt rode up, exposing the bottom hints of pale pink lacy underwear. Wyatt's upper brain stopped functioning as blood rushed south.

Cassie didn't seem to notice the effect she had on him. She walked into the kitchen and poured a cup of coffee, joining him at the small table.

"The ball's tonight. I'm really looking forward to it," she said, taking a sip of coffee. With her bottom half hidden beneath the table, Wyatt could almost control himself. Mostly.

He smiled and nodded, not quite able to form coherent sentences yet.

Cassie frowned as her phone rang from the living room. She'd turned it to do not disturb mode, so at least now the only calls that came through were from select friends or her work. She stood up from the table and walked to the living room, and once again, all of Wyatt's blood rushed south at the sight of her barely covered ass.

"Oh, it's Janessa." Cassie grinned and hit the answer button. "Hey, Janessa. What's up?"

She frowned, looking down at the phone.

"Huh. Must be a bad connection. She hung up." Cassie

shrugged, and came back to the table, setting the phone down so she could sip her coffee. "If it's important, she'll call back."

"I actually have a surprise for you," Wyatt announced, forcing some of the blood to come back up to his thinking brain. It helped that she was sitting again.

"Yeah?" She grinned at him, her face lighting up. "What?"

"I have a spa day arranged for you. And a dress for tonight." He held his breath, waiting to see her reaction.

"You didn't have to do that." She looked surprised but pleased.

"It's your first ball. I thought you should have a Cinderella experience."

She grinned. "Does that mean you'll be my Prince Charming? And dance with me all night long?"

"You and only you," he promised. "And I got the upgraded package where you don't turn into a pumpkin at midnight. You get to stay Cinderella as long as you want."

She leaned across the small table and kissed his cheek. "Thank you. I wasn't sure what I should wear tonight, and this makes it a lot more fun."

"Good. Tonight is about fun. For both of us," he replied. If she had fun, then he hoped she would be more likely to say yes to coming back to the island with him.

"Do you want some breakfast?" she asked, standing up. "I'll make scrambled eggs."

"Eggs sound delicious," he replied, trying not to stare at the hem of her shirt as she walked past him. She saw him looking and wiggled her hips once she was past, subtly arching her back, so the shirt rode up. She knew precisely the effect she was having on him.

Cassie turned on the stove and began cracking eggs into the pan. Wyatt could get used to this. A half-naked woman making him breakfast was a beautiful thing.

Cassie's phone began to ring on the table.

"Will you get that for me?" Cassie asked. "I've got egg all over my hands."

Wyatt hit the green answer button. "Cassie's phone. She's currently unavailable. May I take a message?"

Cassie giggled from the kitchen.

"Hi, Wyatt. I knew there was something special about you. I was right about you all along."

The voice on the other end was not Janessa.

"Lorna?" Wyatt nearly dropped the phone. He checked the caller ID to see Janessa's name.

"You remember my name," she cooed. "I knew you liked me."

"What do you want?" Wyatt put the phone on speaker. Cassie came over from the kitchen, hands on hips.

"You, silly," Lorna replied with a giggle. "I'm such a better match for you. If you want, you can come to the country club. I've heard you've been trapped in your apartment all week. The country club is made for people like us. No one will hassle you there."

"He's not coming, Lorna," Cassie growled. "Back off. He's mine!"

The line immediately went dead. Lorna ended the call.

"Seriously?" Cassie vibrated with anger next to him. "The nerve of that... that bitch!"

Wyatt hadn't heard Cassie use any rough language the entire time he'd known her. Her use of the word bitch was more intense than if she'd dropped a hundred f-bombs.

"Did you mean it?" he asked softly, staring at the phone. She'd said he was hers.

"What? That's she's a bitch? Hell yes." Cassie practically panted with anger.

"No, that I'm yours."

Her body went still, and she turned slowly to face him. "I

guess I did," she said after a moment. She shrugged and offered a smile. "I guess three days of awesome sex will do that to a girl."

Wyatt's heart soared. His confidence for the evening grew higher. He was sure she would say yes now. He was sure they could make this work. They could go back to the island and things could go back to normal.

Cassie went back to the kitchen, stirring the eggs with a spatula and muttering angrily under her breath about Lorna's nerve. She no longer paid any attention to the hem of her shirt, and it kept riding up with her every motion.

It was all Wyatt could do to stay in his seat and not carry her off to the bedroom. He wanted her but knew he needed to wait until she was out of the kitchen. She took her egg cooking very seriously.

"I never asked, but I'm curious," Cassie said after a moment. She glanced over at him, her face no longer angry. "What happened to your old job? The bartending one? Did you just quit? I'm kind of imagining you telling your boss who you were and doing a mike-drop."

He chuckled at the image of him dropping the microphone after telling James off. It definitely would have been satisfying.

"I actually was fired."

Her eyes went big. "What? Why? You were great!"

He shrugged. "An anonymous guest reported that I was at the wedding," he explained. "It was against policy to date guests."

Cassie paused mid-push of her eggs. "You didn't tell me that. You didn't tell me you risked your job to be my date. I mean, I thought it might, but you never said anything. I thought you were okay to come to the wedding."

He shrugged. "It's not like I needed the job."

"But you liked it." She smiled softly. She left her eggs and came over to kiss his cheek. "You must really like me or something."

"Or something," he agreed.

"Wait, anonymous guest?" Cassie scoffed and rolled her eyes. "F-ing Lorna."

"You know you can use real curse words," Wyatt offered. She stuck her tongue out at him.

"Corporate says no foul language," she replied.

"Corporate's not here," he reminded her.

"It had to have been her," Cassie said, ignoring his point. "She would have been the only woman in that entire wedding that would have ratted you out. Everyone else thought you were wonderful."

"Aunt Suzette did say she liked me," Wyatt agreed. "Your eggs are burning, by the way."

"F-ing Lorna," Cassie repeated, making Wyatt laugh as she rushed back to the kitchen to rescue the scrambled eggs.

"Does she do this often? Lorna, I mean, not the eggs," Wyatt asked, twisting in his seat to watch Cassie in the kitchen.

"All the time," Cassie confirmed. "It's basically how she found husband number two. It only lasted a couple of years before he realized what he'd gotten into with her. The eggs are fine, by the way."

Cassie pushed the eggs out onto two plates and returned to the kitchen table. Cassie made the best scrambled eggs. Her eggs were one of the reasons that he hoped she'd come with him to the island.

"I don't want to talk about Lorna," Cassie said, sitting down in her chair. "I can't believe she called like that."

Wyatt shrugged. "I get it a lot."

"Seriously?" Cassie paused with a fork-full of eggs halfway to her mouth.

"I'm a billionaire. Women look at me and see all their dreams coming true," he told her.

Cassie set her eggs back down. "I don't see you that way."

"You mean you don't want me to make your dreams come true?" he teased, liking the way she blushed.

"No, I mean... I like *you*," she explained. "I like the way you think about things. You see things differently than I do, and I like the way you see the world. I mean, the money's nice, and I am completely in love with Maria, but that's not why I'm here. I like *you*. Just Wyatt. Not necessarily billionaire Wyatt."

Cassie flushed a little and went back to eating her eggs.

Wyatt's chest felt like he was filled with helium. He could have floated to the ceiling he was so happy. His request tonight was looking better and better.

Cassie's phone began to ring again. She looked at it with narrowed, suspicious eyes.

"Oh, it's work." She picked it up with a smile. "This is Cassie."

Her smile started to fade. She said several "yes, sir"s and a couple of "I understand"s as well as some "of course"s. With every phrase, her expression fell a little and her voice became softer. Finally, she said goodbye and hung up.

"What's wrong?" Wyatt asked, reaching out to take her hand.

She blinked back tears that she pretended weren't there. "Work. They don't want me back."

"What do you mean? They fired you?" Anger flared up in Wyatt's chest on her behalf.

"No, not fired. Just administrative leave. Indefinitely." She shrugged and looked down at her eggs without touching them.

"Oh, Cassie. I'm so sorry," Wyatt said softly. Guilt tugged at him.

"Apparently the hotel is still swarmed with press and guests that want to have a chance meeting the billionaire," she explained. "They had to hire someone to deal with all the phone calls."

Wyatt's guilt doubled. He had come in like a wrecking ball to try and be with her. Her job was her life. She loved working at the hotel. And he'd taken it from her.

"At least I'm still getting paid," she said, trying to smile. "And it means I can spend more time with you."

"I'm so sorry, Cassie." Wyatt wracked his brain, trying to think of a way he could fix this. The best solution he had was for her to come with him back into the island's obscurity. Was now the right time to ask? Would she say yes with this phone call heavy on her mind?

"It'll be fine," Cassie said, picking up her fork and taking a bite of eggs. "I'm sure this will all blow over soon. Besides, it's a great vacation for me. They didn't fire me, so I still have my job. It's actually a good thing."

She looked up at him and smiled. He couldn't decide if she was faking her smile or if she actually meant it. He decided to wait to ask her. Stick with the plan and ask her tonight at the ball.

The plan was the way to go. Cassie liked plans. Plans worked.

Still, he could barely wait for the ball tonight to follow through on the plan.

27

Cassie

"Have fun," Wyatt said as the SUV came to a halt. "I'll see you at the ball."

Cassie nodded, kissed him on the cheek, and got out of the car.

In front of her was the most expensive salon in the state. She'd heard amazing things about the services, but she'd never even tried to book anything. She couldn't seem to justify spending that much money on just a haircut. Since her hair was usually pulled back for work, it never seemed to matter who cut it.

She swallowed hard and stepped inside. Tranquility washed over her like water, just by stepping through the door. The soft sound of water, the smell of clean linens, and welcoming, comfortable-looking furniture all greeted her.

"Ms. Turner?" the woman at the front desk asked. She smiled when Cassie nodded. "We're so glad you're here. If you follow me, I'll take you to your private room."

Cassie had never heard of a private room for a haircut before, but she happily followed the woman into a beautiful room with hardwood floors. A single comfortable looking chair sat in the center of the room. The sound of water and the soft scent from the lobby still filled the air.

"You must be Ms. Turner," a man said, coming to greet her. He was slender and moved with elegance. His posture was amazing. "I'm Cesar."

"It's nice to meet you," Cassie replied. She held out her hand, and Cesar gave her a gentle handshake.

"Please come and sit," he told her, motioning to the comfortable chair.

And thus began the best haircut of Cassie's life.

If someone had told her that it was possible to feel this pampered and relaxed from a haircut, she never would have believed them. The price suddenly made much more sense. Cesar washed her hair, giving her a luxurious scalp massage. She had cucumbers over her eyes and paraffin wax on her hands as he worked her hair into a lather.

She could feel her shoulders coming down from by her ears as Cesar worked out tension she didn't even know she had.

Then came the haircut itself. Cesar worked quickly and efficiently, cutting her hair and then styling it up. He worked with curls and braids, twists and pins, all the while keeping Cassie comfortable with easy conversation.

When he was done, she looked like something out of a magazine.

Her long hair swept up to a sparkling pin that dazzled against a dark braid. Curls cascaded down her back. Cassie couldn't ever get curls like this, but Cesar had made them look effortless. She looked ready for a photo shoot.

And that was just the hair. Cesar left, and a woman named Katrina came in. Katrina transformed Cassie's face into something smooth and feminine without looking like she wore any makeup at all. Katrina used the same effortless grace as Cesar to create something stunning.

When they were done, Cassie stared at the woman looking back at her in the mirror. She was stunning. Gorgeous.

She looked worthy of dating a billionaire. She looked worthy of a magazine spread, and she was still wearing just jeans and a t-shirt.

Cesar came back in when Katrina finished.

"Do you like the results?" he asked her, a smile saying he already knew the answer.

"Very much," Cassie replied. "Now I just need someone to do this for me every day!"

She meant it as a joke, but Cesar looked thoughtful.

"I could probably work you into my schedule," he mused. "Not the full up-do, but at least the cut. I'm not sure of Katrina's schedule."

Cassie wasn't sure what to say. The idea of having this kind of lavish treatment every day seemed almost absurd.

"But, there is time for scheduling later," Cesar said, waving his hand. "We must get you in your dress. Come with me."

He brought her to a small, intimate room. There were no windows and candlelight flickered from the corners.

"This is usually one of the massage rooms," Cesar explained. "But, it will work as a changing room for today. Your dress is here."

Cesar motioned to a hook on the wall at the most beautiful dress Cassie had ever seen.

Stunning dark red lace covered the bust and made thin sleeves. It then cascaded down into a full and sweeping skirt. Just hanging on the wall, the silhouette was beautiful. Cassie hoped it looked as good on her as it did hanging.

Cesar left her to try on the dress. At first, Cassie was almost afraid to touch it. It was akin to art, and she wasn't sure how to put it on. Slowly, she found her courage and slipped the satin and lace skirt over her head. She then realized she should have stepped into it the moment she had to protect her hair.

She managed to get the zipper most of the way up her back, but she couldn't get the last few inches. But, the dress fit. It clung to her curves, and she loved the soft satin sound the skirts made when she walked.

She opened the door to find Cesar waiting outside. His eyes went wide as he did an up and down of her body.

"Beautiful," he whispered, shaking his head with awe.

"I can't get the zipper," Cassie informed him.

Cesar quickly pulled the zipper the rest of the way up for her. "Come see," he said, stopping once again to admire her. He motioned her to a full-length mirror.

The woman in the mirror was a movie star. She was a model. She was a fairy tale queen who any mortal would fall instantly in love with only a glance.

"Wow." Cassie could scarcely believe it was her. "Amazing what the right dress can do," she whispered.

"The dress only highlights beauty," Cesar informed her. He carefully smoothed a flyaway strand of hair. "The beauty is you."

Cassie blushed a crimson to match her dress, but Cesar didn't seem to notice.

"It's time to get you to the ball," he said. Cassie could only imagine that this was how Cinderella felt. Instead of a pumpkin, it was a black SUV, but Cassie still felt like a princess. She couldn't wait to meet her Prince Charming.

28

Cassie

Cassie bounced her knees with excitement and just a little bit of nervousness as the SUV drove up to the ball. The hotel looked like a castle as they approached, and Cassie couldn't help but stare out the window.

She'd been here once before for a conference. The hotel was a legend with eight pools, two golf courses, spa, and stunning mountain views. The ballroom was the biggest in the state and usually booked out for months. She'd peeked into the rooms during the conference, and the hotel manager in her had fallen in love.

This was bigger than anything she wanted to run. While she enjoyed working at a major hotel, she preferred a more intimate experience. She liked interacting with guests and making the experience personal to them. That was hard to do in a huge hotel.

Still, she loved this hotel. It was like going to Disneyland. It was a chance to see how things were done on a bigger scale with a larger budget. Cassie's hotel only held business events, so getting to see a social event would be new and exciting.

The charity ball was held here annually. Wyatt's company held several of these balls in multiple states across the country. All the proceeds went to charity, and it was usually one of the most significant social events for each individual city. It was pure luck that the Phoenix ball was being held the week Wyatt was in town.

Expensive cars lined the drop-off area in the front of the hotel. A red carpet rolled out from the entrance and into the lobby. Photographers snapped photos as the high society of Phoenix arrived for the charity ball.

Men and women in beautiful clothes stopped and paused for photos as Cassie exited the SUV. Her stomach twisted and churned with nerves. For the first time, she was a guest at one of these events, not a worker.

As an event manager, she knew where the kitchen staff was supposed to be. She knew what table linens and silverware should be out, and that the emcee of the event would keep the schedule.

But, as a guest, she wasn't sure what to do. Should she go to the ballroom? The dinner area? Was there a posted schedule?

Cassie stepped out onto the red carpet and was immediately assaulted by camera lights.

"Are you and Wyatt Landers a couple? Why is he back in town? What's Wyatt Landers doing in Phoenix? Are the rumors that he was working on an island true? What island in the Caribbean were you on? Is this a publicity stunt to launch a new product?"

She didn't know how to answer so many questions thrown at her at once. She shied away from the cameras and hurried inside the hotel. Inside at least, the security kept the press out. Only a few photographers were in the lobby, but they all wore a very clear badge indicating they were associated with the ball. They, at least, asked before taking a photo.

Elegant guests milled around the beautiful lobby, sipping on drinks and murmuring with conversation. The red carpet led directly to the ballroom, where Cassie hoped she'd find Wyatt. They hadn't really discussed where they were meeting, which Cassie was now regretting. The last thing she wanted to do was wander around an event like this without the guest that brought her, so she followed the carpet, feeling a bit like Dorothy trying to find the Emerald City.

Two massive and ornately carved doors stood like guards to the ballroom. Cassie continued to follow the red carpet, trying hard to blend in with the other guests. Despite the dress and the hair, she still felt like everyone could see she didn't belong here. Every time someone looked in her direction, she wished she had on her simple black work suit and had a clipboard and headset.

The ballroom shimmered with light. Crystal chandeliers hung from the ceiling and iridescent fabric draped delicately around the room. It looked like something out of a fairy tale. Cassie stood near the entrance, open-mouthed and smiling as she looked around at the grand display.

"You look amazing."

Wyatt stood in front of her, his expression filled with awe. The look on his face made everything worth it. He looked like he was under her spell.

"So do you," she told him.

He looked good. Really good. The black tuxedo fit perfectly, outlining his broad shoulders and trim waist. He'd slicked his blonde hair back into a sleek style that looked like he'd stepped out of a GQ magazine.

She was Cinderella, and he was indeed Prince Charming.

Wyatt offered her his arm, just like in the fairy tale. She

rested her hand lightly on the stiff fabric of his jacket as he walked her to their table.

They were forced to stop and pose for pictures no less than three times in the fifty-foot walk to their reserved table. Everyone was polite, but she knew that cell phones were snapping photos of them even as they walked past. Wyatt kept smiling and moving them along, staying polite but giving away nothing.

Everyone wanted a piece of the missing billionaire and his mystery woman.

"They're all staring at us," Cassie whispered, feeling dozens of sets of eyes glance their way. Even over the soft classical music, she could hear the whispers as they walked. Wyatt's name echoed softly at every table they passed.

"I can't blame them," Wyatt said. "You are absolutely stunning."

She took the compliment with a smile and a slight shake of her head. He was trying to make her feel comfortable, and it was working. Now that he was with her, her nerves were starting to settle. She felt like she could make it through the night without needing a million drinks. Her stomach still knotted up inside of her, but at least she no longer felt like puking.

"How do you do this?" she asked as Wyatt pulled out a chair for her to sit. They were near the front of the ballroom, near the stage at a prime table. "This ball is a little over-whelming."

Wyatt chuckled. "Why do you think I ran away to the Caribbean?" He shook his head as he looked around the room. "It's beautiful and grand, but... this life is hard in its own way. You must always be ready to perform."

"I feel like we're on display. Like monkeys in the zoo. Pretty monkeys, but still just something to look at." Cassie reached for her glass of water and realized her hand was shaking.

She had a feeling she would never get used to this. She didn't like being the center of attention. She liked working in the background and making sure events like this ran smoothly. This was the exact opposite of what she enjoyed.

"Well, at least you won't be on display on your own," Wyatt told her, motioning with a smile to the guests heading toward their table.

Janessa looked lovely in a strapless purple gown. Kyle had stopped to say hello to another couple at an adjacent table, but Janessa waved and grinned.

Cassie waved back and then smiled at Wyatt. "Did you do this?"

"Brianna is coming too," Wyatt informed her. "I asked Julia, but she had to work."

Cassie's heart melted. "Thank you."

Wyatt shrugged like it was nothing. "I want this to be a good experience for you. And, I want you to know that you can always have your friends with you."

"Thank you." She leaned over and kissed his cheek, breathing in the scent of him. Clean soap with a hint of richness, and somehow a touch of the ocean. Even this far from the water, he still reminded her of where they met.

"This is so beautiful," Janessa announced, coming over to the table. She hugged Cassie and grinned at Wyatt. "I'm glad you told Kyle you were coming. We nearly skipped this year. This is a much better table than we usually get."

Kyle's family was very wealthy. It made sense that they would get an invite to something like this. Kyle arrived at the table and hands were shaken and greetings made.

"Cassie, where did you get that dress? It's amazing. You look like a princess." Janessa grinned at her.

Cassie blushed a little. "Thanks. Wyatt got it for me."

Janessa turned to Wyatt. "You are now allowed to pick out my wardrobe as well."

Wyatt chuckled. "I wish I could claim credit. I hired someone. My expertise is in surfboards, not women's clothing."

The group laughed, and Cassie could feel herself relaxing. With Janessa, Kyle, and Brianna here, she wouldn't feel like an outsider.

"Wyatt, there you are!"

A woman in a sleek blue dress hurried over to him. Her short blonde hair was modern and chic. She looked like she belonged here.

"Olive." Wyatt grinned and stood up to greet her. The hug he gave her sent a small shot of unnecessary jealousy through Cassie's chest.

"Wyatt, I'm so glad I found you," Olive announced, taking the empty seat next to him. "I'm in a pickle."

Wyatt frowned, concern creasing the edges of his eyes. "What's wrong?"

"Our emcee for the auction is sick. Do you know the band, The Tones? We were supposed to get the lead singer to run the auction for us, but he's lost his voice," Olive explained. "We need an emcee."

"Oh, no. Not me," Wyatt said, shaking his head. "Find somebody else."

"Wyatt, it's your company that's putting this on," Olive told him, sounding like a mother reminding her child to do his homework. "It's kind of your responsibility."

Wyatt sighed and slumped in his chair. "Fine. When you put it that way."

Olive grinned. "Thank you. I'll go get everything set up. It'll be easy. Promise."

She flashed him one more grin and then disappeared.

"Who was that?" Cassie asked, trying to keep her voice neutral.

"That's the charity manager," Wyatt explained. "She is responsible for running the whole ball."

"Oh." Cassie still didn't like the green envy sliding through her ribs. Olive was attractive. She knew how to navigate this billionaire world. Even though Wyatt hadn't done anything other than greet the woman, Cassie still felt like Olive had something she didn't.

"Oh, here comes Brianna," Janessa announced with a happy smile. Her smile then faltered. "And Lorna."

The mention of Lorna's name made Cassie's stomach sour. She suddenly wished she had a stronger drink. Lorna was the last person in the world Cassie wanted to spend this evening with.

Cassie turned to see Brianna in a black halter-dress walking toward the table. She also wore an uncomfortable look as Lorna hung off her arm. There was no way Lorna was letting go of Brianna and going to a different table.

Cassie wondered if she could just crawl under the table and hide. It was that, or possibly punch Lorna in the face.

Neither seemed appropriate for a fancy ball.

29

Cassie

"Look who I found on my way in," Lorna announced as they arrived at the table. "I'm so glad I found her. Otherwise, I would have been sitting at the wrong table all night. Here's where the party is, right?"

Lorna wore a poison-apple-green skin-tight dress. The mermaid tail flared out at the knee, but the rest was practically painted onto Lorna's body, highlighting her trim figure. While stylish, it was also loud and over the top, much like Lorna.

Brianna smiled weakly.

"You sit next to Kyle, and I'll sit at this spot here," Lorna said, practically pushing Brianna at Kyle. Lorna took the empty seat next to Wyatt.

Cassie tried not to bristle. She decided not to let her anger and jealousy rise to the surface. She could be the bigger person. Tonight was for charity after all.

"Brianna, I'm sure Cassie wants to catch up with you. Trade me seats?" Wyatt asked, looking innocently at Brianna.

"Sure." Brianna hopped up, and the two switched seats. Cassie felt a surge of smug pleasure at the way Lorna's face twitched with annoyance. She was now seated as far away from Wyatt as possible.

"I'm so sorry," Brianna said softly to Cassie. "She ambushed me. I feel like a mountain lion stalked me. I'm not even sure she actually has a ticket. She just grabbed onto me as we walked in the front door."

"It's fine," Cassie told her, trying to believe it herself. "She's just being Lorna."

"Excuse me for a moment. I see a business partner I need to speak with," Kyle announced. He nodded around the table and then left.

"So, Wyatt, tell me, how has Phoenix been treating you?" Lorna asked, putting her chin on her hands and blatantly showing off her cleavage to the person sitting across the table from her. She was definitely making lemonade out of her lemons.

Wyatt cleared his throat. "It's been a great city," he replied. His eyes went to Cassie and warmed. "It's exactly what I was looking for."

Little tingles of energy rippled down Cassie's arms with his smile. He wasn't looking at Lorna's cleavage. He wasn't interested in Olive's fancy haircut.

He liked her. He'd come back for her. Not them.

"I'd love to show you around town," Lorna tried again. She shifted her shoulders so that her chest somehow stuck out just a little bit more. The green fabric struggled to stay attached at the seams.

"I'm good, thanks." Wyatt gave her a polite smile, making sure that his gaze wasn't where she wanted it. "If you'll excuse me, I need to go prep for the auction."

Wyatt stood up and instead of leaving directly, came over and kissed Cassie's cheek. He made it sweet and sensual, and slightly possessive.

"I'll see you soon. Don't bid on too many of the bachelors," Wyatt teased, his hand grazing a bare patch of skin on Cassie's back. She shivered with the touch, wanting more.

"Sure," she replied, feeling a little dazed from the kiss. She wasn't sure how a kiss on the cheek could be more sexual than one on the lips, but Wyatt had definitely done it. He winked and disappeared behind the stage. The goofy grin on her face stayed for a moment before fading. "Wait, bachelors?"

"After a kiss like that, I'm not surprised you can't think straight." Brianna chuckled, knowing that Cassie's brain was still in kiss mode and unable to function properly.

"The auction is a bachelor/bachelorette auction," Lorna replied, her voice haughty. "Didn't you even look at the invitation?"

"Did you even get one?" Brianna shot back. Lorna just rolled her eyes.

"He's not listed on the auction page," Janessa assured Cassie. "They do it every year. All the single socialites and local celebrities put themselves up for a date. Last year, we even had that actor from the vampire show. He got a ton of money."

"The blond one or the really tall one?" Brianna asked, leaning forward. "Because if it's the blond one, I will use my life savings." She paused and then grinned. "Well, to be honest, I will use my life savings for either one of them. They are so good looking."

The conversation between Janessa and Brianna on the workings of their favorite vampire show took over the table. It was light and easy, with a shallowness that was easy to navigate. Cassie was glad she didn't have to hold up the conversation.

As much fun as getting dressed up was, this wasn't her thing. She wasn't a high-society kind of person. She would much rather be curled up on the couch with Wyatt watching reruns of the Twilight Zone. She had a feeling he would rather be on the couch as well.

"You doing anything interesting this weekend, Cassie?" Lorna asked. She smiled, looking almost innocent. Unfortunately, Brianna and Janessa were deep in conversation, leaving Lorna with only Cassie to talk to.

"Um, just staying in. Wyatt and I are planning on trying a new restaurant tomorrow," she replied. "He says it will be super romantic. Then we'll just go back to his place. Like we have been all week. It's fabulous."

Cassie knew it was shallow. She knew she was being petty, but she didn't care. She wanted to rub it in Lorna's face that Wyatt was with Cassie.

"How lucky for you." Lorna's sour face turned away, and the conversation thankfully was over.

The lights dimmed, and Olive came out on the stage.

"Ladies and gentlemen," she announced. "It's time to begin the auction."

A drum-roll filled the ballroom as guests hurried to their seats. Lights flashed and the stage filled with swirling lights. Stage smoke rolled across the floor, and Wyatt stepped out, looking like he was made for TV lights and being the center of attention.

"Ladies and gentlemen, it's a pleasure to have you," Wyatt said into the microphone. He walked casually across the stage, smiling and handsome. "We're about to auction off some very exciting dates. If you're single and looking to mingle, or even if you just want a chance to talk business, here's your opportunity. All proceeds will be going to the

House For Home charity, so be generous and brave with your bids."

Lorna sat with her lip between her teeth and fawning up at the stage. Cassie knew the same look was on her face. Wyatt held the stage wonderfully. He was a natural, even though Cassie knew he would rather not be the center of attention.

Cassie didn't bid on anyone. She didn't need to. Brianna put in a bid for a date with a professional football player but was quickly outbid. Lorna only bid once, and not very much. It made Cassie slightly nervous that the money and status hungry woman wasn't throwing dollar bills up on that stage to get dates. It seemed like it would be the perfect opportunity, yet Lorna wasn't taking it.

"And that's our last date," Wyatt announced. "I'd like to thank everyone for their generous bids, and the bachelors and bachelorettes for the donation of their time."

Olive walked out on stage and took the microphone from Wyatt.

"Can I get a hand for our emcee, Wyatt Landers?" She held open her arms to loud applause. She waited for it to die down. "But, I'm afraid Mr. Landers is incorrect. We have one more date to auction off."

Confusion filled Wyatt's face as he looked down at his notes. It was apparent he didn't see any more names listed for auction.

"For our last date, we'll be auctioning off a night with the recently returned billionaire, Wyatt Landers!" Olive announced. The crowd went wild. Lorna looked ecstatic.

Surprise flooded Wyatt's features. Cassie could clearly see him mouthing "no" to Olive, but she just pressed on, ignoring his unhappy reaction.

"Do you want to know where Wyatt Landers has been hiding out the past few years? Ask him as he takes you to Sur la Table, where the chef will prepare a romantic dinner for just the two of you. It can't get more romantic and intimate than this, folks. Bidding starts at two thousand dollars."

Time moved in slow motion. The bids were far more than she could afford. Even if she cashed out her 401K and took out credit card loans, she couldn't afford the prices people were shouting out.

"I have twenty-eight thousand dollars," Olive called out. "Going once... going twice..."

"Thirty thousand," Lorna called out, standing up. Her voice shook slightly.

Olive beamed on stage. "The record bid for our auction is twenty-eight thousand, five hundred and I now have thirty thousand! Going once... Going twice..."

Cassie closed her eyes, wishing this moment could end. Wyatt looked panicked up on stage. Brianna squeezed Cassie's hand under the table.

But there was nothing she could do. She didn't have anywhere close to thirty grand. Especially not to drop on a single date. Cassie thought she might throw up.

"Sold!"

Applause filled the room. Lorna sauntered from the table and up to the stage to get her certificate. She posed for the camera, flaunting her curves and wealth as they praised her for her generous donation to charity.

Only it wasn't generous. It was selfish and cruel. Cassie could have dealt with just about anyone else winning a date with Wyatt. But Lorna?

Cassie wanted to punch her in the face.

Wyatt hopped down from the stage and came back to the table. Lorna tried to follow him, but she was diverted to follow Olive to write the check for the date. At least Cassie got a bit of satisfaction from the annoyed look on Lorna's face as she was forced to hang back.

"We'll think of something," Brianna promised. "Let me talk with Janessa. We'll come up with a plan. It'll be okay."

The sentiment was sweet, but Cassie knew there wasn't much her friends could do for her. Brianna gave her a quick hug and then got up and went to sit next to Janessa to hopefully plot something out.

"I'm so sorry," Wyatt said as soon as he was close. He took Cassie's hands in his and kissed them. "I swear I didn't know she was going to do that."

Cassie believed him. The look of shock was too real to be faked. "It's okay," she replied. "Maybe you can just put it off forever."

Wyatt chuckled, but there wasn't much mirth to it. "Why didn't you bid on me?" Hurt filled his green eyes.

"I don't have that kind of money." Cassie shook her head. "I don't even think I have a credit card with a limit that high."

"You could have used mine. I would have paid you back," he told her.

Cassie closed her eyes and felt the fool. "I didn't think of that."

"It's okay." Wyatt squeezed her hands. "Maybe I can convince her to bring you along."

Cassie laughed at the idea. Lorna would do that the day pigs flew and the sun set in the east. She had a feeling that even if Wyatt offered to buy her out, she wouldn't take it. Lorna wanted this date. She wanted Wyatt and was willing to do just about anything to get him.

Cassie kissed Wyatt's cheek, and they both sat down. Dinner would be served soon.

"Well, hello my date," Lorna purred, coming back to the table. She wrapped her arm around Wyatt's shoulders.

Wyatt shrugged her off, but Lorna didn't seem deterred. She sat down in the seat next to him.

"We're going to have so much fun." Lorna purposefully thrust out her chest and looked up at him through her eyelashes.

Cassie had to wonder if Lorna had back issues from arching her back that much. It certainly didn't look comfortable.

"I'm actually rather busy for the next few weeks," Wyatt replied. "There's lots of business for me attend to. And then I have some traveling. You'll have to talk to my assistant about scheduling."

"Well, if you're going to be busy, I understand." Lorna nodded thoughtfully. She looked a little crestfallen, but understanding. Cassie thought Wyatt was doing an excellent job of putting her off. Cassie nearly believed him.

"I'm glad you understand." Wyatt gave Lorna a flat smile. Cassie squeezed his hand under the table, telling him he was doing a good job.

"I just had the best idea," Lorna announced. "If you're going to be busy, then we should have our date right away. I'm sure Cassie will be alright with giving you up tomorrow night. She said you had a romantic dinner planned. Just switch the two of us out."

Lorna giggled. Her eyes met Cassie's, and Lorna's grin was sinister.

"I really don't think that's a good idea..." Wyatt began.

"Of course it is. You can pick me up at six. There, see? It's settled. And this way, you can get this date off your schedule. I am *very* accommodating." Lorna ran her tongue across her upper lip. "I can do *whatever* you want."

With Lorna's focus on Wyatt, across the table Brianna was miming over the top sexual faces at Wyatt, underscoring the ridiculousness of what Lorna was saying and how she was saying it. Brianna licked her lips the way Lorna did. She made kissy faces and outrageous winks. She fluttered her eyelashes and opened her mouth as if she might orgasm at any moment.

Wyatt was having a hard time keeping a straight face. His mouth kept thinning as he held back a smile. Cassie had to pick up a napkin to hide her smirk. At least her friends could make her feel better, even if they couldn't stop the date. She had a feeling that tomorrow night, Brianna, Janessa, and Julia would be showing up at her front door with ice cream and movies to keep her distracted.

Lorna glanced across the table, and immediately Brianna schooled her face into a polite smile. The motion had Cassie in silent stitches. Janessa had to pretend a cough to contain her laughter.

"Well, since it's settled, I'll see you tomorrow," Lorna said, turning back to Wyatt. She ran her finger seductively across his lapel, biting her lip and giving him huge bedroom eyes.

She got up slowly, making sure to move in the most seductive manner she could. Everything was arches and curves as she paused to give him a good view of her ass.

"Remember, I'll do whatever you want." Her voice was low and seductive as she wiggled her hips slightly to make a point. She then sauntered away, her hips swinging with every step.

Cassie made eye contact with Wyatt, and then with Janessa, and finally Brianna. Brianna batted her eyelashes and blew a kiss. Cassie couldn't help but bust out with laughter, and the whole table followed her into giggles.

"At least she gave thirty grand to a good cause," Brianna said, clutching her chest and wheezing with laughter. "If nothing else, she actually did a good thing."

Janessa nodded, trying to take a sip of water. "I will definitely give her credit for that. I have no idea where she got the money, but I'm glad it's going to a good cause."

"And don't you worry, Wyatt," Brianna said turning to him. "We'll take good care of Cassie tomorrow."

"Yeah, just don't get too comfortable," Cassie added on. "You're supposed to be with me."

Wyatt leaned over and kissed her cheek, making her heat from head to toe. "Don't you worry, Cassie. I know where my favorite person is."

Love and warmth washed through Cassie in waves that made her blush. The other two girls aww-ed from across the table, but Cassie didn't care.

Wyatt was hers. Not even Lorna stealing a date from him could change that.

Even though she was sure, she couldn't figure out why she had such a horrible nagging feeling that this was going to lead to nothing but trouble and heartbreak?

30

Wyatt

"Well, other than the auction fiasco, I think the night was a success," Wyatt announced, kicking off his shoes at the door of his apartment.

Cassie followed him in, adding her heels to his shoes. He liked the way they looked tumbled together.

"I had fun," Cassie said, walking into the kitchen and pouring a glass of water. She grinned at him. "Thank you for inviting me. I don't know if I want to do it again, but once was fun. It was definitely different."

"You want to live the billionaire lifestyle all the time now?" he asked, loosening his jacket and tie.

"Hell no." She shook her head. "I'm exhausted mentally, and I didn't have to do anything. All those people? I just want to curl up with you and not move for a week. My brain is totally and completely fried."

He thought about asking her to come to the islands. Now

was the perfect time, only... she just said her brain was fried. Asking a huge decision right now was going to end poorly.

Maybe he was just afraid of rejection, or perhaps he sensed something about the night, but she didn't want to ask. He blamed it on Lorna's purchasing of him. He knew that it grated on Cassie.

So, he didn't ask.

"You look so amazing," he said, staring at her in the kitchen. Her red dress pooled around her feet and her hair was slowly coming out of its perfect curls. She looked absolutely stunning. He couldn't imagine a more beautiful woman.

She was perfect.

She grinned at him. "You look pretty good too," she replied, setting down her water. "But, you have too many clothes on."

It was his turn to grin. Instead of asking her to run away with him, he just took the most beautiful woman in the world to his bed and showed her what his words couldn't find the way to say.

The next morning was dark and cloudy. It matched Wyatt's mood well. He was not looking forward to this evening. Not even a little bit.

"I've heard that the restaurant is amazing," Cassie said, sipping on her coffee. She looked over her phone at him.

"What restaurant?" he replied, shrugging and pretending that he wasn't already dwelling on the date.

"I know you're thinking about tonight," she told him. "You've moved the salt and pepper shakers around a dozen times, yet you've barely sipped your coffee. You usually have had two cups by now."

He looked up at her. "You noticed that?"

She smiled, and it was like the sun had come out. "Yes. I notice a lot about you. Like how you frown, right here, when you're worried about something."

She leaned across the table and gently pressed her fingertip into his brow. "When it's something you don't want me to feel bad about, you get these little lines near your eyes. Right now, you have both."

"Come here," he said, motioning to her. She grinned and happily settled into his lap. He loved the way she felt against him. He wrapped his arms around her and nuzzled her shoulder, breathing in the soft scent of her.

She smelled like flowers and his soap. He loved the way she smelled like him. Like she was now a part of him.

"You smell so good," he murmured. He nuzzled her shoulder with another kiss.

"I need a shower," she replied with a giggle. She turned in his lap and grinned. "Care to join me?"

As if he could say no.

In a smooth motion, he picked her up and carried her into the bathroom. She giggled and clung to him, wrapping her arms around his shoulders. He loved the sound of her laughter. He loved the way she felt in his arms. He loved everything about her.

And he was going to show her just how much in the shower.

"I wish we could just stay like this the rest of the day," Cassie murmured. Her hand drew lazy circles on his bare chest as they lay tangled in bed sheets. Her breasts pressed against his ribs, reminding him she was there with every breath she took.

He'd already had her in the shower, and then again now in the bed, yet, with her breasts touching him like that, he was practically ready to go a third time. With Cassie, he felt like a teenager. She made his body feel young.

"I would like that," Wyatt agreed. He tried to ignore the clock on the nightstand. It was almost time for his date, and they both were avoiding it. With every moment that ticked closer, dread settled a little more firmly around his shoulders.

"Brianna says the hotel is finally losing some of the photographers. Lenny has been telling them I'm not there all week, but then he loves to preen for the camera and tell them all about how our hotel attracted such a big name." She shook her head. "I hope I can go back to work soon."

"You don't have to, you know," he said, trying to keep his voice neutral. He didn't plan on asking her to the island just yet, but if it was a natural question...

She sighed. "I know. I just miss my old life." She stilled and then sat up on her elbow to look at him. "I mean, I love having you here. I do. I just miss being able to go to the grocery store. I miss working and being busy. This has been great, but I don't think I could live like this forever."

Wyatt nodded. He took a deep breath. He could ask her now.

"Anyway, that's not really important right now." Cassie smiled down at him. "You have to get ready. I don't want Lorna complaining because you were late. Knowing her, she'd just say that means she gets to keep you for double."

Wyatt let out the breath. He would ask later. In business, timing was everything. If you asked a client for something too soon, you would lose the deal. It paid to be careful and make sure that the client was in a mood to say yes before offering a contract.

Slowly, reluctantly, he rolled out of bed. Cassie kept her eyes on him, watching him dress. He loved the wicked gleam in her eyes and the way she looked at him.

He dressed in dark blue slacks with a matching business

jacket. No tie. He wanted to look presentable to the restaurant, but casual at the same time. He didn't want to give Lorna any ideas that this was anything more than a pre-arranged meeting.

"Now, don't forget me," Cassie said, coming out from the bed. Her naked form stole his breath as she sashayed up to him. She went to her tiptoes and planted the sexiest kiss he'd ever had on him. There was something incredibly hot about being fully dressed while she was bare.

"As if I could," he whispered. His body was begging to go another round with her. He didn't know how she did it to him. She just kept turning him on, and his body kept responding. With Cassie, he felt like he would never run out of sexual energy for her.

She grinned and pulled her hair back. "It won't be that bad. At least you're going to have good food."

He kissed her, pulling her soft skin into his clothed body.

"You should get dressed," he told her, keeping her close to him. "Your friends will be here soon."

She gave him one more small kiss and then pushed him away. He didn't want to go. He would rather go have a root canal than spend a romantic dinner with a woman that wanted him only for his money.

Slowly, he left the apartment and the woman he wanted to spend the evening with behind.

31

Wyatt

The ride to the restaurant didn't take long, but Wyatt moped the whole way there. He knew it was childish and that he was a full grown man, but since no one but Thor would see him, he pouted.

When the car door opened to get out though, he wore a polite smile.

Lorna was waiting for him at the table. She wore a tiny black dress that showed massive amounts of cleavage and left little to the imagination. Wyatt had to admit that she was very beautiful, but he much preferred Cassie's simple but elegant style. He liked having something left to the imagination.

"Hi, Wyatt." Her voice was low and breathy. She stood up sensually and stepped toward him.

"Hello, Lorna," he greeted her. He held out his hand and made it a point that he was shaking her hand, not giving a hug.

She stared at his hand for a moment and then shook it with a surprised smile. "How professional."

He was a perfect gentleman. He had a plan to get through this. He pulled out her chair and helped her sit before going to his own seat.

"So, Wyatt, tell me about yourself." She leaned forward, showing off cleavage along with her eager smile.

"I'm sure you've read most of it online," he replied. "Or that Cassie's told you."

Her smile faltered slightly at Cassie's name. "Well, tell me about the boat you have at Cannes. I've heard it's amazing."

"I sold it," he confessed. "I'm rarely in Cannes. It's too rich for my blood. I've found I much prefer being out of the spotlight. It's something Cassie and I share."

Lorna's eye twitched slightly again at Cassie's name.

"Oh, look, the waitress is here." Wyatt quickly scanned his menu. "I'll take the lobster special, please."

"What do you think I should have?" Lorna asked him. "What do you want for me?"

"I don't know," he replied. "Cassie always picks her own food. You should too."

Lorna's smiled dropped, and she glared at the poor waitress. "I'll have the lobster too. And the recommended wine."

The waitress left, and Lorna fixed her smile back. Wyatt could tell that this wasn't going the way she'd planned.

Wyatt knew what she was trying to do. He'd been on so many dates like this. Women saw his wealth and wanted it. They would go to dinner, wearing something revealing, and ask him to talk about himself. They would say that everything he said was funny or clever.

He'd fallen for it a few times before discovering that it was all fake. Women would say or do whatever they thought would make him like them. It was ironic because that was precisely the last thing he wanted. He liked that Cassie spoke her mind. He liked that he didn't have to order for her. He liked that she didn't always laugh at his jokes.

"I heard you have the most amazing beach house in California," Lorna tried again. "Will you tell me about it? I bet you get invited to the best parties."

"When I lived in California, I spent most of my time at the office. I didn't get to enjoy the house or the parties." He hadn't enjoyed that part of his life at all. It had been all work all the time. It was a big part of why he'd left. To bring it up showed that she didn't know him at all. "I honestly could barely tell you what the kitchen looks like. I was basically never there."

"That's a shame," Lorna replied. "You must be so proud of your business. I love it when a man finds something he's passionate about."

"You know that I quit, right? I left my business." Wyatt frowned slightly.

"Oh, right." Lorna blushed. She'd gotten caught up in the yes-man routine. "I mean, you were passionate about being in the Caribbean, too. Right?"

"Where I met Cassie. Yes." Wyatt took a sip of his water. He was determined to bring up Cassie wherever he could.

He didn't feel bad about it either. Lorna knew he was with Cassie, yet she was choosing to pursue him anyway. Lorna was supposedly Cassie's friend, yet she was choosing to try and break them up. The only thing she knew about Wyatt was that he was rich. They'd never had a real conversation. Even now, she was asking him about things that related to his wealth, not to him.

If anything, he felt pity for her. She wasn't going to get him, no matter how hard she tried.

"Lorna, tell me about yourself." He decided to let her talk for a while. "I'm sure you must have some sort of interesting hobby."

Lorna's face lit up. "I play golf and tennis," she explained excitedly. "Do you play? I'm sure you must, being a billionaire and all."

"I actually don't," Wyatt admitted. Golf had been his father's game. Wyatt much preferred swimming and surfing, and he'd never had the time to get good at tennis. "But, tell me about them."

"You don't play golf?" She frowned slightly but then smiled. "I'd love to teach you. I'm a very patient teacher. I can show you moves that will blow your mind. I'm really good at handling balls."

Wyatt sighed internally. Sex wasn't a selling point for him either. Especially not so blatantly. He wondered if this had worked on other men because it certainly wasn't working for him. Lorna seemed to be oblivious to his discomfort.

"I'm not interested in your 'ball handling,'" he said, pointedly. "It's really unnecessary. I just want to have a normal conversation."

Lorna giggled. "Of course you do. I just want to make sure you know what I'm offering. It's more than Cassie can offer, I assure you."

She bit her lower lip and looked down at her ample bosom, shaking her shoulders slightly to show off.

"Tell me more about tennis," he said, trying to get her back on a topic. "Do you play recreationally or on a league?"

"I happily play doubles," she replied with a wink. "If you know what I mean."

Wyatt sighed and felt like banging his head against the table.

This was going to be a very long dinner.

32

Wyatt

Fifty-seven minutes later, Wyatt was beyond relieved that dinner was over. They'd had their meal. They'd had dessert. They were done.

He'd started counting the number of times Lorna made an inappropriate sexual comment but stopped counting after thirty-seven. He told her several times that he wasn't interested, but she ignored him.

Lorna was not kind to Cassie. The insults were never blatant, but there. "I bet Cassie doesn't do this" or "Cassie is too busy to do that" and even "you can do so much better" came out multiple times during the conversation.

It only made Lorna look spiteful. The woman was beautiful with her trim body, large breasts, and shiny hair, but her soul did not match the outside. She was shallow and cruel. She was willing to throw Cassie under the bus for a chance at a billionaire's heart.

He sighed with relief as soon as the check came.

"Thank you for this date," Wyatt said, setting the check down and standing up. "And thank you for your kind donation."

It was time to escape. He turned and could see the light through the door. Freedom.

"You don't want to stay and talk some more?" Lorna asked, painting a sad pout onto her face.

"I'm afraid I have other plans," he replied diplomatically.

She pouted, but then stood up. "At least walk me to the valet." She blinked up at him through long fake eyelashes.

He looked to the door. It was only a few feet away. He'd survived this long. This wouldn't be that much more.

She took his arm, pressing her body into him and gazing up adoringly. He tried to pull away, but she clung to him like a burr.

He walked quickly, sensing freedom as soon as he could reach the sunlight.

He held open the door for Lorna, they stepped out, and he was free.

Only, he wasn't. As soon as they were clear of the door, Lorna jumped up and wrapped her arms around his neck, planting a kiss on his lips.

He spluttered and pushed her off, angry that she would do such a thing.

And then he saw the photographers. The lights were flashing, and the cameras were rolling. Lorna grinned up at him, her lipstick smudged on her self-satisfied smile.

Anger flared up white and hot. He couldn't see straight.

"What have you done?" he growled at her, wiping his mouth with the back of his hand. It felt dirty.

She smiled sweetly. "What you should have done in the first place." She turned and smiled sweetly for the photographers. "If you could give us some privacy, I know we'd both appreciate it. We're working things out."

Wyatt saw red. "How dare you!"

"Oh, dear. I know that things are rough right now, but I forgive you. That other woman tricked you. I love you. We can still be together. I forgive you completely." Lorna fluttered her eyelashes at him.

The click of cameras filled the air, all of them tuned on Lorna.

"That's not true," he said, trying to keep his voice calm.

"Darling, I know that we've had some rough spots, but we can work things out. I want to work things out. I won't let that other woman lie to you. That's all she's done. You and I are meant to be. Don't be angry with me for making you see the truth. I'm only trying to help you."

Wyatt stared at her. The words she was saying made no sense, yet the paparazzi were eating it up.

He realized no matter what he said, it would be misreported. Right now, she had the upper hand.

There was nothing he could do to fix this. Better to disappear before she could catch him in any more drama. The less pictures that existed, the better. Besides, he was too angry to think straight. Staying would mean giving the photographers more fuel for their tawdry fires.

He turned and pushed his way through the photographers, leaving them to snap pictures up as he went. He wanted to hit something. He wanted to throw and destroy every camera there, but he knew it wouldn't do any good.

The damage was done.

A picture of Lorna and Wyatt kissing passionately existed in the world.

Wyatt's head hung in shame as Thor in the SUV skidded to a stop in front of him. He climbed in, already dreading telling Cassie. He knew she would understand, but at the same time, it was one more incursion into her world.

If she were dating a regular man, this wouldn't be a problem. She wouldn't see her boyfriend kissing another woman as front page news if she was dating anyone but him.

This was the part of being a billionaire that sucked. He had no privacy, and everyone wanted something from him.

It was not the way that he wanted to live. If given the option, he would happily trade his billions for a more normal lifestyle. He didn't want to live in poverty, but the idea of merely being a multimillionaire without fame sounded like heaven.

The walk up to his apartment was long. He dreaded having to tell Cassie what had happened. He hated knowing she would see this picture. He knew she would understand, but that didn't change the fact that she had to deal with it. She would take it with grace and understanding, as she seemed to take everything his world threw at her. She would smile and tell him it didn't matter while her eyes grew distant and her mouth lost its smile.

He knew it dragged on her. She disliked this celebrity status as much as he did. It was one of the reasons that they got along so well. They matched one another in their desire to remain private and didn't need the general public to validate their decisions.

He took a deep breath before opening up the door. Inside he could hear laughter and the sound of music.

It made him feel more guilty. He was going to come in and ruin their fun. He gave serious thought to just going to the gym or on a run, but he knew Cassie would worry. She expected him home around now from the date, and if he didn't show she would worry that Lorna had somehow seduced him.

It was laughable, but then there was the picture showing the lie could look possible.

He opened the door, trying to keep a positive look on his face.

Inside, Cassie and her three friends sat on the couch, a bottle of wine and glasses on the coffee table. Old pop music he recognized from his high school years filled the room, and they were laughing as they talked.

"You're home!" Cassie shouted, jumping up with a smile. Her eyes shone with relief that he was back and no longer in Lorna's clutches. She ran to him, wrapping her arms around him.

Even though the kiss was not of his doing, he felt like he was contaminating her with his touch.

"How awful was it?" Brianna asked, standing up and picking up the empty wine bottle. The other two women helped her pick up and put the dishes in the kitchen.

"It went exactly as you'd expect," Wyatt said. He turned and looked at Cassie. "I need to talk to you."

Concern filled her beautiful brown eyes. "What happened?"

He glanced over at her friends, but they were in the kitchen. He could hear them talking quietly as they put the dishes in the sink.

"Lorna kissed me." His voice was flat.

Cassie's eyes went wide for a moment. "What?"

"I didn't kiss her back," he assured her. He sighed. "But, she made sure to do it in front of the photographers."

Cassie's eyes narrowed. "Of course she did. And I bet she made it look good, didn't she?"

Wyatt nodded, shame creeping up the back of his neck. "I swear to you Cassie, I didn't kiss her back. I didn't give her any indication that it was wanted or--"

"I know you didn't," she cut him off. She put a hand to his cheek and smiled up at him. "You look too damn miserable about it."

"It's going to be in the press," he told her.

She sighed, dropping her hand. "I know. That's Lorna's

style. She's relentless and incredibly selfish. I half expected something like this from her. She probably paid half the photographers to be there."

Wyatt felt the balloon of fear inside him start to deflate. Cassie wasn't angry. He'd suspected she wouldn't be, but it felt good to know he'd been right.

"We're going to head out," Janessa announced. Wyatt turned to see Cassie's three former roommates standing by the door with their things and shoes already on.

"Thank you guys for coming over," Cassie told them. She leaned against Wyatt.

"Any time. We should do this more often anyway," Julia replied with a grin. "Wyatt, you're going to have to go out on more dates."

She said it with a wink and a laugh, but Wyatt had a hard time cracking a smile.

"Thanks for having us," Janessa quickly said, reading the mood of the room. She smiled and pushed the other two out before they could make any more inappropriate jokes.

The songs of the past still played in the living room, filling the silence after the guests had left.

Cassie sighed and went to the living room, turning off the music. She went to the kitchen and got a fresh glass of wine before throwing herself into the couch and taking a big sip.

"Are you okay?" Wyatt asked. He really meant to ask if *they* were okay.

She gave him a weak smile and patted the couch beside her.

"I'm just having a hard time adjusting," she admitted when he sat down. "My life was boring before this. It was just work. I followed Corporate's rules, and my life ran smoothly. Corporate doesn't have any guidelines on what to do when dating a famous billionaire. I looked."

"I'm sorry," he said softly.

She sighed again. "It's not your fault," she replied. "Not really."

"What if we went back to the Caribbean?" Wyatt hadn't planned on asking now. He still wanted everything to be perfect, but the longer he waited, the more the question pressed on him. He didn't want to be in the city anymore. He wanted to go home. He was so tired of being here that he asked the question without it being perfect.

"That would be great," Cassie replied. Her whole body relaxed. "I could go for that."

Wyatt's heart nearly burst from his chest. It had been so much easier than he'd been afraid of. He'd been worried over nothing.

"This should all be blown over in a couple of weeks," Cassie continued. She smiled as she planned in her mind. "Then we can come back, and we won't be followed by cameras everywhere. I can go back to work. I can go back to my apartment and get clothes."

Some of the elation ebbed away. "What? Why would we come back?" Wyatt asked.

A mix of surprise and confusion pulled Cassie's brows together. "Why wouldn't we? The islands are just a vacation... right?"

"No. The island is home. Our home."

Cassie fell silent for a moment. She shifted away from him.

"This is my home." Her voice was soft but stubborn. "This is where my life is."

"What life?" Wyatt asked. Anger flared inside of him. He was so tired from the day. He'd used up all his emotional reserves dealing with Lorna. He could feel anger starting to form inside of him. He just wanted to go home. To leave all this behind and go back to the life that he loved.

Her eyes narrowed. "This is where my life is," she

repeated. "My house. My job, my friends. I don't have anything in the Caribbean."

"What house?" he snapped. "You live in a tiny apartment. Your job? You've basically been fired. And your friends? I've seen what your *friends* do. They assault people to get what they want."

Anger flooded Cassie's pretty features. Her cheeks flushed, and her chest started to heave.

"How dare you," she hissed. "My friends are good people. Lorna isn't my friend. You chose to go on that date. You know that Lorna isn't a *friend*."

Wyatt didn't even care that he knew he was wrong. He was angry now. He was so tired of being here. He'd come here for Cassie, but she wasn't willing to do the same for him. She wasn't willing to give them a chance as he had.

He'd come to her home, but she wouldn't come to his.

"You don't have anything for you here," he said, sounding logical and reasonable.

"It's my life," she replied, drawing further away from him. "And it was just fine before you came and wrecked it. You're the one who dragged me into this mess. This is all your fault."

She crossed her arms and lifted her chin defiantly. Her eyes flashed with fury, and her cheeks flushed with emotion and wine.

Wyatt vibrated with unleashed anger. He was here for her, yet she was ungrateful and unwilling to try. Guilt only added fuel to the fire consuming him.

"It's been a long day," he said, rising to his feet. "I think it's best if I go to bed."

"Yeah, that sounds like a good idea," she said the words with bitterness.

He tried to walk calmly to the bedroom, but he felt like stomping and swearing the entire way.

Nothing was going as planned. Nothing was working the

way it was supposed to. He'd thought they would be already in their happily ever after, but Cassie showed no signs of leaving. She obviously didn't care for him as much as he did for her.

Heartache, guilt, and anger all fought in his chest as he flopped into bed. Sleep took a long time coming, especially because Cassie never joined him in bed.

She left him to sleep in his own anger. She wanted nothing to do with him.

33

Cassie

Cassie's neck hurt the next day, and her back had a cramp that she couldn't stretch out.

The couch was not nearly as comfortable to sleep on as she'd expected. After a few hours, the once soft couch became too soft to be supportive. The blanket was too light, and every time the air conditioning kicked on, she got cold. The pillows were too small and decorative to be useful for actual sleep.

She'd nearly gotten up and gone to the bedroom several times, but each time her pride and spite got the best of her.

The fact that Wyatt would call Lorna her friend rankled. His dismissive attitude toward her job infuriated her. Sure, she wasn't a billionaire. She was just a hotel manager, but she had worked hard at it. She'd followed the rules. Didn't that mean something?

Why did *she* have to give it all up?

It wasn't fair. She wanted to be with Wyatt, but she didn't want to give up her life to do it.

She pretended to be asleep when Wyatt left the bedroom in the morning. He came out wearing a suit and tie. He paused as he approached the couch and stood there for a moment before sighing and then leaving the apartment.

Cassie wasn't sure if she should be angry or sad. She wasn't sure what she wanted anymore.

The longer she was with Wyatt, the more her priorities shifted. She wasn't the living, breathing embodiment of corporate policies anymore, but she wasn't free of her desire to make something of herself either.

She didn't want to just disappear into the Caribbean and live her life on the beach. It sounded nice for a while, but she knew she'd get bored. She needed something to do. Something to give her life meaning that wasn't made out of daiquiris.

The apartment echoed with empty loneliness without Wyatt. She suddenly felt like a guest here for the first time during her stay. The silence was a weight on her soul.

She dressed and left the apartment. She went to the only place that she felt like she belonged. Work.

The reporters were still at the hotel. There were fewer of them now, but she still went in through the back to avoid them.

Her office was unchanged, yet it felt cold and empty. It was apparent someone had been in here working while she was away, yet it looked the same. The thought that she'd become such a corporate shill that anyone could replace her without changing things hurt.

She sat at her desk, trying to come up with a plan. She went to look for her manager's notes and found they weren't where she kept them. They were probably at the front desk where Corporate wanted them, she realized.

Where she couldn't get them because the reporters would see her.

She sighed, sliding down her chair and pouting.

"What are you doing here?" Lenny stood in the doorway, his round features unhappy.

"I just wanted to get some paperwork done," Cassie explained. "I know I'm on leave, but the monthly reports are due."

"The reports are done," Lenny replied. "They were due yesterday. You shouldn't be here."

"I need to do something," Cassie explained.

"You can't be here," Lenny repeated. "Especially after what you've done."

"What I've done?" Cassie asked, confused. "I haven't done anything."

"You brought a philandering man into our hotel," Lenny hissed. "You've damaged the brand. Do you know the phone calls I've been getting from Corporate about you?"

Cassie stared at him. "I literally have no idea what you're talking about."

"Wyatt Landers. I'm sure you thought seducing him into staying here would improve your career, but Corporate does not want the StarTree brand to be a place where people go to cheat on their spouses!"

"Spouses? Cheating? What in the world are you talking about?" Cassie stopped slouching in her chair.

"Wyatt Landers was happily engaged to another woman," Lenny informed her. "But I'm sure you knew that. You would have had to in order to get him to stay here. His fiancee lives in town. Why else would he stay in our hotel and not with her?"

"Wyatt isn't engaged to anyone," Cassie informed him, shaking her head. "He's never been engaged."

"Tell that to his fiancee." Lenny shook his head in disgust.

"You're a homewrecker."

A terrible suspicion started to form in the pit of Cassie's stomach.

"Did this fiancee just suddenly appear yesterday?" Cassie asked. "A pretty blonde woman? Local? Named Lorna?"

"You do know about her!" Lenny exclaimed, pointing a finger. "You knew, and you brought him here!"

Rage flared up hot and white. Cassie seriously considered finding out how much hiring a hit man to take out Lorna would cost. At this point, she had a feeling Wyatt would help her pay for it.

"She was never his fiancee, Lenny. She made it up."

"There's a picture of them kissing at a restaurant," Lenny informed her. "It doesn't look like it was made up. Here, I'll show you. Turn on the computer. I was just reading about it."

Cassie turned on the monitor of the computer in front of her. It hummed to life and flickered to show a gossip website. Front and center was a picture of Lorna with her arms wrapped around Wyatt and her lips plastered to his.

Cassie thought she might be sick. She read the headline, her eyes going wide with shock:

Abandoned Fiancee of Billionaire Reveals All! Read the shocking story of how a local businesswoman, Lorna Frankson realized that the love of her life was being stolen away in the Caribbean!

"That bitch," Cassie whispered as she read the article. Lorna painted herself as the love of Wyatt's life until Cassie the homewrecker came in and swooped him up. It was Cassie's fault that Lorna was heartbroken, but she was willing to forgive Wyatt and let him come back to her.

"We don't use that kind of language here," Lenny chastised.

"This isn't true." Cassie pointed to the computer. "Not a single word of it. You know me, Lenny. Does this sound at all like something I would do?"

"No," Lenny admitted, sounding a little bashful. "But that's not what Corporate is worried about."

"What is Corporate worried about then?" Cassie asked, suddenly exhausted.

"This isn't good for the hotel's image," Lenny told her. "And as you know, our image is a top priority. Guests stay here because of our image. The image is a number one priority."

Along with cleanliness, politeness, and a good experience. Everything was a number one priority for StarTree Corporate.

"And?" Cassie asked, already fearing the worst. This wasn't something Corporate was going to let slide. This wasn't putting her notebook in the wrong place or having extra oranges out in the morning buffet.

Lenny shifted. "Corporate understands that this isn't a normal situation. They appreciate your years of excellent service and the excellent rating the hotel has earned in the city. However, the recent press creates a problem." Lenny spoke as if reading from a script. Most likely he was. Corporate had scripts for everything.

"And?" she asked again. "Cut to the chase, Lenny."

"You are asked to relocate to another manager position in a different city."

Cassie sat back in her chair, the wind knocked out of her.

She was basically being fired. She was no longer going to be the manager of the Phoenix StarTree hotel. They would put her in a different state. She would be hidden from view until this blew over, but she had a feeling she would have a black mark on her file for the rest of her days. StarTree never forgot anything. That was also a number one priority for them.

"And if I don't want that?" she asked weakly.

Lenny shifted his feet again. "I am authorized to give you a generous severance package if you resign voluntarily. StarTree would like to avoid any more negative press."

Cassie nodded. She was glad she was sitting down because it felt like the floor was falling out from under her.

This hotel was her life, yet she was no longer welcome here. This wasn't an option anymore.

"Give me a little bit to think about it," Cassie said softly.

"Of course. I'll give you to the end of the day." Lenny went to the door. He narrowed his eyes, still not trusting her despite the fact the gossip article wasn't true. "Don't touch anything in here. Please take your photos and go out the back when you leave."

He shut the door, and Cassie promptly made sure to touch everything on the desk. She touched the stapler twice just because she could.

What was she going to do? This job was her life. She'd sacrificed years to get here. This job had been the only thing that kept her going after her divorce. Would she be happy working in a different state? A different hotel?

She looked around the office, seeing how little her presence had mattered here.

She went to a shelf and picked up the lone photo of her and her friends. It was the only thing in the entire room that was truly hers. The awards were all in the hotel's name. The books were all hotel manuals and policies. There was nothing except one picture in the entire room that was a reflection of Cassie.

Was this what she wanted? She had to admit, the past couple of weeks being free had felt wonderful. She no longer dreamed of following rules. She hadn't read the StarTree Manual since before the trip, and she found that she didn't really want to reread it.

She didn't care about her job as much as she thought she did. She didn't care how many oranges should be in the breakfast display. Or what the correct scripting for greeting a customer should be. She liked not having to ask everyone if they wanted a credit card offer.

The past week had changed her. Wyatt had changed her.

It was a little shocking, but she didn't want this job anymore. She loved managing a hotel, but she didn't enjoy managing a StarTree hotel. She liked the work, but not the rules. In fact, she was happiest when she had to work around the rules and do what needed to be done for the guests.

She liked the safety and stability of her life with this job. It was predictable and safe, but she realized she wasn't truly alive. She was just going through the motions. It wasn't Star-Tree that she loved. It was this hotel, its staff, and its guests. If she couldn't have this hotel, she didn't want to work for the company anymore.

She turned on the computer and found the StarTree template for a resignation. She filled in her name and the appropriate words into the premade letter and printed it out.

She left it on the desk. And that was the end of her job at StarTree.

Cassie slipped the photo into her purse and left the office. She felt numb as she escaped down an employee hallway and out into the bright morning light. She walked along the sidewalk to her car and sat down in her sun-warmed car.

What was she going to do?

She sat there for a moment before starting the engine and driving. She drove without thinking, just letting her hands and feet take control. She didn't have a plan on where to go. She just drove.

And wound up in front of Wyatt's apartment.

Suddenly, things made sense. It was like putting on glasses for the first time. Things that she always assumed were made of blurs suddenly had texture and resolution.

She knew what she needed to do.

She needed to leave it all behind. She needed to escape.

34

Cassie

Tires squealed as Cassie slid into a parking space in front of Brianna's apartment. She barely had the engine off before racing up the stairs to Brianna's apartment. She needed to do this before she lost her nerve.

Cassie banged on the door. Brianna opened the door, looking surprised. She still had her pajamas on and Cassie could hear Netflix in the background. It was Brianna's day off, so she was at home relaxing. Ian was at school.

"What's up?" Brianna asked. "Are you feeling okay?"

"I just got fired."

Brianna's eyes went wide. "I'm so sorry, Cassie. I really am. Come on in. I've got ice cream." She ushered Cassie inside, shutting the door behind her.

The apartment was dark but comfortable. Brianna hadn't done much to the space to make it her own, yet it still felt like Brianna. The paintings were simple and bright. Books covered nearly every surface and at least three mugs sat half-filled with tea in the small kitchen. Toy cars littered the floor in front of the TV and kid drawings plastered the fridge.

"How are you doing?" Brianna asked, going to the kitchen and turning on an electric kettle. Cassie didn't really drink tea, so there would be another half-filled mug of cold tea joining the others soon.

"I'm actually better than I expected," Cassie admitted. "Did you know that I haven't read the corporate manual since we got back?"

"You haven't? No wonder they fired you," Brianna teased. She tensed and looked over at her friend. "Too soon?"

Cassie shook her head. "You can joke about it," she told her. "I actually feel like a weight has been lifted off of me. I didn't know just how afraid I was to break the rules."

"And now?" Brianna plunked two tea bags into two mugs.

"I think I have a plan," Cassie replied. "But, I'll need your help."

"Anything," Brianna assured her.

"Will you check my mail once in a while?" Cassie asked, holding out a small mailbox key. "I need to get away from it all for a while."

Brianna carefully took the key. "Does this have anything to do with what Lorna did?"

"A little," Cassie admitted. "She's actually part of the reason I was fired. The hotel doesn't want any kind of drama."

"But it wasn't your fault!" Brianna brought her hand down hard on the counter.

Cassie shrugged. "Corporate doesn't care. They never do. I pretended like corporate was this caring older sibling. That they were looking out for me while getting the job done. Except they aren't. They don't care at all. I don't matter, even though I thought I did."

"You going to be okay?" Brianna asked. The electric kettle

bubbled and rumbled. Brianna carefully took the hot water and poured it into the cups.

"I think so, actually." Cassie smiled. She had a plan. Even though it was crazy, the longer she thought about it, the better it was.

Brianna handed Cassie a steaming mug of tea. Cassie nearly spilled it all down her front when someone else started pounding on Brianna's door.

"Apparently I'm popular today," Brianna joked, setting down her own mug and going to the door. She'd barely pulled it open when Janessa stormed in.

"I'm going to kill her," Janessa shouted. "Murder. Torture. Make her go to the back of the line at the DMV!"

"Whoa, slow down there, Satan," Cassie replied. "Who are you destroying at the DMV?"

"Lorna," Janessa hissed.

"Oh, well in that case, I'm happy to help," Cassie said. "I'm down to tell her to bring the wrong forms too. And then put her in the wrong line again."

"I am so sorry she did that to you, Cassie." Janessa hurried over and hugged Cassie. "I can't believe she did that."

"What happened?" Brianna asked, confusion filling her face. "I know that Lorna is awful, but purposefully giving the wrong forms at the DMV bad?"

"Here." Janessa handed Brianna her phone and Cassie watched as confusion faded to shock which twisted into fury.

"That bitch," Brianna murmured. "How anyone doesn't see through this is beyond me."

The phone chirped with an incoming message. Brianna quickly handed it back to Janessa.

"It's Lorna," Cassie explained. "She just does that to people. No one sees her evil side."

"I think people are seeing it," Janessa announced. She

stared down at her phone, her mouth starting to curve into a smile. "I just got a message from Kyle."

"Kyle?" Brianna asked. "What's he going to do about his cousin?"

"I always thought that he was blind to anything bad Lorna could do," Janessa explained, scrolling through the message on her phone. "He's furious about this. About what people are saying about you, Cassie."

"That's sweet of him," Cassie replied. "I appreciate the thought."

"Oh, it's way more than just a thought," Janessa assured her. "He's telling his uncle. Lorna's getting cut off from the family."

"Seriously?" Brianna looked shocked.

"Yeah. Apparently they were funding her since her alimony dried up," Janessa continued. "No one in the family is happy that she's putting the family name in a bad light."

"It's not quite DMV level cursing, but I think it's fair," Cassie said.

"She deserves way worse. May her fake boob pop," Janessa spat. She turned and frowned at Cassie. "What are you doing here? Aren't you supposed to be with Wyatt?"

Just the sound of his name made Cassie's heart clench. She realized that she was behind schedule.

"I'm leaving town for a little bit," Cassie told her friends. "Things aren't the way I want them with Wyatt. I need to make some changes."

"You going to be okay?" Janessa's voice was soft and full of concern.

Cassie forced a smile. "I sure hope so."

"If you need anything, you let us know," Brianna told her. "We're here for you."

Cassie smiled for real this time. She had good friends.

"I need to get going," Cassie told them. "But, I really appreciate you guys."

"Good luck with whatever you're planning," Janessa replied.

Cassie needed to get going again, before she lost her nerve.

"Thanks. See you guys later," she replied, heading for the door. She had places to be. There were things she needed to do before she could leave, but at least she'd been able to say goodbye to her friends.

35

Wyatt

Wyatt walked in the front door of the apartment ready to apologize to Cassie. He had reservations made at a fancy restaurant. He had flowers in hand and jewelry was set to arrive later this afternoon.

The business meeting this morning had been long and arduous. He thought he'd escaped the corporate world by moving to the island. Being a peon for a holiday resort was easy. He just had to do what he was told and pour drinks. Now he was back to being the boss and he hated it. He had less freedom at the top of the chain than he did at the bottom. He was beginning to think that he would always be stuck with corporations telling him what to do with his life. It didn't seem to matter where he went.

He'd spent his entire miserable meeting thinking of Cassie and how he could fix things between them. Of how he could give her what she wanted and what she deserved. He was willing to do whatever it took to keep her.

The longer Wyatt stayed in billionaire mode, the easier it was to stay here and lose his happiness. News of his return was spreading, and everyone wanted a piece of him. New business ventures beckoned, and old ones were ready to be revitalized.

All he had to do was say yes, and he could be back in the world of business.

Except that wasn't what he wanted. All he would be working for was time to relax on the beach. He was happy with his simple life. Why sacrifice and struggle when he already had what made him happy?

Except it was Cassie that made him happy. If he stayed here, he would fall back into his business life, but he would have Cassie. He was considering it, and at the same time afraid of what it would cost him. But, it was something he was willing to do to keep Cassie in his life.

He would find a way to make his billionaire status no longer matter. He would join the business world again until he was expected and normal here. It wasn't the life he wanted, but he was willing to do it for Cassie.

He just needed to tell her he was sorry. That he was going to make things right so she could stay here and have her life. He needed to apologize for the things he'd said the night before. He'd been tired and angry. The strain of being under a microscope was hard on them both.

He set the flowers down on the coffee table and called her name. There was no answer. Wyatt frowned and began to look for her.

Except, the apartment was empty. There was no sign of Cassie.

Wyatt checked his phone but didn't see any messages. He went to the bedroom and found the bed neatly made in Maria's signature fashion.

With shaking hands, he checked the closet and found that Cassie's things were gone.

Her suitcase, her shoes, everything.

There was nothing in the bathroom. There was nothing in the bedroom. There was nothing left of her in the apartment.

She'd left him.

He stumbled slightly, his hand going to the kitchen counter to catch himself. He wanted to rip his heart out of his chest and throw it against the wall. Anger, hurt, and loss dug their talons into the center of his bones and threatened to rip him apart.

She couldn't handle the fame. She wanted her life back, and he couldn't blame her. She'd escaped from this life she didn't want. The media intrusions, the arguments, the cruel words he'd said- he couldn't blame her for leaving.

Tears flooded his eyes. He hadn't cried since he was a boy, yet he felt he would explode with tears. Everything inside him felt shattered and ready to fall apart like a house of cards.

For the first time in his life, he didn't have a plan. He'd always had a plan. Even if the plan was merely to be a beach bum bartender who did nothing but bang tourists, he'd had a plan. There was always a plan.

Except, without Cassie, he didn't have a clue what to do next.

If she couldn't handle the billionaire life but didn't want to return to the island, he was forced to face the prospect of losing her or giving her up.

He wasn't sure he knew how to do that.

Wyatt sat down hard at the kitchen table, his head in his hands and his heart in tatters.

He almost didn't see the note.

It sat on the kitchen table, written in Cassie's neat script. It was just a small white card with his name. He almost didn't want to open it. He didn't want to have his worst fears confirmed. He didn't want her leaving to be real. He didn't want to believe that he'd lost her.

But the note beckoned and taunted him.

With shaking hands, he read the small, neat words.

Dear Wyatt,

I'm sorry for last night. You didn't deserve my anger. My jealousy was something I hadn't counted on. I am not used to this life.

Wyatt's heart fell. This was how a breakup letter started. There were only a few words left, but he was having a hard time finding the strength to look at them. He didn't want to feel the heartbreak he knew was coming. He took a deep breath, telling himself just to get it done and over with. Just finish reading.

Come and find me. I'm waiting for you. I'm waiting for us to be how we should be.

-Cassie

Wyatt frowned. That wasn't a breakup at all.

An address followed that he didn't recognize.

He sat in the brightly lit kitchen, feeling like he was still in the dark. He reread the note, forcing himself to put his emotions aside and focus on her words.

...how we should be.

. . .

He stared at the note, hoping that he understood its true meaning. Hope started growing inside of him, small and fragile, yet increasing with every passing second.

... how we should be.

She wanted them to be together. That was the only explanation.

He couldn't take the thought that he might be wrong. That path led to heartbreak and madness. Without letting himself think or worry, he went to the car.

He had somewhere to be.

36

Cassie

Cassie hoped she was doing the right thing.

Doubts assaulted her. Had he gotten the note? Had he understood? She should have been clearer. She should have left better instructions. She should have waited at the apartment.

But she'd been afraid if she waited she would chicken out. She would change her mind or that he wouldn't want this anymore. She was afraid if she stayed at the apartment, things wouldn't work out the way she hoped.

Besides, she wanted to do this here. She needed to show him she was serious.

She paced nervously in front of the airplane hanger. Her packed suitcase sat by the entrance. She'd spent nearly all the money in her bank account. The flight left this evening. There was no return flight scheduled.

What if he didn't come?

She tried not to think about it. She tried not to think

about how she was about to change her life completely. Change terrified her. She liked knowing what was going to happen, but this had two very different endings. If he came, her life would change. If he didn't, it was still going to be different. There was no going back now. She wasn't in control anymore.

Though, to be honest, her life had changed the moment she met Wyatt. Nothing could be the same after him. This was just her realizing that fact and accepting it as truth.

She'd tried to pretend that her life would go back to normal. She'd tried to pretend that she could be happy with her old life. Except she knew it wasn't true. Her old life paled in comparison to her life with Wyatt. She would never be happy unless it was with Wyatt at her side.

So now she waited to see how life would change. She waited to see what letting go would get her.

She paced. She chewed on her nails. She tapped her toes, and she tried not to throw up.

Every black car that passed got her hopes up. Every dark SUV that turned the corner had her hopefully smiling and coming to the curb. Every time, she was disappointed.

Until one.

Time moved in slow motion as the black SUV slowed and finally stopped at the curb. Cassie held her breath as the car door opened and a handsome man stepped out.

He still wore the suit he'd left in that morning. His hair was messy as if he'd run his hands through it a million times. His green eyes were sharp. His shoulders held tall with confidence.

Cassie's heart stuttered and almost failed. She hoped there was someone nearby that knew CPR because there was an excellent chance she was going to need it, especially if he turned her down. If he said no, her heart would stop in her chest forever.

His steps slowed as he approached her. He looked calm and professional. She was reasonably sure that despite the fact she'd checked her hair seventeen times and fixed her clothing twenty-eight times, that she looked a mess. She felt frazzled and out of control. She just hoped she didn't look it.

"Cassie?" His voice cracked slightly, the only indication that he might be as nervous as she was. He frowned slightly. "Where are we?"

"This is a private runway," she explained. She held out two fluttering pieces of paper. "These are tickets. For us."

He frowned slightly, his green eyes going to the tickets. Carefully, he took them and read them over. She watched his face, waiting for a reaction.

Slowly, so slowly that her heart nearly gave out, a smile started to appear. It started with just a twitch upward on one side and gradually spread across his mouth as it filled and grew until he was grinning at her.

"I think we should go to the Caribbean," she announced. "I think you're right. I think it's the place that we're supposed to be. The place that we're supposed to stay. The place that's home."

"Really?" His beautiful eyes came to hers, searching her face. "I don't want you to regret this. I want you to be happy."

Cassie's heart melted around her ribs. She reached out, taking his hands in hers. They were warm and steady beneath her fingers. Just touching him made her breath catch with desire and emotion.

"Wyatt, I love you." She looked up at him, her eyes wide and smile nervous. "I love you, and I want to be with you. If you think we can be happy in Antarctica, I will go there."

"Antarctica?" He looked bemused.

"I'd need to pack different clothes, but I'd go."

"You love me." He smiled as he said it as if he could barely believe his luck.

Cassie nodded. "I was stuck on my old life, but you weren't a part of my old life. You're a part of my new life. And that's not here. We need to go to where we belong."

"You love me," he repeated, a little bit of awe in his voice.

She couldn't help but smile. "Yeah."

He wrapped her up in his arms, his fingers sliding into her hair as he pulled her into a kiss. He kissed her with an intensity that told her his emotions better than his words ever could. His embrace told her that he needed her as much as she needed him.

"I love you, too," he whispered, holding her into him as if she might disappear in a puff of smoke. "So, so very much."

Cassie's heart sang. Her body thrilled, and she felt like laughing and crying at the same time. She felt like she could fly. She wanted to dance and sing, shout and explode, jump and clap all at the same time.

She kissed him, emotion overwhelming her completely. Wyatt held her, the two of them laughing and crying.

Soon they'd be escaping to the Caribbean to start their new lives.

EPILOGUE

Wyatt

Wyatt stepped out onto the deck of his new boat and stretched in the morning sun.

Life had never been this good.

Wyatt couldn't imagine how he'd once thought being a bartender had ever been enough. He couldn't believe that he'd ever been happy without Cassie.

They were home here. Blue Caribbean waters were a balm to weary souls. The white sand called to them, and the warm sunshine banished worries.

Cassie and Wyatt didn't go back to the resort. Wyatt didn't have a job there anymore, and after hearing how he'd been treated, Cassie had refused to go to such an establishment. Besides, Wyatt didn't need to tend bar and live a bachelor lifestyle anymore. He didn't want that life.

So they bought a sailboat. It wasn't the biggest or flashiest boat in the world, but it was comfortable, and it got them where they wanted to go.

Today, it was taking them to a very special island.

Wyatt checked the rigging and made sure his route was plotted in the computer. The island wasn't far, but he wanted to make sure they arrived there with plenty of time left in the day. He had a surprise, and he wanted to make sure that Cassie would be able to make the most of it.

He peeked in the cabin to make sure Cassie was still asleep before going back up on deck. He pulled out his phone and dialed his assistant.

"Is everything set for our arrival?" he asked Amanda when she answered.

"All set, boss," she assured him. "The caretaker has prepped everything, and you're good to go. The kitchen is stocked, and the grounds are ready for viewing."

"Good." Wyatt still felt nervous though. The last two weeks had been heaven. He wanted to make sure that they stayed in this Heaven.

"Oh, and I have news for you," Amanda continued. He could hear the smile in her voice. "You remember that charity date you went on while in Arizona?"

As if Wyatt could forget Lorna and her terrible kiss. He was glad he knew how to disappear in the Caribbean, and that they were on a boat that no reporter knew about. It made avoiding anyone wanting answers about his supposed "fiancee" much easier.

That and his lawyer's cease and desist letters had really cut down on the annoying phone calls.

"What about it?" Wyatt asked, almost afraid of what was coming. Anything to do with Lorna spelled out trouble.

"The check bounced."

"Wait, what?" Wyatt asked, surprised.

"The check bounced. She didn't have the funds to cover her donation," Amanda repeated. "It's a mess. But at least she's stopped talking to the press. I have a feeling it may be due to the fact she's facing criminal charges for writing that large of a bad check."

Wyatt nearly burst out laughing. It was only fair that her tricks come back to bite her. He knew she'd been kicked out by her family and recently one of her ex-husbands had come forward with damning information. Lorna had sown her own future with her choices.

"Make sure to up my donations to compensate," Wyatt told Amanda. "I don't want the charity to suffer because of that woman."

"I figured you'd say that," Amanda replied. "I've emailed you new consents. Send them back to me whenever you get the chance."

"Thanks, Amanda."

"Anytime, Boss," Amanda told him. "Enjoy the new island. Let me know whatever you need."

Wyatt hung up the phone and grinned. The day was already going better than expected.

"Who were you talking to?" Cassie asked, coming up on deck. She wore short shorts and a thin t-shirt that didn't hide her curves. She had no idea what the sight of her body did to him. Suddenly, he lost the ability to think in cohesive sentences as he stared at her chest. She wasn't wearing a bra.

"Amanda," he grunted.

"Tell her I say hi next time," Cassie replied with a smile. "Where are we going today?"

She didn't seem to notice how his lower body was reacting to her as she walked across the deck. Her hips swayed with the boat, and Wyatt felt himself harden.

"It's a surprise," he told her. "We'll get right underway after I do something first."

Cassie turned, a slight frown on her face. "Do what?"

"You."

And he took her in his arms and showed her what seeing her sexy body did to him.

They got to the island later than Wyatt had planned, but he didn't mind. The morning had been worth it. Every time with Cassie was worth it. Especially because now she sat humming on the deck, glowing and looking pleased.

"Look at that," Cassie said, shading her eyes and coming to her feet. "It's beautiful."

White sand beaches gave way to palm trees and grass before a huge white colonial looking mansion.

"That's where we're going today," Wyatt explained, loving the grin she gave him. "The dock is just over here."

The large white house sat near the beach. It was more mansion than house, but that suited Wyatt's plans. The house originally belonged to a media mogul. There were more rooms than Wyatt knew what to do with, three pools, a mini-golf course, miles of beach, and a professional grade kitchen.

Wyatt docked the boat and secured it. As he was finishing, a man with a broad smile walked down the dock to greet them.

"Mr. Landers, I presume?" the man called.

"Please, call me Wyatt." Wyatt hopped off the boat to shake the man's hand. Cassie was right behind him. "This is Cassie."

"A pleasure to meet you, miss," the man replied. "I'm Franco. I'm the caretaker here. Let me show you to the house."

Franco led them up a carefully tended path away from the beach. Cassie's eyes were wide with delight with every step. Wyatt's excitement grew. This place was perfect for what he had planned. It was better than the brochures promised.

The house beckoned them to enter. Cassie hurried to the doorstep.

"Wait," Wyatt said, catching her. He bent over and swooped her into his arms. "Let me."

Cassie giggled but didn't fight him as he carried her over the threshold. "You're so romantic," she told him, kissing his cheek.

The house was everything Wyatt had hoped it would be. The rooms were more spacious, the kitchen better than expected, the view to die for, and the town and airport closer than he thought.

All in all, it was perfect.

"Wyatt, this place is beautiful," Cassie told him after Franco left them to get settled. They stood out on the master bedroom's balcony overlooking the ocean. "I feel like I should wear a corset and say I'm the governor's daughter."

"The governor's daughter?" Wyatt asked, not following her train of thought.

"Like in a pirate movie," she explained. "This place feels like it belongs as a set in 'Pirates of the Caribbean.' This place is a palace."

"Do you like it?" he asked, feeling his heart start to speed up.

"I love it," she told him. She smiled. "I could see this place being an amazing hotel. It would be small, but intimate. The town is close, and it wouldn't take too many renovations."

"Already dreaming," he said, watching her light up as she planned her ideal hotel.

"I can't help it. Hotels are what I know. They're what I'm good at." She blushed a little and then pointed to the beach. "Right there would make a perfect spot for a coffee cart with comfy chairs. And there's a spot we walked past that is made for guests to relax."

"Then this place is yours," he said. "Turn it into a hotel."

She turned back to him, her smile unsure. "What?"

"Turn this place into a hotel," he told her. "That's why I bought it for you."

Wyatt was rewarded with seeing Cassie's jaw hit the floor. "You bought it?"

"Amanda saw it and had me look at it," he explained. "It's just like you said- a perfect hotel."

Cassie's hand went to a wall, touching it gently and with awe. "So you bought it? For me?"

He nodded. "I bought it for our future."

Her eyes were bright with happy tears as she looked at him. "*Our* future. I like that."

She came to him and kissed his lips, gently and sweetly.

"Thank you, Wyatt. And yes. I say yes."

"You're skipping ahead," he teased her. "I'm supposed to ask if you'll marry me before you say yes."

She laughed and kissed him. "Then ask me before I can't stop kissing you."

"Cassie, will you marry me? Escape with me to this island and live happily ever after?" Wyatt's heart thudded in his chest, even though she'd already said yes.

This wasn't quite his plan, but he'd learned that with Cassie, he didn't need a plan. He just needed her.

"Yes. Yes to everything."

And they lived happily ever after.

IF YOU LIKED THIS BOOK...

An American Cinderella: A Royal Love Story

"I'd give up my whole kingdom to be with you. I want to be your Prince Charming."

Aria has a big heart but bigger problems. Her whole life is a mess thanks to her controlling stepmother. But when she's knocked over- literally- by the hottest man she's ever had the pleasure of tangling up her body with, everything changes.

Henry Prescott, second-string rugby player for the Paradisa Royals, is funny, sweet, charming, and oh-so-sexy. He's got a rock hard body and tackles her in bed as fiercely as he tackled her in the park. Knowing nothing about rugby, but absolutely intoxicated by his accent, she finds herself falling for him.

There's only one problem: Henry Prescott doesn't exist.

The man she thinks she loves is actually Prince Henry, second in line for the throne of the nation of Paradisa. He's the man who Aria's entire department has to impress for trade relations. And that makes Aria's stepmother's plans even more dangerous.

He's the man who could destroy her world or make all her dreams come true.

He lied about being a prince... did he also lie about being in love?

NYT Bestseller Krista Lakes brings you this brand new sweet-and-sexy royal romance. This standalone novel will have you cheering for an American princess's happily ever after.

An American Cinderella: A Royal Love Story

ABOUT THE AUTHOR

New York Times and USA Today Bestseller Krista Lakes is a thirtysomething who recently rediscovered her passion for writing. She is living happily ever after with her Prince Charming. Her first kid just started preschool and she is happy to welcome her second child into her life, continuing her "Happily Ever After"!

Thank you for supporting an indie author. Anything you can do, whether it be writing a review, or even simply telling a fellow reader that you enjoyed this, helps me out immensely. Thanks!

Krista would love to hear from you! Please contact her at Krista.Lakes@gmail.com or friend her on Facebook!

Further reading:

Bad Boys and Babies
    Family Doctor's Baby
    The Billionaire's Baby Arrangement
    Crime Boss Baby

Kinds of Love
    A Forever Kind of Love
    A Wonderful Kind of Love
    An Endless Kind of Love

Billionaires and Brides

Yours Completely: A Cinderella Love Story

Yours Truly: A Cinderella Love Story

Yours Royally: A Cinderella Love Story

The "Kisses" series

Saltwater Kisses: A Billionaire Love Story

Kisses From Jack: The Other Side of Saltwater Kisses

Rainwater Kisses: A Billionaire Love Story

Champagne Kisses: A Timeless Love Story

Freshwater Kisses: A Billionaire Love Story

Sandcastle Kisses: A Billionaire Love Story

Hurricane Kisses: A Billionaire Love Story

Barefoot Kisses: A Billionaire Love Story

Sunrise Kisses: A Billionaire Love Story

Waterfall Kisses: A Billionaire Love Story

Island Kisses: A Billionaire Love Story

Other Novels

I Choose You: A Secret Billionaire Romance

His Every Desire: A Billionaire Seduction

Wolf Six's Salvation: A Shifter Love Story

Burned: A New Adult Love Story

Walking on Sunshine: A Sweet Summer Romance

An American Cinderella: A Royal Love Story

Mr. Darcy's Kiss: A Contemporary Pride and Prejudice